"You said you wanted to ask me out."

"I do." He set his glass down. And somehow managed to move a little bit farther away as he turned toward her and took her hand. "I really do."

"So? Why is nothing...happening?"

He didn't say anything. Just studied her.

"Ethan's usually around." His answer, when it came, was a huge disappointment. And a relief, too.

Only because he was confirming an excuse she'd already come up with.

"He's not around tonight."

Her father had not taught her to be a woman who threw herself at men. To the contrary, he'd beaten her bloody the first time a boy had kissed her on her front step after a date and the great fire chief had witnessed the unremarkable occurrence.

Buzzkill. Maybe this wasn't a good idea after all.

"I'm afraid that if I touch you, I won't stop."

Tad's words brought her head up. She saw the truth in the light in his eyes.

"Who says you have to stop?" she whispered.

* * *

If you're on Twitter, tell us what you think of Harlequin Romantic Suspense! #harlequinromsuspense

D0970824

Dear Reader,

Oh my word. I am just so happy to be here with you. I've been writing romantic suspense my entire career, and I am finally, with this, my ninetieth book, writing them for Harlequin Romantic Suspense! The line wasn't even in existence when I started my Harlequin career and, thankfully, Harlequin Superromance happily published my suspense titles. I am very thankful that you, the Harlequin Romantic Suspense family, invited me into your fold.

So...welcome to The Lemonade Stand, where secrets are safe. Always. This series is integrally a part of me. It hits home. It's personal. I created The Lemonade Stand several years ago, at the request of a Harlequin editor. I had no idea the impact it would have on readers, or on me. The Stand is a unique resort-like women's shelter off the coast of California. And the stories that happen here...they stand alone. They're individual stories of individual women and men whose lives have been impacted by this wonderful facility.

This book...I feel it down to my core, and I hope and pray that you do, too. It's intense, but I promise you an ending that is real and filled with hope.

If you like this book, you can find the first fifteen Where Secrets are Safe stories, published by Harlequin Superromance, at all online retailers, including Harlequin.com, or by ordering them through any of your local retailers. And for future ones, just sit right here with me. They're already on the way!

I love to connect with my readers. Please find me at www.tarataylorquinn.com, www.Facebook.com/tarataylorquinnauthor, on Twitter @tarataylorquinn or join my open Friendship board at www.Pinterest.com/tarataylorquinn/friendship.

Happy reading,

Tara Taylor Quinn

HER DETECTIVE'S SECRET INTENT

Tara Taylor Quinn

HARLEQUIN®ROMANTIC SUSPENSE

Recycling programs
for this product may
not exist in your area.

ISBN-13: 978-1-335-66216-3

Her Detective's Secret Intent

Copyright © 2019 by TTQ Books LLC

HARLEQUIN®
www.Harlequin.com

Printed in U.S.A.

Having written over eighty-five novels, **Tara Taylor Quinn** is a *USA TODAY* bestselling author with more than seven million copies sold. She is known for delivering intense, emotional fiction. Tara is a past president of Romance Writers of America and is a seven-time RWA RITA® Award finalist. She has also appeared on TV across the country, including *CBS Sunday Morning*. She supports the National Domestic Violence Hotline. If you need help, please contact 1-800-799-7233.

Visit the Author Profile page at Harlequin.com for more titles.

For Drake Winchester, the brand-new little guy for whom I'd give my life.

I am so thankful you're in the world.

Chapter 1

Detective Tad Newberry—currently on leave from the police force in Charlotte, North Carolina—walked into the pediatric examining room in Santa Raquel, California, forcing a big smile. In addition to the exam table, some plastic chairs, a counter with drawers and glass containers of various cotton supplies, the room boasted zoo animal prints in shades of blue and green. The floor was gray tile, eight-inch squares, and the lights were ceiling-mounted fluorescent bulbs.

After giving his surroundings a quick glance, cataloging every aspect out of habit, he focused on the seven-year-old boy dressed in jeans and a yellow T-shirt sitting on the edge of the table, swinging one of his legs back and forth—a nervous gesture, Tad surmised, not a happy or excited one.

The boy's mother, in jeans and a navy hoodie with a light green shirt underneath, stood beside him, hand about an inch behind her son on the paper-covered cushioned mat. As though she was ready to grab him at any moment. Tad glanced at her, having been prepared ahead of time, and still felt bile rise in his throat when he saw the red-and-purple puffiness taking up one entire side of her face.

Marie Williams wanted to be kept safe from her abusive husband, but she didn't want to press charges against him. She truly believed that once they got through their divorce, she'd be fine; he'd no longer be a risk to her. At the same time, she didn't want to ruin his life.

Tad had heard the entire report. He didn't get it. But it wasn't his place to judge.

"Danny, this is Tad, the man I told you about," said the third woman in the room that sunny April morning, the one Tad knew and by whose invitation he was there. Pediatric physician's assistant Miranda Blake could easily steal Tad's entire focus if he allowed himself to relax. Something he could never do around the lovely brunette.

"Hi, Danny," he said, his gaze on the boy as he approached. "I hear you've had a bit of a tough time." Pulling up a chair, not the doctor's stool Miranda had pushed his way, he settled half a foot below the boy's eye level.

Chin almost to his chest, Danny nodded.

The boy, a beefy little guy, though not overweight, wouldn't meet his eyes.

Tad had never been married, had no kids, but he knew human nature. Leaning down, he tried to catch the boy's look. Danny turned to his mother, burying his face in her chest.

"Tad's not going to hurt you, Danny." Miranda's tone not only held authority, but that incredible sense of nurturing that had captivated him from the first time he'd heard her speak. The woman radiated caring. Not that he required it for himself.

He had other matters on his mind. Giving all his attention to the boy, he made a guess. "I'm not mad at you, son. You aren't in any kind of trouble. And I'm not a doctor or anyone in the doctor business. I'm not here to look at your injuries. I'm just here to talk."

He was there as part of an individualized plan designed by the High Risk Team in Santa Raquel—a team comprised of various working professionals who shared domestic violence information with the single goal of preventing domestic violence deaths. The current plan had been devised to protect Danny and his mother. His role, strictly volunteer, was to keep an eye on Danny anytime the boy wasn't with his mother or teachers. Specifically he was to do multiple drive-bys a day to see that all was well. Miranda, a frequent visiting member of the High Risk Team, had come up with the idea for the two of them, Danny and him, to actually meet. Her reasoning—if Danny knew him and knew he was close by, he'd be more apt to reach out if he was in trouble—was sound.

But it was only going to work if he could get Danny to trust him.

Not an easy feat for a man who'd had few dealings with kids until recently, and a little boy who'd had his trust in men destroyed by the one man he should've been able to count on—his father.

The boy didn't turn to him as Tad spoke. Danny's tennis-shoe-clad heel on his good leg was no longer lightly bumping the table. It hung completely still beside the leg he could hardly move.

That caught Tad's attention.

Danny didn't have to know or like Tad for Tad to keep an eye on him. But maybe he could do more here than help prevent further physical harm. Maybe he could help the little guy heal in other ways.

As someone who was attempting to heal himself, he found that the idea appealed to him.

"Ladies, if you'll please forgive any impropriety and feel free to turn your heads, I'd like to show Danny something on my leg." He tore the paper from the top half of the exam table, wrapped it around his waist. Then, looking at Miranda and Danny's mother for an okay and receiving nods, he awkwardly—using one hand, as though performing some kind of comic routine—managed to get his loose-fitting jeans undone and dropped them to the floor. He was a boxers kind of guy, dark blue that day, and even without the paper all pertinent parts were fully covered. It wasn't the pertinent parts that were relevant right now.

Pulling the paper up on his waist, high enough to expose his upper thigh or, more accurately, the jagged, puffy and discolored seven-inch scar slashing across the front and around the side of his leg, he said, "It doesn't look as gross now as it did. And yours won't look nearly as bad because it was a straight line, and that makes a big difference."

Standing there with his pants around his ankles, Tad might have felt embarrassed. Or inappropriate. All he felt was that he had to reach this little guy on his own level. Dealing with what was foremost on the boy's mind.

And it appeared to be working. Danny, having sat upright, was staring at the scar. Boys must still be somewhat the way he remembered himself being—fascinated by gross things.

"I fell, too," he said, leaving out the part about the explosion that had sent him flying. Just like he didn't mention that he knew Danny had been running from his enraged father when he'd tripped and impaled his leg on a plant stake in the backyard.

"It hurt like heck to move my leg for a while," he added, because he knew Danny had months of rehab ahead of him as the muscle that had been cut in his upper thigh healed.

"I go to the gym at least twice a day, three days a week, to make it stronger, and now I can walk without any limp at all." Unless he was overtired. Then a tilted gait came back to remind him of what he'd done.

He moved his leg enough to flex the muscle, which made the scar jump. "See, it works just fine now."

Glancing briefly at the two women on either side of the exam table, he asked if they'd mind turning around so he could get himself put back together. He did so in record time, except for tucking in the blue cotton polo shirt. Going strictly on instincts, as he watched the boy watching him, he lifted his shirt a few inches, showing Danny his back. "I got burned, too," he told the boy. "So, you see, I'm just here as a guy who got hurt, wanting to help another guy who got hurt."

Danny didn't speak. But he didn't turn away, either. He watched Tad. And maybe that was enough.

"What happened?" Danny's mother asked. Tad looked up and saw the compassion on her face. He chose to think of it as that, as opposed to pity, which he could not abide. He'd made a stupid choice.

But it had brought the best result possible—saving a little girl's life. Something that might have been done with less damage—to himself and others—if he'd followed protocol by waiting for the hostage negotiators and SWAT to arrive.

Or little Lola could have been hurt far worse than the minimal bruising she'd suffered from Tad's falling too heavily on her when he dived to protect her body from the blast.

"A guy was angry with me," he said, vetting his words carefully with Danny in mind. "He had something that didn't belong to him and when I went to get it back, he… hurt me."

Lola's's father had rigged a homemade bomb to go off if anyone pushed open the antiques store's back office door, behind which he held the child hostage. Unaware that the girl was there, Tad had gone to the business, not yet open for the day, to question him about some things he'd been selling in his shop. Stolen things.

"Did they get the bad guy?" Danny's voice was surprisingly strong as he looked Tad in the eye.

"Yes, they did," he said. The man had been prepared to kill himself and his daughter, too, apparently, rather than face arrest. The child wasn't supposed to have been there. Her mother, who'd had shared custody of her and no idea that her soon to be ex-husband was in any kind of trouble, had dropped her off with him because she'd been called into work.

He'd dragged her into the back office, telling Tad and his partner to get out or he'd hurt her...

"So, anyway, if you want to come to the gym with me sometime, have your mom call me," Tad said. Marie Williams already had his cell number. "You might see me hanging out, too," he added. "You can talk to me or not, your choice. I just wanted you to know who I am and that I'll be around."

Danny said nothing more. Tad took the boy's choice at face value and left the room.

Miranda didn't hurry through the rest of her appointment with Danny and Marie Williams, but as soon as they were out of the exam room, she finished the last of her administrative responsibilities for the day. Then she was out the back door of the clinic where she worked for pediatric specialist Dr. Max Bennet, and heading to her car.

The white Chevy Equinox blended in with a million other similar-sized and -shaped white mini SUVs, which was why it fit her perfectly. She had an hour before she had to pick Ethan up, and Tad Newberry was waiting for her at a coffee shop halfway between her office and the school.

The balmy sixty-five-degree weather was perfect for her white cardigan and cartoon-spattered scrubs.

Heart pounding in an entirely new way, she drove five miles over the speed limit, switching lanes when necessary to weave past slower cars. All the while, she thought about those minutes in the exam room with the off-duty, out-of-state detective who'd shown up at a High Risk Team meeting six weeks before.

He'd dropped his pants. The move had been calculated, out of the ordinary, a somewhat shocking attempt to get Danny's attention—and build trust, too. She understood that. Admired the hell out of it, actually. He'd known that Danny felt particularly vulnerable, so he'd made himself seem—and perhaps feel—just as vulnerable.

All of that aside…she'd peeked. She shouldn't have. It had been completely unprofessional. Completely, 100 percent out of character. And she'd done it. Seen…a lot.

Blue boxers. Dark hair on legs that were tight and firm. Even now, driving to discuss the afternoon's event and how it played into the care plan the High Risk Team had developed to prevent Devon Williams from ever hurting Marie or their son again, she shied away from thinking about the ugly facts of life, and found herself picturing those jeans pooled around Tad's ankles instead.

Watching him with a very definite feminine reaction.

Wrong. It was just plain wrong of her. On so many levels.

Parking in the coffeehouse lot, seeing Tad already inside sitting at a table for two with a couple of steaming cups in front of him, she pulled herself together. Having very private fantasies was bad enough; allowing them to invade the space she shared with others was prohibited.

Period.

"That went well."

Miranda heard the sarcasm in Tad's greeting as she sat down. She felt herself immediately tuning into him.

"It did go well," she assured him. "I can't tell you what was said after you left—" he knew about her legal restrictions with regard to medical confidentiality "—but it went well. Marie asked me to tell you thanks. She feels much better knowing that you'll be adding extra drive-bys to the ones the police are already going to be doing."

Tad's next comment was angry. "Devon Williams should be in jail."

"Agreed. But since he hasn't actually physically hurt anyone—that we can prove—since Marie dropped those charges against him last year, and still insists that her current bruising comes from a fall, there's not a lot the prosecutor can do."

He knew that, too. Santa Raquel's assistant prosecutor was a new member of the High Risk Team.

"At least the judge granted her restraining order," Miranda added, wishing she was only thinking about the woman who'd just left her office. Truth was, she saw more abused children and their mothers than she'd like. She suspected that at least five of the fifty families she saw on a regular basis dealt with that insidious disease.

"And you know as well as I do that those orders are ignored more than forty percent of the time in these kinds of cases," Tad countered.

And often victims invited the abuser back into their lives. Yeah, Miranda knew that, too. Which was part of what made the situation that much more frustrating.

Unknown to Tad, though, she wasn't just aware that it

happened, she understood *how* it happened. In the most personal way possible.

"I don't get it," he said. "How can a woman marry a man after he's already abused her? It makes no sense to me."

He was talking about Marie, whose boyfriend had hit her a couple of times back in high school. Once, he'd also shoved her up to a wall with his hands around her neck.

He'd also loved and adored her when no one else had, making her vulnerable to him, and he'd scared her into thinking that marrying him was the only way to keep herself safe. And happy.

The incidents had been isolated. She'd understood that he hadn't been himself for various reasons—usually involving alcohol. But she'd believed him when he promised never to lift a hand to her again when she'd dropped charges against him the previous year.

She'd hoped.

Right up until he'd been thundering behind their son, trying to catch up to him to give him a spanking for not packing a suitcase as he'd instructed. He'd panicked Danny, who tore out of their house so fast he'd tripped and fallen on a stake she'd just put up in her garden.

"Our job is to follow the safety plan and do what we can to see that Devon doesn't have a chance to hurt either of them again," she reminded him. "You heard Chantel. As soon as he violates that protection order, his ass is in jail."

Chantel Harris Fairbanks, a Santa Raquel detective on the High Risk Team, might be married to a millionaire banker and live in one of the town's most impressive mansions, but she was all cop when it came to her job. Even to the point of keeping her previous small apartment in town so she didn't ever lose sight of who she was and what she knew. So she wouldn't ever forget where she came from.

Miranda envied her—being able to keep her old self

alive. Nothing about Miranda's former self lived on with her. Not even her name.

"And then the prosecutor can call for a dangerousness hearing," she said. It wasn't technically called that in California, but it meant that if Devon was arrested and was considered a danger, he could be held without bail.

The man had threatened to kill his wife. Twice in the past eight weeks since she'd told him she wanted a divorce. He'd actually told her how he'd dispose of her body. He'd been drinking again. And quit his job. When he'd gone to their house the week before to insist that Danny come to his apartment and stay with him for the weekend, the boy suffered his fall. And then he'd blamed his wife for that, too, taking his anger out on her face. On a list of nineteen risk factors pointing to the danger of death, Devon Williams ranked at thirteen. It only took eight for the case to be referred to the High Risk Team.

Marie was changing her routine, her working hours. Her newly married sister and brother-in-law were moving in with her for a while. She and Danny were going to stay around crowds when they went out. She wouldn't be going to her usual church, grocery store or hairdresser. Not until Devon was under control.

It wasn't just to keep her and Danny safe, but because she truly wanted Devon to succeed. She wanted him to come through this. To find a good life for himself. To be happy.

She loved him.

And that was the part Miranda got that many others, most others, couldn't. How a heart could still feel love for someone who beat them.

The secrets she held close inside kept her emotions in check during that afternoon coffee with Tad Newberry though she desperately wanted to talk to him about them.

She couldn't. She wouldn't.

No matter how badly she hurt.

Ethan's life depended on her keeping her secrets to herself.

And the second she'd given birth to him, his life had become more important to her than her own.

Chapter 2

Miranda was fine right up until Tad walked her out to her car. His, an older-model black SUV, was parked down the street. He'd bought it used, he'd told her during one of their coffee sessions with a couple of others after a High Risk Team meeting. He was only in town for a year while he was on leave from his detective job back east. Michigan, she figured. That was where he'd said he'd grown up. A suburb of Detroit.

He was using his time off, he'd said, to learn more about the High Risk Team with the thought that he could help implement a version of it in his hometown.

Other than that, she knew so little about him.

And wanted to know much more.

Almost as soon as they drew up to her car, that vision of his pants around his ankles hit her again—like there was some kind of mental video player attached to her vehicle. Maybe she should buy a new car; maybe that would fulfill her wants, if not her needs. The inane thought came and went.

To be replaced by a sense of panic. Tad was different from any man she'd ever known. The way she responded to him was different.

But she couldn't be an honest half of a partnership. Any partnership.

When she'd run, the idea of having a lover, or a boyfriend, or anything along the lines of a male companion, hadn't even entered her mind. She spent two years in a women's shelter outside of Santa Raquel before moving to the city four years ago, and it hadn't been a problem since.

But now it was.

She didn't want to live the rest of her life alone.

Did she have a choice?

"Ethan's, what, six?" Tad asked, startling her out of her reverie.

"Yeah," she said. She must be tired. Working too hard. Spending too much time identifying with Marie.

The woman's case spoke to her on a personal level more than most. Probably because of Danny.

"He's in the first grade," she said, forcing herself back into the moment. Tad had met Ethan twice. Brief introductions both times.

After the second time, her son had teased her, saying she should go out on a date with Tad. They'd run into Tad at the grocery store one evening and she'd stopped to chat. Ethan's reaction had surprised her. She'd never thought of her son as thinking about her personal situation. She was Mom. That was all.

But maybe it had been her son's grinning little push that was her problem here. Was he missing a male figure in his life? Had that prompted his teasing remarks?

And was her current fascination with Tad merely reaction to that?

Just thoughts that Ethan's comment had put in her head?

Yeah, if life were that simple.

"Could I take the two of you out to dinner?" Tad asked, while her mind continued to fly off course.

Her stomach flip-flopped. She almost dropped her keys. Struggling to find a way to say no when what she wanted to do was ask how soon, she said nothing as he continued. "I'd like to spend some time with Ethan, since he's so close to Danny's age. Just to observe. It would help me get a better feel for things. In case I ever need to speak with Danny again. Dropping my drawers was a little extreme and I don't think it would work a second time."

She nodded, trying to school her features—feeling she managed, at best, a cross between a frown and the grin that was trying to break through.

Dinner was all he'd asked. To observe her son. No big deal.

And complicated as hell.

"I'm sorry about that, by the way," he said when her feelings continued to flay around inside. "The dropping of the pants thing. And thank you for not mentioning it."

"It was unconventional, not to mention unexpected, but I thought the idea was brilliant," Miranda spoke the complete truth. Probably because she could. Her tongue needed to fly along with her brain waves, but most of them weren't traveling in the same atmosphere.

"And… I like you in blue."

What? Had she lost her mind? *I like you in blue?*

Oh my God. She was flirting with him?

Dinner was definitely out.

"I'll keep that in mind." Tad's tone was so easygoing,

her raging blood settled a little. A lot, actually. She felt completely put in her place.

Which meant that… "Dinner would be fine," she said, sane again. He needed her help with Danny. And Ethan would be with her. She was clearheaded every second of every day that she was with her son. She was all he had in the world, and she was conscious of that fact first and foremost. "When?"

"Tonight? Unless you have other plans? I'm already on Danny duty and am eager to get what help I can so I don't blow it with him."

His "duty" entailed a few minutes a few times a day, driving by wherever the boy was, according to the schedule Marie would text him each week, with nightly changes if there were any. Marie could call or text him if she got in a bind. Miranda knew, because she'd been sitting at the table when the plan was devised. She knew what every participant in the plan was doing—including their medical office. They were all on alert. And careful to make sure that only handpicked personnel were alone with Danny any time he was in for treatment.

That brought her back to this morning. Tad in the examining room.

She was dying to know what had happened to him in the past. The details.

But she didn't ask. Instead, she agreed to meet him at Uncle Bob's, a hamburger diner on the beach with a sandbox for kids to play in, at six.

She didn't have time to stand around and chat right now. Ethan would be out of school in ten minutes, and unlike Marie, she didn't have a team of experts watching out for her son.

Because, unlike Marie, she'd escaped her past. She was safe.

As long as she kept her mouth shut.

In his rented apartment with a view of the ocean, Tad took a long, hot shower, turning the water to cold when the heat failed to relax him.

He was supposed to be recovering, and in the interim, doing a man he respected a favor as a private way of repenting for the wrong turn his career had taken. He was supposed to be getting his shit together, not losing it over the woman he'd been sent to find.

Pulling on a pair of black jeans one size larger than he normally wore, to accommodate the thigh that was still painful sometimes and had a tendency to swell, he took a T-shirt from the top dresser drawer. He followed that with a button-down white shirt from the closet, careful to line up the empty hanger in its proper place, and yanked open the little side drawer on the dresser for a pair of socks.

The arrangements in his apartment weren't all as he would've preferred them, but the place had come furnished and that was what he cared about. His clothes back home in North Carolina were in the house he'd purchased the previous year in an upper-middle-class neighborhood.

Reaching inside one of the socks he'd retrieved, he pulled out the burner phone that had traveled across the country with him six weeks before. Fridays were call days. North Carolina was three hours ahead of California and he didn't know how late he'd be out.

"Chief O'Connor." North Carolina's newly appointed state chief fire marshal always picked up on the first ring.

"Just checking in, sir. I told you she's working as a physician's assistant in a pediatric office and I had a chance to see her in action today. Like you, she's not afraid to think outside the box. I think you'd be proud of her." Maybe it made him a bit of a wuss that he always tried to find a way to comfort the older man during these conversations, to make him feel less alone.

But if it wasn't for Chief O'Connor's quick thinking at a scene that hadn't even required his presence, Tad and a couple of his fellow officers could well be dead.

"And the boy?"

"Other than those two brief meetings I told you about, I haven't seen him." He'd meant to tell the chief about his dinner engagement. Didn't.

Wondered why the hell not.

He didn't like the predicament he was putting himself in.

"Yeah, best to go slowly." The older man's voice came firmly over the wire. "The last thing I want to do is tip her off…"

"I was going to ask you about that. With her ex gone, is there really a need for this secrecy?"

The question had been bothering him for a while, particularly since the Marie Williams case had sprung up that week. Miranda Blake, real name Dana O'Connor, had no way of knowing that she was out of danger. Surely she'd welcome the knowledge—and the chance to go home to the friends and family she'd been forced to leave behind when she'd changed her identity to escape a madman.

"I know my daughter, young man. This is *my* operation. My call. Dana doesn't like change. She doesn't like having her world upended. If she's happy there, in that life, I want to know about it. I'll need to figure that into how I approach her. And I'll need to figure out how I might fit into that life so I can make the transition easier for her."

Okay. Sure. But…

"Her ex…he might have family," the chief went on.

"Someone who'd want contact with the boy. I've got a guy looking into that. Good investigator. I need to be absolutely certain, before I have any contact with her, even through you, that I'm not putting her in any danger or in any way making her life more difficult than it's already been. I'm not going to put my selfish need to have her back in my life ahead of her needs."

Nodding, respecting the man all over again, Tad wandered into the living room, to the window looking out toward the Pacific Ocean two streets in the distance.

"I'd be more than happy to check into any in-law family that might exist." His detective skills had earned him the right to make his own calls on the job—until he'd made a call based as much on emotion as skill, one that was so far from protocol that he'd almost gotten himself and others killed.

He'd saved the girl, though.

There was that. Always that. Every single time he relived the horror of that morning three months before.

"Forgive me for being set in my ways, but I learned a long time ago not to put all my eggs in one basket," Chief O'Connor said. "I have someone else following that lead. Someone who has no idea that you, or your job for me, even exist. I'm paying you to use your highly touted skills to find my daughter and grandson, which you've done, and to be fully focused there, to keep me informed. It's been years since I've had any word of my daughter and these weekly calls of ours…well, let's just say they're the best moments I've had in all those years. And I won't risk having any searches for her coming from the town in which she lives. There can't be anything connecting our investigation too close to her."

Tad nodded, understanding. He'd succeeded in tracking her down, via the access he continued to have to law enforcement databases of various kinds. He'd learned a great deal about her.

But he still wasn't satisfied. He didn't even know Dana's ex's name. The cop in him needed to be certain, especially after witnessing from the sidelines the Devon Williams nightmare that week, that he was working with complete and accurate information.

In his entire career, he'd always double-checked facts himself. He wasn't a "rely on others" kind of guy.

"You're one hundred percent certain her ex is dead." His voice could be intimidating, too, when necessary.

"Yes. I have definitive proof. I give you my word on that."

Then there was nothing more to be said. He'd accepted the job. He respected the man. Hell, all of North Carolina respected him if such a thing was possible. Heroes didn't come around every day, and when they did, they didn't shine as often or as brightly as Brian O'Connor had. Again and again, over the course of a lifetime, he'd risked his life, and volunteered his time, too, to save and enrich the lives of those in his community. And his state.

If he'd grown a little eccentric over the years, Tad figured that was his right.

He owed him the news that Tad would be having dinner with his grandson in a few minutes. That he could call back later with a report the chief had been waiting for.

He owed him. And he reneged.

He'd figure that one out later.

First, he had a date to keep.

In a manner of speaking...

Chapter 3

"So…are we like…on a thing?" Ethan glanced between Miranda and Tad, his eyes rimmed by the dark-framed glasses he'd chosen because he thought they resembled the ones worn by Clark Kent, Superman's alter ego—the Superman of earlier days that Miranda had shared with him. If her son had been grinning, teasing, she might have been able to brush the moment aside.

"No." She reined in the rest of the blurted response that almost came out, changing it to a mildly firm denial. "I told you, Tad and I work together."

They'd just ordered their burgers, and all three had glasses of soda with straws sitting in front of them. The minutes they'd be waiting until their food was delivered suddenly seemed interminable.

"On a committee." Ethan nodded. "You said you work together on a committee." He looked at Tad. "Do you like my mom?"

"Of course I like your mom. Why would I eat dinner with someone I didn't like?"

"Exactly," Ethan said, pushing his glasses back up his nose. "Do you know the game *Zoo Attack*?"

Breathing a sigh of relief, Miranda took a sip of soda and let her son have at Tad. After all, the off-duty detective had asked for the meeting to get to know Ethan better.

"No. I don't know that game," Tad said, elbows resting on the arms of his chair.

"It's really cool," Ethan said. "You get to be in the zoo, taking care of animals, and then danger comes and you have to solve puzzles to save the animals…"

As she listened to her son's in-depth and enthusiastic description of his favorite video game, Miranda wanted to relax. To enjoy the moment.

There was much to enjoy. In spite of everything, she'd raised a boy who was confident enough, trusting and outgoing enough, to take charge of a conversation with a virtual stranger. A male stranger.

And she was sitting with a man who, in another lifetime, might have been someone she'd feel passionate about. Watching Tad as he seemed to give Ethan his full focus, engaging in conversation as though the conversation mattered to him, she felt again that peculiar bounce of joy inside, as though she was with someone special.

"I'd like that," Tad said, and she tuned back in, realizing, too late, that Ethan had just invited him to their house over the weekend to learn how to play *Zoo Attack* in two-player mode, which meant that they'd be racing against each other to get puzzles solved to save animals.

Tad *couldn't* come to their home. Ethan would ask, "Why not?" She could hear his voice inside her head, asking. No simple or credible-sounding reply presented itself. But the answer was unequivocal. He could not come into their home.

Home was her safe place. The only space she could be herself without fear…

"Jimmy from school is over there, Mom. Can I go play in the sandbox?"

She had to nod. To let him go. She wanted him to be independent. But she did not want, at that moment, to be left alone with a man who was getting way too far into her.

"This isn't a thing," she said as soon as her son was out of hearing range.

He nodded. "I know."

"It can't be a thing." She was sounding like an idiot. Had to get herself together.

"You seeing someone, then?" Tad asked easily. She didn't like how his total attention was suddenly on her. Eyeing her with some kind of understanding or something. She didn't like how warm that made her feel.

She was hot enough already.

Tempted to lie to him, she hesitated. Santa Raquel wasn't all that big. And her son's conversational filters were sadly untrustworthy.

"No, I'm not seeing anyone."

"Coming off a bad breakup?"

That might work. Except that Ethan seemed unusually focused on her dating situation. Could it be that now that he'd started school, he was noticing they were missing a part of their family? Was he needing that male figure in his life? Granted, there'd be plenty of kids without dads at his school and some without mothers. But many had other family, siblings, aunts and uncles, grandparents, cousins…

She'd known this time of reckoning would come. Had worried about it to no avail—figuring she'd have to let the future take care of itself on that one.

"No, I'm not coming off a breakup." She prayed he'd leave it there. Or that their food would arrive and Ethan, who always seemed to know when there were goods to shove in his mouth, would descend upon them once again.

When Tad glanced in the direction of the boys playing outside the sandbox with little cars Jimmy must have brought, Miranda guessed he was seeking a way out of their awkward moment, as well.

He looked so good, his dark hair, thickening shadow of whisker growth and brown eyes giving him a rakish aura in an oh-so-masculine form. She knew his legs were lean and strong. She'd seen them firsthand…and was he still wearing his blue boxers? Or had he showered since she'd seen him at work that morning?

"So you don't date at all, or is it just me?"

So much for the idea that he was looking for an out. He'd just slammed them right smack-dab in the middle of *too complicated.*

"You're only here for your leave." She blurted what immediately came to mind, as though that explained everything.

He didn't argue, and again she hoped she was off the hook. At least with him.

She still had to deal with herself and her deepening feelings for this man. And she would. She'd only known him six weeks. It wasn't like it would take a lifetime to get him out of her system.

Unless… What if, for the first time in her life, she was really and truly falling for someone? As in…the real thing?

Of course, that didn't matter in the long run. Her life wasn't open to *real.* Her goal was to give Ethan a chance at a good life, a life of his own. He wouldn't have to lie to anyone he met in his future. The life he lived now was his only known reality.

"You don't ever talk about Ethan's dad."

"It's not like we've had a lot of time for private conversation."

Not entirely true. They'd fallen into the habit of having coffee after every High Risk Team meeting. At the moment, as the team became a stronger force in Santa Raquel and the surrounding communities, they were meeting weekly. And she'd volunteered to go in place of her employer, Max, every single week.

Partially because of Tad, she was ashamed to admit to herself.

"Ethan's father is dead." She dropped it out of the blue. There were some truths she could tell, at least in part. Clearly everyone would realize Ethan had had a father. "He died before Ethan was born."

With no name, there'd be no chance to find a death record. To trace her to any young man who'd died during their last year of college. Or even to trace her to a particular college. Or to identify a girl who'd been friends with a boy who died. No way to discover who she really was.

"Wow. I'm so sorry."

So was she. Jeff had been one of the greatest guys she'd ever known, and he hadn't deserved the blows life had dealt him. "I miss him every day," she said, allowing one more piece of her real self through. Jeff had been the only one who ever knew the whole truth about her. The only one in her past life she'd told.

"That had to be hell, to lose him and be pregnant at the same time."

She shrugged. "You'd think so, but being pregnant, knowing that Ethan was part of him, and a new part of me, a whole new life… I'm sure that's what saved me." In more ways than Tad could ever imagine. If it hadn't been for Ethan she might never have had the strength, the clarity of mind, to get away.

Jeff, who'd been a foster kid, had believed in her, trusted her to raise his child—even knowing the truth about her life.

Tad's brows had been drawing closer together as she talked, giving Miranda the impression that she was coming on too heavy. She was suddenly aware that she wasn't in their own little cocoon, with her son playing safely in the distance. Instead, she—and Tad—were in a noisy diner with Friday-night happiness going on all around them.

She tried to think of a way to change the subject.

But she didn't manage before he asked, "How long did you know him? Ethan's father?"

"Four years."

"You were obviously close…"

Obviously. She'd had his son. Though not close in the way Tad would assume. "We were best friends." And that was all they'd been. Friends. Not a "thing." *Best friends*. With Ethan, she'd given her best friend his dying wish—a child who would always be part of him, carrying on a life that had been cut far too short.

"How long were you married?"

Her mind went blank. What did she say? Would the truth give her away somehow? She tried to think of everything she'd been told. By the lawyers who helped her legally change her identity. By Lila and Sara at The Lemonade Stand, the unique women's shelter in town that had founded the High Risk Team. Everything she'd heard during her time with the team about the ways information could travel to the wrong people.

Marriage meant records.

The haze of panic receded. "We weren't married." She

told him the truth. No one could find what didn't exist. She was safe.

And no one knew that Jeff was Ethan's father. She hadn't named him on the original North Carolina birth certificate, and their new identities certainly didn't name him. To begin with, she'd kept the secret to protect Jeff from her father's wrath; Jeff had so little time to live and she couldn't bear the thought of bringing more tension into his life. And when he'd died before Ethan was born...she'd just kept the secret.

Tad sat back, adjusted his knife on the table. Took a sip from his straw. What was he thinking?

Surely, in today's world, he didn't respect her less for having a baby outside of marriage?

She wanted to tell him that they knew Jeff was dying. That they'd decided not to marry so there couldn't be any legal chance she'd be held responsible for any of his medical bills.

It seemed to be taking an inordinately long time for their dinner to arrive. But then, it was Friday night and the place was packed. Ethan had glanced their way a few times, but was still happily engaged with Jimmy. The two were in the sandbox now, trying to plow roads for their cars around the other children playing there.

All in all, less than ten minutes had passed. It just seemed like forever.

"I haven't dated anyone since Ethan was born." She had to tell Tad something that would get them out of this awkward mess. "A conscious choice I've made." For reasons she'd never tell him, no matter how badly she wished she could.

Tad wasn't asking her out, but she was guaranteeing that he wouldn't, although her heart was clamoring for a chance to see what life with him would be like.

Even if just for the months he was there.

Because it was only for however many months he'd be there. There'd be no risk of having to live a whole life of lying to him… It would be a question of living in the moment for the few months he was around.

Which her heart was telling her would be better than nothing.

It would be great, actually, to have such a memory to take with her into the future. To hold close. A good secret to combat all the bad ones…

"In honor of his father?"

"No. But…" She searched for an explanation that would shut him down. And yet she didn't allow anything remotely credible to surface. Would it be so wrong to get to know him better? He wouldn't be staying, had an entire life, an important job, to return to.

"I haven't had the time," she finally said, wondering if leaving a door open to him was emotional suicide. Or maybe it was the only personal bliss she'd know in her life. "I'm a single mother, and not all men want to take that on. Added to that, until last year I was in school full-time and working, too." While becoming a PA had only taken two years of additional schooling, she'd been unable to take her college degree with her and had to earn that all over again, too. Thankfully she'd been able to test out of more than two years of that, having to pay just for the class equivalent, not actually retake the classes.

"So now that you're fully accredited and have more time…"

Oh, God. Was he going to ask her out? Flooded with heat, she felt she was possessed by something stronger than herself—this desire to get closer and closer to him.

She shrugged when he didn't complete his sentence.

He nodded, as though her lack of a definitive "no" was interesting.

She smiled.

He nodded again.

And dinner was served.

What in the hell was he doing?

Walking the dark streets of Santa Raquel sometime after midnight, hunched in his department-issued coat with the collar turned up, Tad warded off the thirtysomething-degree chill of California ocean air. He'd intended to head over two blocks to the beach, but had only gone one and then turned, choosing sidewalk instead of sand.

If it hadn't been for dinner arriving, he was pretty sure he would've asked out his client's daughter. The subject of his current job.

If he ever hoped to work in law enforcement in North Carolina again, he couldn't be pissing off the state's chief fire marshal—a man with more connections, both law enforcement and political, than Tad could ever hope to have.

Did he hope to go back to some form of law enforcement work?

He'd quit his job.

The department had refused to accept his resignation, so officially, he was on administrative leave for the year they'd agreed upon.

Time for the department to fully investigate, review and further discuss his last case or, more accurately, the one really bad decision he'd made in a career of relatively great ones. His solved-cases record was better than that of anyone in the department.

They wanted to keep him on.

They also wanted him to take some time to get his head

on straight. To show them that he'd be able to regain any trust he'd lost with his peers.

But…did he hope to go back?

Noting that he'd crossed the fourth block with at least two largely cracked cement pieces, he thought about Santa Raquel's finances. Figured fixing cracks in the sidewalk of a seasonal tourist town should be on the radar. Someone could trip. Fall. Sue the municipal government.

The town, which was more resort-like than not, didn't seem to be hurting for money. Based on the number of large, well-maintained homes in the area, he supposed the town was doing just fine. Sidewalks didn't last forever. They cracked.

And a detective was bound to make one bad decision in his lifetime.

But what if he made two?

What if he asked out the daughter of his client? A woman he'd been hired to find? And keep watch over?

In his line of work, there'd been more than one occasion when the means justified the end.

Would that be the case here? Could he convince the chief that dating his daughter, casually, of course, was the best way to stick close to her? To spend time with her son?

And what about Miranda? What right did he have to mess with her life? As if she hadn't already been through enough?

She knew he was only in town for a matter of months. Their conversation that evening had gone in an unexpected—and much more personal—direction. Thanks to Ethan, who'd put the simmering tension between him and Miranda right out there.

So…if she was potentially interested in spending more time with him, say, one-on-one, knowing that it couldn't last long, would he be wrong to give it to her?

The thin line he walked was going to trip him up. He knew it.

Just as he'd known, when he made the choice to barge into that back office without waiting for SWAT and the hostage negotiators to arrive, assess the situation and do their jobs, that he was crossing a line.

He'd practically gotten himself killed. Had put every other officer on the scene at risk.

But he'd saved the girl.

It always came back to that for him.

He'd saved the girl.

Could he help save Miranda and Ethan, too?

Chapter 4

The thing about having a kid was that you couldn't just make up your mind about something and count on having it happen. When Ethan was a baby, Miranda was in charge. Or at least she'd felt she was. From the twos on, though, he'd been pretty adamant about having his own say in anything and everything, and she'd had to rethink her approach. A process that seemed to happen every day since. She had to foster his independence. And above all, keep him safe. So her mantra had become that if it didn't involve his safety or health, he could decide—which, in their world, meant he could have his way.

If it did have any kind of impact on his well-being, they did it her way. The line used to be clearly delineated. At least in her mind. And her boy had been good about accepting her decisions once she explained them to him.

That Saturday after dinner with Tad, Ethan woke up talking about *Zoo Attack*, about a new animal kingdom he was going to create and then show Tad. He'd said he'd come to their house and so, to Ethan, that meant he was coming.

Her moment to object to that idea had already gone.

Tad's, too, apparently, at least according to her son.

And Miranda was left with the task of explaining to her son that sometimes adults said things they didn't really mean.

A concept he wasn't willing to accept.

"Call him, Mom, he'll come, you'll see," Ethan said for the umpteenth time that morning. Standing in a pile of dark clothes on the kitchen floor by the laundry room, he kicked up a sock to emphasize his point.

She threw the last pair of white underwear in the dryer and bent to pick up their darks before he kicked them any farther.

"He's a grown man, Ethan," she told her son. "I'm sure he's got more important things to do than play video games this weekend."

As soon as she heard the words, she wanted to retract them. Implying that her son's engagements weren't important wasn't what she'd intended to say.

"He said he *wanted* to," Ethan insisted.

But *she* didn't want him in her home. Hadn't let any man visit since she'd made the first home for her and Ethan.

Their little rented cottage was her haven. She didn't have to be as careful there to hide her secrets. Or to worry that someone might be watching her. Looking for her. Or him. Keeping their home private was paramount to her peace of mind, to her belief that she could keep them safe.

None of which she could explain to her son.

"Call him, Mom, please? You'll see, he'll come."

She took her time loading the washing machine. Pouring the soap. Filling the little ball dispenser with fabric softener and dropping that in. What should she tell Ethan?

She'd promised herself that Ethan wasn't going to grow up in fear. Jeff had trusted her with his son.

Turning, she saw him still standing there, his big blue eyes imploring her.

"Okay," she heard herself say. "You go put the clean sheets on your bed like I showed you, and I'll call him."

"Yes!" Ethan jumped up in the air and he was off.

Miranda had a knot in her gut as she pulled her cell out of her pocket. Tad was in her contacts, as were all the High Risk Team members.

She'd told Ethan she'd call.

"Miranda?" He picked up on the first ring. "Everything okay?"

"Of course," she lied, listening to the washer fill with water, the clinking of a metal button on a pair of white pants in the dryer. "Why wouldn't it be?"

"Just making sure." He didn't really sound worried and she figured he was merely being polite—not reading her mind.

"I'm sorry to bother you, but I told Ethan I'd call. He hasn't let up on me all morning about that *Attack* game."

"He's going to give me my key to the animals."

"You were being nice to him, and I appreciate that, but I'll get you out of it. The thing is, he wasn't going to take no for an answer until I called." So she did. Because she didn't have a logical reason to give Ethan that he'd understand.

"I don't want out of it." His response sent her heart thudding. "I meant to solidify something before we split up last night and forgot."

"You don't have to come here and play video games with my kid," she told him, hoping her chuckle sounded genuinely unconcerned. Although it wasn't.

"I want to…unless you have some reason for *not* wanting me to?"

What was it with these two guys? It was like they were plotting together against her. One she loved with all her being, and the other…she really liked Tad.

She was intrigued. Curious. She wanted to explore further.

Her life didn't support that choice.

At least not long-term.

"I mean, I know you're busy and—"

"I'm on leave," he reminded her with a laconic drawl. "In a town where I know very few people. Other than my daily exercises, High Risk Team meetings and checking on Danny, my day is free."

Looking around at the fairly large but still cozy living and kitchen area—all open so she didn't have to worry about anyone lurking in a corner—she tried to figure out what to do. This was why she didn't let people get too close, why the only "friends" she had were at work or The Lemonade Stand.

Not only did it keep life manageable, safe, but she'd also realized that if she ever had to run again, having no one close, in any sense, would make it easier. Less complicated.

"Or we can do it another time," Tad said, his tone as relaxed as always. Hard to believe this laid-back guy was a decorated detective. In her experience with law enforcement personnel—and she had a lot of it growing up with her fire chief father—first responders were an intense bunch. Work hard, play hard.

Get mad just as hard, at least in her father's case.

"I'm cleaning house this morning," she said. What was she going to say? What reason could she give for not having him over that didn't make her sound crazy?

She'd been told, during her identity-change counseling,

to stick to the truth as much as possible to avoid mistakes. But the truth was, there was no real reason she couldn't have people over. Her counselors had also told her to live life as normally as possible.

She was…scared.

"But it's not a big place," she continued. Hallway, bath and the two bedrooms left to sweep and mop. "If… How does one sound?"

He offered to bring lunch.

She tried to demur, but failed. He offered Mexican. She and Ethan loved Mexican.

Clicking off her phone after giving him their order, she didn't feel hungry at all. In fact, she felt nauseous.

She pushed through the sensation. Picked up her broom. Took nice, even strokes down the hall.

She'd invited Tad Newberry further into their lives.

She was doing this for Ethan.

Who better than a man who was already protecting another little boy from domestic abuse to have around her son? To help fill the male void she'd been noticing. He'd been talking about Jimmy's father a lot.

The decision to have Tad around, just for a short time, was a good one for Ethan, she told herself as she finished with their small bathroom and moved into her bedroom, listening to her son sing a goofy rendition of a kid's song blaring from the player she'd given him for Christmas.

But she could only have Tad around if she made absolutely sure that Ethan understood that the detective was only in town for a while. And kept herself constantly apprised of that fact, as well.

Tad barely had a few seconds inside the quaint little cottage not far from the beach. The front door opened to him and he was whisked through a living area and out to a back patio before he'd even had a chance to say hello.

The place smelled like disinfectant mixed with lavender. The brown leather sectional had a patched spot on one arm; the recliner and coffee and end tables were dust-free but mismatched. Wall art, generic. Floors, ceramic tile with throw rugs. Nothing out of place. Kitchen off to the left, complete with a top-of-the-cupboard microwave and built-in dishwasher. All spotless.

"Hey, Mr. Newberry! Mom says we can play on my Windows tablet, which is so cool 'cause we can pass it back and forth, instead of the computer where I usually have to play." From a too-big chair at an outdoor table for four, the blue-eyed boy stared up at him, his brown hair shaggy and cute, not quite long enough to hang in his eyes. As before, he was in blue jeans and a T-shirt.

"That's *Detective* Newberry," Miranda said from right behind Tad. "What would you like to drink?"

Ethan had a glass half filled with red liquid in front of him, and a hint of pink mustache to go with it.

"I've got tea, bottled water or punch."

He chose the tea and, taking a seat on the eight-by-eight tiled patio, dug into the bag of food he'd brought, dispensing items according to the orders placed—burrito minus the sauce for Ethan, taco salad with sour cream for his mother. From the family-run taco joint down by the beach.

Tad went with the house specialty. Tacos.

"That's Mom's seat." Ethan's voice was softer than normal as he unwrapped his burrito.

Tad's fingers slowed on his own paper-covered food. "What?"

"You're in Mom's seat. She always sits there, and if I do, she makes me move."

He'd taken the seat with his back to the wall of the

house. He could see the door to the living area, and the small, nicely manicured, walled-in yard, too.

That was probably why she'd chosen it as her own. A woman who'd been scared enough to take on a new identity could experience a need to keep her back to the wall.

As quickly as possible, he moved, managing to resettle himself before Miranda returned.

Maybe what he was doing—ingratiating himself into their worlds—was duplicitous. Making him untrustworthy. He liked Miranda. Really liked her. More than he could remember ever liking a woman in such a short time. He couldn't tell her the truth about his mission, not yet, anyway. Not until he knew that his news wouldn't ruin her life again, upend her and cause her to start all over. From scratch. With a six-year-old child.

On the contrary, his goal was to make her life better. To take away her fear. To let her know she could live safely, free of the past.

He just wasn't at liberty to do that yet.

And didn't even want to think about it until he knew for certain that her ex-husband was dead. If he believed her, the man had been dead for years, but it wasn't like she was going to tell the truth. She'd told him the rehearsed story attached to her assumed identity. But as much as he trusted her father—his current employer—he wasn't a man who relied on the word of others. You never knew if someone had been given falsified proof.

He'd seen enough twists and turns in his career to make him wary. As recently as his last case—a man putting his own daughter's life at stake, preparing to kill the child while she stood there in his arms, crying…

"You need to watch me do this, Mr. Newberry," Ethan's young voice brought Tad fully back to the moment just as Miranda came outside with their drinks. "That way you'll learn for when you do your own and our animals can fight sometimes, too."

"Sorry, I had to brew more tea," Miranda said on the tail end of Ethan's words. "I added extra ice."

Which was quickly melting.

"And it's Detective Newberry, Ethan," she said again, sitting in her chair, unfolding a napkin and dropping it in her son's lap.

"I'd prefer Tad, if that's okay with you," he told her. Who knew if he was going to stay on as a detective when his leave was through?

Although he couldn't see himself being happy doing anything else.

"Is it okay, Mom? Can I call him Tad?"

Looking over the boy's head, Tad smiled at her.

She smiled back.

And lunch was good.

Chapter 5

It clearly wasn't Tad Newberry's first video game.

Nor had it seemed in any way a hardship for him to have his time engaged with Ethan's *Zoo Attack*. Miranda had lunch cleared away, the laundry finished, the dishwasher emptied, and brownies made before either of them seemed to notice that she'd left the table on the patio.

She only had one Saturday off a month and had to make it count—couldn't just sit and watch the "boys" play—but she caught herself smiling a few times as she heard the deep male voice coinciding with her son's little-boy enthusiasm. And heard the friendly dissension as they disagreed and ended up in battle. She was grinning from ear to ear as her son, with compassion in his voice, claimed victory.

She wasn't smiling so much that evening, though, when Ethan hit her up with a request to take his training wheels off his bike the next day.

"I'm done being a baby, Mom," he told her, his brow

furrowed as he gazed at her with those big blue eyes. Jeff's eyes. She'd never been able to resist Jeff's pleading. And the man definitely lived on in his son. "I'm the only kid in first grade with training wheels."

The fact that she'd known it was time didn't make her acquiescence any easier. Training wheels were a safety net. Miranda was already living more boldly than was comfortable for her. More risks weren't on her agenda.

You didn't get to choose when life handed you challenges. Jeff had certainly been proof of that. He'd been her best friend. The only person on earth who knew about the beatings. He'd been her rock. And when life had turned on him, she'd been his rock, too.

Which was why, at nine o'clock Sunday morning, after breakfast and dishes and making beds and washing up— and anything else she could come up with to stall—she was outside on the driveway of her rented haven, a screwdriver in hand, granting Jeff's son's request.

Jeff couldn't do it, so she had to.

Somehow. She'd had the wheels put on at the store two years earlier when she'd bought Ethan the bike for Christmas. They must have used a frickin' machine.

"Can't you do it, Mom?" Ethan asked, squatting down beside her and pushing his glasses up on his nose, as though staring at her incompetence would somehow get the baby wheels off his bike.

"Of course I can," she told him. "I just need some oil." Or some of whatever it was that helped loosen bolts. She'd read about it…

"Maybe you could call Tad," he said. "Or I can if you gimme the phone."

She wished it was the first—or even the fifth—time she'd heard the detective's name since he'd left the day before. But no…all afternoon, all night long, even that morning, Ethan had been talking about him.

Warning bells had been sounding so loudly in her head, it was a wonder she'd even heard her son's request—let alone finished the grocery and necessary-item shopping and then managed a trip to the movie theater with her son, followed by the fried chicken that he loved.

Trying to get his mind off Tad Newberry.

Didn't help that even when Ethan wasn't mentioning the guy, Miranda's mind was jabbering on about him.

Bike on its side, with the back wheel lodged between her feet, Miranda sat in the driveway and pulled on the wrench with all her might. It slipped off the bolt and slammed her in the knee.

She didn't swear out loud. Nor did she give up. She couldn't afford to do that. She stood. "Let's go." She got her keys and headed over to her car. Driver's license and credit card were already in the back pocket of her jeans.

She never stepped outside without the means to run, to take Ethan and disappear, if she had to.

"We going to take the bike back?" Ethan asked as she wheeled the bike out of their way.

"Nope, we're going to the store to find something to help us with the bolts." She'd look up on her phone what she needed when they got to the hardware store.

"Or we could just call Tad," Ethan said, under his breath and with a touch of belligerence.

She let that go, choosing her battles. "Tad's only going to be in town for a while, Ethan. I told you that already. We can be friends with him, but we can't ask for his help with stuff."

How did you explain life's hideous complications to a six-year-old?

"You could date him and then maybe he'd stay around."

"No, he wouldn't." *Make no mistake about that, little man.* Because she couldn't let him stay.

"He has an important job to go back to as soon as he's healed enough. Remember?"

Looking out the window he could barely see over, Ethan crossed his arms and harrumphed. "He doesn't act like he's hurt."

"Well, he is."

"How do you know?" She could feel those blue eyes turned on her.

"I'm a doctor's assistant. I'm trained to know." She almost mentioned having seen Tad's scars, but thought better of it. Remembering Danny's reaction, she couldn't take a chance that Ethan would share the seven-year-old's seeming fascination and ask to see for himself.

"But we can be friends," he said.

"Yep." Somewhere over the past six weeks, maybe even during the past twenty-four hours, she'd made that choice.

More like, it had been made for her.

"But we just can't need him, like, to fix my bike, right?"

"Right."

"Okay. Cool."

Tad had been burning with anger after he watched Miranda and Ethan drive away from their house. Livid with a man who'd father a child and then beat that boy's mother to the point that she'd feared for her life and run away from everyone she'd ever known or loved just to keep the two of them safe.

Anyone she'd have called to help when she couldn't get the training wheels off her son's bike had been left behind in North Carolina.

He hoped to God that Miranda's husband really was dead, as the chief had testified. For Miranda and Ethan's safety, first and foremost. And, he had to admit, so he wasn't tempted to go for the man's throat himself.

Out of his car, he was halfway between it and the bike leaning up against Miranda's little house, intending to get those training wheels off and be out of sight before she got back, when he stopped.

He was still a newcomer to the world of domestic violence, but after six weeks as an honorary member of the High Risk Team, in addition to all the reading he'd been doing since agreeing to work for Brian O'Connor, he knew he shouldn't fix that bike. A woman in Miranda's position, a woman who'd lived with daily fear, would be more likely to panic at the idea that someone had been on her property, messing with her stuff. The fact that this person knew she'd been struggling to get training wheels off her son's bike would tell her he'd been spying on her. Chances were she wouldn't see her benefactor as a Good Samaritan, but rather, someone who'd found her and intended to control her again. Someone who was letting her know he was stronger than she was. That she needed him.

If the panic was too intense, that act, something as simple as fixing a bike, could even prompt her to run again.

He was being paid to keep Miranda and Ethan in sight. To keep them safe. Not to fix bikes.

Back in his older-model SUV, he drove away before he had any other stupid ideas.

Miranda saw Danny again on Monday. She'd removed his stitches on Friday and Marie was worried about a puffy redness on one end of the incision that had been made during the surgery, which was done to repair the muscle tear he'd sustained during his fall.

"I'm fine," Danny said, when Miranda asked him how he was doing.

As soon as she had a look at the incision site she knew what the problem was.

Fear. Marie's fear.

Not infection. Or further physical damage. The scar area was pink, not red. A healthy pink.

Asking a nurse to come and stay with Danny in the exam room, and giving the boy a handheld learning-game device with the permission of his mother, Miranda led Marie down the hall to her office, closing the door behind them.

"What's wrong? Is it infected or is the injury worse than we thought? Does he need more surgery? Should Dr. Bennet take a look at him?"

Max Bennet, the pediatrician who'd hired Miranda as his PA even before she'd completed her training, would be a good person for Marie to talk to. But not about her son's leg.

"Danny's incision is fine, Marie."

"But shouldn't Dr. Bennet take a look, just in case?"

Picking up her phone, Miranda sent a quick text to Max, who responded immediately.

"He's going in now, if you'd like to meet him down there," she said to the worried mom.

Her furrowed brow smoothing out, Marie shook her head. "He'll let you know if there's a problem, right?"

"He'll text either way."

"You called me in here to talk to you—separate from Danny—and since there's nothing wrong with his incision…" The other woman's words trailed off.

Miranda nodded, words tripping over themselves as they fought for release, while, for the most part, she was forced to remain silent.

For the most part.

"Danny's leg hurting…we know it's going to." She started

slowly. "Surgery let us put the fibers back together, but there'll still be scars. We talked about how the nervous system sends messages when muscles have been compromised, inflaming the area to protect weak fibers, shortening the fibers…"

Marie gave a quick nod. "Rehabilitation is all scheduled, and we'll be there on time, every time," she said.

"Good."

"I just… I'm so scared, you know? Danny—he's all I have. I should've gotten him out sooner and now he's hurt, and Devon might try to take him from me and… I'm sorry. I shouldn't have wasted your time today."

Marie was in daily counseling through The Lemonade Stand. She didn't need Miranda to work through all the issues with her. Nor was Miranda professionally qualified to do that.

"I know," she said now, making a silent choice that she prayed she wouldn't regret. But what was the value of her life if she couldn't use her experiences to help others? She'd needed to speak to Marie since she'd first heard her story. "And that's why I called you in here. Fear is insidious. The thoughts it drives can consume you to the point of interrupting your ability to cope with daily life. The stronger those thoughts get, the more real they seem…"

Danny was only a year older than Ethan.

If Miranda hadn't left when she did, her son could so easily have been that little boy sitting down the hall. Or worse.

Her father had been after Ethan, just as Devon was after Danny.

"I know I'm being paranoid, and I'm sorry…"

"No, no, don't apologize," Miranda said, leaning forward with both hands on her small desk, in her small office, as she looked at the woman in the folding chair across from her. "What I wanted to tell you, still want to tell you, is that I understand. And that…anytime you have a concern, even if you pretty much know that it's just fear, you're welcome to call me. At home."

Taking a card from the holder on the front of her desk, she wrote her cell number on it. "Anytime," she said, handing Marie the card. "Sometimes you have to hear a professional opinion to stop the fear," she added. "You couldn't trust your own mind because you knew that someone else had manipulated it, that it played with you.

"I don't want you to put off calling the doctor, or to have to wait for the office to open, nor do I want you to run up medical expenses with urgent care and emergency room visits. Of course, if it's an emergency, go! But if you're not sure, even if it's the middle of the night—call me."

Staring at the card, looking like she was fighting tears, Marie didn't reach for it. "I can't do that," she said instead. "I can't bother you like that."

"I want you to." To communicate how intensely she meant those words, she laid her hand on Marie's, then turned both hands over and placed the card in Marie's exposed palm, closing her fingers around it.

"I have to do this on my own…" Marie's words were a trembling whisper.

"Some of it, yes." Miranda knew she might be overstepping a line between professional and personal, but she wasn't sure that mattered.

Not in this case.

"But you also have to know when to accept help," she said, realizing that she was speaking to herself, as well.

"Why?" Marie's eyes were moist as she looked at her. "Why would you do this? You've got your own life. You don't need patients, or mothers of patients, waking you up in the middle of the night because they're afraid…"

Miranda told herself to come up with some platitude. Quickly.

She couldn't break the promise she'd made to herself never to screw up again.

Couldn't speak of the past she'd left, ever. Doing so could expose her to someone talking to someone else who happened to be talking to someone who'd once known a woman named Dana and was looking for her...

"Just please...if your mind starts to play tricks with you, if you start getting paranoid that something's wrong with you or Danny, if he sneezes and you worry that he could be getting pneumonia, don't get scared. Don't let fear take over your senses. Call me instead."

"I don't..."

"Think of me as your weapon in that particular battle," Miranda said, finding strength out of nowhere. "Fear seems all-powerful, but the truth is, it buckles and evaporates when you stand up to it. Calling me is the way you look that particular fear right in the eye."

Marie needed an arsenal. She'd collect it one weapon at a time, to face down one fear at a time.

Just as Miranda had.

And she'd need to carry it with her for the rest of her life, too. Because although fear slithered away, it always waited, out of sight, to strike again.

Chapter 6

The Santa Raquel High Risk Team was meeting every Tuesday in a conference room at the police station—for those who could make it or had news to share. Eventually the meetings would taper back down to once a month, but while the team was building, they were keeping in close contact.

In jeans and a striped shirt, with the sleeves rolled to his elbows, Tad sat and listened. He wasn't an official member of the team, although he had his moment to report that during his dozen drive-bys of Danny Williams, he'd noticed nothing untoward. Everyone, including Danny's mother, Marie, was following established protocol.

Sara Havens Edwin, a licensed professional clinical counselor, head counselor at The Lemonade Stand, looked relieved, and Tad nodded in her direction. In a private conversation, Sara had informed him that one of the biggest concerns in a situation like the Williamses', one of the greatest threats to life was Marie herself. She not only loved her husband, but she'd been manipulated by him since high school. She was driven from within to keep him happy.

Miranda had her turn, too, telling everyone about Marie's visit to her office the morning before, leaving out specific medical information that wasn't pertinent to the case, but letting them know that while Marie had been concerned about her son's wound, the boy's healing was completely on track. There'd been no sign of any other injury. Sara took notes on that, too.

A few minutes of administrative discussion took place then. A new email loop was being set up; contact information was dispersed. Funding was mentioned, finances appropriated. He listened, but found himself paying more attention to the little park benches with primary-colored rainbows over them that dotted the scrub top Miranda was wearing.

They dipped and fell with the shape of her breasts and he knew he shouldn't be noticing that. Tried not to. And looked again.

Her breasts weren't the only ones in the room. And he wasn't the type of guy who generally went around noticing them in any case. A shapely, curved butt was his more usual distraction. But those rainbow-covered breasts across from him... They were so captivating. Like the woman.

Miranda's ability to nurture flowed from her with every breath. And he kept wondering how it would feel to lay his head on her breasts.

Wrong. Wrong, Newberry. Wrong. Wrong. Wrong.

They'd be soft, with hard nipples. Womanly softness with a core of strength.

And they'd smell like flowers.

Because she did. Something in her soap, probably. Or whatever lotion she used.

When he started envisioning himself rubbing lotion onto her back, into her shoulders and the sensitive parts of her neck, he sat forward. Brought his thoughts to a screeching halt—to catch her watching him stare at her breasts.

Their charged gazes held for a second.

How could something so not good feel so great?

Tad wasn't feeling too great half an hour later as he sat with Miranda over coffee in a shop they'd visited several times before. Others had been there with them, the last of them just leaving.

"Let's move to a smaller table," he suggested when she didn't get up with the others. He was pleased she'd stayed, but the look on her face didn't bode well. Something was bothering her.

And since she'd been fine until the others left, he was pretty certain that something had to do with him.

Or rather, his wandering eyes. He'd screwed up. Badly. Bringing sexual awareness into the workplace. He of all people. Back home, at the station, he'd developed a reputation for being the one guy who hadn't fallen under the spell of a young female cop who'd apparently joined the force to find herself a husband in uniform, not to serve and protect.

He'd also refused friendly advances from a forensic specialist he'd actually liked a lot because he knew better than to bring sex into work.

Letting Miranda pick the table, he followed her to a two-seater in the far corner, and his mood dropped another notch. He was supposed to be gaining her trust, not losing it. For her own safety. And because he'd given his word to a man he trusted.

It wasn't about the money. It had never been about the money for him—not one day of his working life.

He had to fix this.

"I'm sorry," he said the second they were seated across from each other at a table so small he had to turn so his knees weren't touching hers.

Absolutely *no* touching. He had fences to mend, not further destroy.

"I was completely out of line, but I swear to you, I've never, ever had a problem keeping personal and work separated."

Miranda's frown made her look smart rather than confused. Assessing rather than seeking. "I'm sorry, did I miss something? What are you talking about?" She sipped from her half-full cup of latte, which had to be getting cold.

His straight-up black had been gone a quarter of an hour after they'd arrived. An espresso sounded good. He wasn't used to all the sitting in his car staring out at life that he'd been doing these past six weeks. If nothing else, the time off was letting him know that much as he loved detective work, he wasn't cut out to be a private investigator.

He was more of an action type of cop. Following leads. Hunting down the bad guys.

Not being one of them. "You and I… I appreciate the chance to learn about the High Risk Team, to help out while I'm here. I might have crossed a line and—" He stopped. "Uh, I want to tell you that—"

He broke off as she shook her head, and then looked him straight in the eye. "If anyone crossed a line, it was me, Tad. Letting my son talk you into playing video games with him…"

"I thoroughly enjoyed myself. I was kind of hoping for a rematch," he said. She thought *she* was the one being inappropriate?

"He is, too," she said. But she wasn't smiling. So he wasn't getting his hopes up. Or his worries, either.

He had to talk to her father. His current boss. To let him know he could be developing feelings for his daughter, so the chief had a chance to get him off the case before anything happened between them.

And then he'd lose his reputation for good. Lose any chance of resuming his career in North Carolina, and possibly anywhere else depending on how the internal investigation into his last case went down.

"I told Ethan I'd talk to you about it," she said, surprising him further. "But...this is all so awkward, you know? You haven't even asked me out, or hinted that you wanted to, and it feels like we're having 'the talk' or something."

"I'd say apologizing for possibly crossing a line could be construed as a hint." What the hell was he doing?

"So maybe it's a little complicated, huh?"

"Maybe." He should be walking away. Instead he was leaning in. Smiling at her. "I'm attracted to you."

He wasn't going to lie to this woman any more than he had to. She'd had enough hell in her life. Had already had a man betray her trust in the worst possible way.

"Yeah." She glanced away, licked her lips in a completely natural manner that turned him on, although it clearly wasn't meant as a come-on, and looked back at him. "I told you I haven't been on a date since Ethan's father died. What I didn't tell you was that..."

He waited, not even breathing. Was she going to tell him that the man had beaten her so badly, terrorized her so horrifically, she'd had to change her identity to get away from him?

Would she tell him the man's real name so he could verify his death and know for himself that she was safe?

He couldn't tell her who he really was without her father's say-so, not at that point, but if he could at least be certain that the fiend who'd hurt this woman was definitely gone, he'd be a whole lot happier.

"Well, the truth is, I haven't even been attracted to anyone…"

Becaauuusse…

"Which is probably why I'm behaving like such an imbecile right now," she finished, running the rim of her finger around the edge of her coffee cup.

Had she just told him she was attracted to him? Replaying the last minute or so without his own inner dialogue, he was pretty sure she had.

And while he was disappointed that she wasn't confiding in him, he was relieved, too. Anytime she spoke to anyone about her past, she opened herself up to the possibility of being found.

He was glad to know that Miranda was taking good care of herself and Ethan.

"We're attracted to each other," he said, adding a lightness to his tone he didn't feel. "We should drink to that. Can I get you another coffee?" He stood, needing that espresso in the worst way.

"Another latte?" she asked, gazing up at him, as though she'd just asked for a whole lot more and was confident he'd deliver.

He wanted to.

But was equally sure he couldn't. Not yet.

One thing was for certain. His weekly call with the man paying his rent couldn't come fast enough. Maybe he'd break protocol and move the conversation up by a few days.

Maybe.

Standing at the coffee bar, Tad was mostly just eager to get back to the beautiful woman waiting for him at the table in the corner.

Miranda's stomach was in knots. Her hands shook. It didn't seem to matter that she'd made up her mind two days ago to have this talk with Tad Newberry, or that she'd rehearsed how it would go.

He'd looked her in the eye and told her he was attracted to her. Okay, not a major occurrence in the larger scheme of things, but in her world, it was a huge first. A guy she had the hots for thought *she* was hot.

In her old life, that had never happened. After all the counseling she'd had, she understood that the feminine part of her, the part that controlled things like budding sexual attraction, had been shut down by her father's abusive treatment. Her defenses against men, against trusting men, had been acute ever since.

And now?

Now she had to have the conversation she'd set out to have. Regardless of how her belly flip-flopped and her crotch got warm as she watched Tad walk back to her.

She thanked him for the coffee. Took a sip to distract herself while he sat down. No need for her to glom on to his fly while it hung there at eye level.

This situation was not going to get out of control. She couldn't let it.

Wouldn't let it.

"I'm not looking for a relationship," she said as soon as the sting of hot coffee subsided from her tongue. "No matter how I feel about someone, I'm not going to hook up, period. At least not until Ethan is older."

There. She'd done her deed. And if it meant he walked

out of here and avoided her the rest of the months he was in town, so be it.

All the better, really. Meant she didn't have to be on her guard around him. Constantly fighting the insane need she had to feel his lips on hers.

To know how his tongue felt against hers.

When she and Jeff had conceived Ethan, they'd tried to kiss first, but had ended up laughing, instead.

Tad was still sitting there. Studying her. "Good to know," he said, leaving her with a strong desire to be privy to every single one of his thoughts.

"You're only here for, what, another nine months, at most?"

No. That hadn't come out right. As though, if he was willing to hang around, she might change her mind.

There could be no hint of possibility here. No cracks in any doors or windows through which he might slip.

"At most," he told her. He'd leaned back in his chair, was sitting partially sideways so that one arm was on the table, the other hanging off the corner of his chair. As though he didn't have a care in the world.

But the way he watched her…assessing…made her nervous. Like he was seeing more than she could ever allow.

This was a bad idea. Worse even than she'd feared.

What if she let something slip? Some little nugget of a fact that made him curious…

No.

She stopped that thought, too. She was *not* going to let paranoia take over again. She'd won that battle. Wasn't going to let fear and suspicion get close enough to have to fight them again.

At least not if she could see it coming.

Since returning to the table, Tad had contributed nothing to their conversation. If she wasn't still humming inside from his admission that he was attracted to her, preceded by an apology for "crossing a line," and followed by his backhanded admission that he wanted to ask her out, she might be able to convince herself that they had nothing to talk about.

That she'd been worried for nothing.

"I told Ethan we can be friends, the three of us, you and me, you and him, but that we can't *need* each other for things. Or rely on each other," she said in a rush.

Half hoping he'd miss the "you and me" part of that. And yet fearing he would.

"I'd like to be friends." He rested both arms on the table again, and she could hardly comprehend how relieved she felt. Almost giddy with it. Like she had to laugh out loud. And maybe cry a little, too.

"All three of us, me and Ethan and you and me," he added.

And she started to tremble.

Chapter 7

In the spirit of friendship, with a phone call to North Carolina lurking in his very near future, Tad asked Miranda how her weekend had gone.

He knew she'd gotten the training wheels off Ethan's bike. The boy had been riding like a pro when Tad had checked on them later that afternoon. He'd found a place around the corner from them where he could park and still see their house between the other houses. And when he drove down the street behind them, he could keep tabs, too.

At first, watching them had felt good. Righteous. He was keeping them safe. But the more he got to know them, the less great he felt. The cause was important.

Still, did the end always justify the means?

The sixty-four-million-dollar question of his life these days.

The question Internal Affairs was pondering on his behalf.

"Ethan kept asking me to call you on Sunday." She'd been talking about a movie she and her son had seen and that Ethan had wanted him to see, too. With them.

"You should have."

"I'm sure you have things to do."

The things he was being paid to do were much easier when he was spending time with her.

"I do a lot of sitting around," he told her. "In meetings, in my car... I'm finding I'm not all that good at it."

"You want to be out saving the world," she said. He noticed a difference in her tone. Not necessarily negative, but...different. *Aware.*

And he figured he understood why. "You know someone like that?" he asked.

Her father.

The man, a true hero, must have been an incredible parent. Growing up with someone who was willing to take risks over and over again, to fight the hard fights selflessly, must have been remarkable. Such an inspiration. With Tad's father's defection from their family when Tad was just a baby, Tad had been the man in his family his whole life. He'd been all his mom and older sister had for protection.

And he'd failed them.

Just as Miranda's husband had failed her.

"Not personally, I don't," Miranda said, with no hint of subterfuge. "But since you were hurt on the job, I'm guessing you didn't make your living sitting at a desk. I imagine that for someone like you, who usually works in dangerous situations, it would be difficult to have, as the highlight of your day, driving around checking up on a little boy."

Her blue eyes were filled with warmth, and they directed her nurturing to him; he sucked it in like a man dying of thirst.

"But you must realize that what you're doing is far more than being ready in case Danny's in trouble," she continued. "You being out there, watching, gives Marie extra strength, too. And it reminds her that she can't give in and contact Devon because everyone would know and he'd be the one in trouble if he came around. She might not be able to protect herself, but she's been programmed to protect him."

The insight struck him hard. He'd been doing a lot of reading on domestic violence over the past three months. And gained more understanding in five minutes of conversation with Miranda. Her experience spoke to him.

Probably more than she knew.

Or maybe because *he* knew.

"She's at possibly the most critical point in her life," Miranda was saying, her voice low as she leaned closer to him. Tad could feel her intensity.

"If she makes it through this total break, if she can stay out from under Devon's mental control long enough to free her own thoughts from him again, to counteract his voice in her head, then she'll be able to work on recovery and building a new and happy life."

He felt like he'd just slipped a bit deeper into Miranda's own psyche. Wanted to be there. But only with her permission.

"I'll do whatever I can to help," he told her. And added, "If there's more I can do, please let me know."

He'd do whatever it took to help Marie stay out of harm's way. To help her win this victory over evil. And if he got any insights into how he could help Miranda as well, all the better.

"I will," she said. "I know that when you came to see Danny at the office, that really helped."

Dropping his pants, she meant. He'd relived that one a

dozen or more times in the days since, mostly with mortification.

But he wasn't sure he'd do anything differently…

Ends and means and all that stuff.

"If I tell you something, do you think you can keep it to yourself?" she asked.

"Of course." What else could he say? The more of her secrets he knew, the better he'd be prepared to protect her.

Not that she was in any danger. He'd just feel relieved knowing firsthand that her husband was really gone.

"When Marie was in the office the other day I gave her my personal cell number," she told him. She sipped from the coffee he'd pretty much forgotten was there. But she met his gaze—standing up for the choice she'd made. Standing by it.

"Paranoia can be a lasting result of being a victim of domestic violence. When your trust is betrayed on such an intimate level—"

She broke off, and he needed to take her hands in his, or preferably, take her in his arms, let her know he'd die before he allowed anyone to hurt her again.

"I'll keep an eye on her, too, if you'd like." There was only so much he could do for Miranda at the moment. But he could help Marie get through the things he hadn't been there to help Miranda with. The first steps of the difficult journey to freedom.

Surprisingly, Miranda shook her head. "If she found out, it could do more harm than good," she said. "The point is for her to learn to trust herself. To be able to rely on herself, on her own strengths. To discern the difference between being dependent and asking for help. No one's good at everything. She needs to do all she can, and to know when she needs help and then ask for it."

He got that. More than he ever had before.

And thinking of her son's training wheels two days before, he wondered where Miranda was in the process.

"That's why I gave her my number," she told him. "It's not illegal or wrong or anything for me to do that, but it does go outside normal medical protocol. I just saw a chance to give her a tool to help her fight her demons and knew I had to do it."

And she was telling him this because…

She didn't trust herself all the time? Would she ever?

Even when you won the battle and became a survivor instead of a victim, did you ever fully lose the sense of having been there once? Did anyone?

Life shaped people. Changed them.

"I think it's great that you did that," he told Miranda now, meaning the words. She'd been dealt a horrendous hand, and she'd saved herself.

So much for needing the protection he kept trying to assure himself he was giving her. Truth was, maybe he needed to give it to her more than she needed to get it from him.

"I just hope she uses it," Miranda said, and then smiled at him. "This is nice," she added. "Being friends."

"You want to have a friendly dinner sometime this week? Maybe give me another shot at becoming a zoo-keeper your son can't easily obliterate?"

She hesitated, and he fell a little flat. "Or not."

"No." Miranda sat up straighter, took a visible deep breath. "I mean, yes, let's talk about that. I… I'm pretty odd about my house," she said. "I…don't invite people over. I know, it's weird, but being a single mom , you never know who you can trust, and I've always kept our home a safe place. You know, where it's just the two of us."

He remembered the way she'd rushed him through to the backyard on Saturday.

"I could invite you to my apartment," he told her. "It's not much, but there's a kitchen and a TV where we could hook up the game."

"No. I'm just being…"

Paranoid?

"Maybe it's time to open up Ethan's world a bit more. To expose us both to a society that's been good to us. Let me check my schedule and get back to you with a night. Would that work?"

Let me think about it, he translated.

"Sure," he said with a shrug. "I'm available."

"Do you like baked spaghetti?"

"Who doesn't?"

"It's one of Ethan's favorites. I'm off early on Thursday because I work Saturday this week. We could do it Thursday night."

"Does this mean you've already checked your schedule?" He grinned at her.

She grinned back. "Smart-ass."

Miranda had to go back to work, and he wanted to get in a workout at the gym before heading over to Danny's school for his afternoon watch. He walked Miranda to her car, moved on down to his own, but didn't unlock it until he'd watched her drive out of the parking lot and out of sight.

He'd never admired a woman, wanted a woman, as much as he did her. For the first time since his sister was murdered, something mattered to Tad more than getting the bad guys off the streets.

Suddenly, seeing a woman—and her young son—happy was what mattered more.

Marie and Danny's safety mattered most, certainly. Absolutely.

They had an entire team of people helping them. He was proud to be among them.

But his mission was much more personal, too.

It was time for Miranda Blake to be free to become Dana O'Connor again. To return to the father who adored her. The life she'd been forced to leave behind.

To be free from the past that clearly still haunted her.

She'd won her battle; now it was time to come home from the war.

Chapter 8

Miranda waited until Wednesday night to tell Ethan that Tad would be coming for dinner on Thursday. Purely for self-preservation. She needed to have her own thoughts securely in place before dealing with her son's barrage.

Was she doing the right thing? Could she have someone in their home without somehow revealing any piece of their past that might help someone find them?

Would someone approach Tad in town, someone he thought she knew, and ask him some innocuous question? He might well answer, unknowingly, with something that could expose her. Her father's superhuman ways opened any possibility.

She'd been told to live a normal life. Had saved nothing from her past. Nothing. No pictures. Not even the fourteen-karat gold heart charm Jeff had given her the day she'd told him she was pregnant. A symbol of the love he felt for her, and the love she'd given him. The love they'd created in their baby, through their baby. He'd told her that whenever she doubted her worth or questioned herself, to hold on to that charm and talk to him—promising that he'd hear her from wherever he was and find a way to answer her.

The night she'd run, she'd taken a side trip back to college and buried the charm alongside Jeff's grave, thinking that maybe, someday, when Ethan was grown, she could take him there, tell him the truth about the wonderful man who'd fathered him and give him the charm.

Was it wrong to steal a moment of happiness for herself by inviting Tad over again? Was she risking Ethan's life?

Or was she hurting it by keeping them cloistered? Would her son grow up being afraid of the world?

He'd gone to bed ecstatic Wednesday night. And had jabbered about dinner the next evening, wanting to know what she was going to make, suggesting that she bake brownies, too, and asking if he could have a night off from homework.

She'd made the brownies as soon as she got home on Thursday. Crossed her fingers that there'd be no homework, and if there was that they could get it done quickly. She was smiling as she waited in her usual spot outside Ethan's school that afternoon. As she'd cooked and cleaned her way through the early afternoon, she'd had a long talk with herself. And maybe with Jeff, too. Listening to his voice in her mind, telling her how smart and capable she was.

Of all the friends he could've had in college, he'd chosen her—a normal-looking, quiet, shy loner—to hang out with. Jeff had always seen something in her she'd never seen herself.

"I don't like Tad and I don't want him to come over for dinner." Ethan's words were spewing out before he'd even climbed into the front seat beside her. His glasses made his eyes look bigger as he turned them on her. "You have to call him and tell him he can't come," the boy said, and then shoved his backpack on the floor at his feet and sat there, arms crossed, with his lower lip jutting out like it did when he was trying not to cry.

Heart thumping, Miranda went immediately into calm mode. "Why? What did he do?"

"I thought he was *my* friend. Our friend. But he's friends with any old boy."

"I don't understand," Miranda said, her tone filled with the love the little guy drew from the depths of her. She ignored the other cars and kids milling around outside her vehicle.

"I saw him," Ethan said. "He was here, on the other side, where they play baseball. At recess. I thought he came to see me, but when I started to run over to him, some other kid went over and Tad didn't even see me. Or wave. He just talked to that other kid for our whole recess and then... I don't know what. Maybe took him for ice cream or something."

"What other kid?" Miranda's senses were on alert for an entirely different reason now. She'd known Ethan and Danny Williams went to the same school; it was a big school and the boys were in different grades.

"I dunno." Her son's chin was down by his chest, and she had to fight the need to pull him close and rock him against her as she had when he was smaller.

"I'm sure, since the other boy was at recess, too, he couldn't just leave school. Do you really think Tad took him for ice cream?" she asked, seeing so many complications and not knowing what to tackle first, or at all.

"No."

"So you think Tad shouldn't have any friends but you?"

"I dunno."

"But you know, people care about more than one person. Jimmy likes more kids than just you and you like more than just him."

"He's only a little kid like me."

"You liked Tad, and that didn't mean you didn't still like me, right?" As she tried to assuage her son's hurt feelings, it occurred to her that she'd failed him in a way she hadn't seen coming, focusing only on her work and on him, giving him unrealistic expectations of the adults in his life. Few as there were…

"I dunno," he said again. "I thought he was *my* friend."

Kids' feelings got hurt. It was all part of growing up.

Maybe some of them were better acclimated by the time they were six. More exposed to human interaction. Probably most of them had to share the caregivers in their lives. And they'd likely had more than one.

In an effort to keep Ethan safe, she'd sheltered him, figuring he'd have his own interaction with others when he started school. When he was old enough to protect himself. Or at least tell someone if he was hurt or afraid.

She'd had it all planned out. Had him prepared and…

You'd think, given that, he'd be jealous of sharing *her*, not jealous of Tad being friends with another boy.

The way he'd taken to Tad—the first person she'd shown real warmth to in front of him, other than the professionals with whom they came in contact…

Could be this wasn't so much a relationship thing as it was a "daddy" issue. Having a man around.

She had no idea what to do about that at the moment. How to explain…any of it.

"You said you wanted me to go on a date, right?"

"Yes, but not with him. Not anymore."

"It's a little late for that," she told him. "I already invited him over. And he's planning to be a successful zookeeper tonight." Dealing with children was her forte. Not only because of her training, but because it somehow came naturally to her.

Still, she felt completely, uncharacteristically, lost.

"Can you do me a favor and be nice to him? Just for tonight?" Give her time to figure out how to handle the newest bump in their road. She'd known bigger bumps were coming. Had been as prepared as one could be when facing the unknown.

"I dunno."

"He wants to see you, Ethan. He really likes you."

When Ethan looked at her, she could see tears in his eyes. "Then why didn't he notice me?"

"Did you ever think about asking him? You say you want to be his friend, but what kind of friend just gets mad and cuts you off without at least asking you about what hurt him?"

She had to text Tad. Give him a heads-up. Maybe sort this one out between the two of them before he arrived for dinner.

Telling Ethan the truth—that Danny was a victim of domestic violence, that his own father had threatened to kill Danny's mother and had tried to force Danny to leave with him, that Tad was on the team that was protecting him—was out.

Shouldn't be such a hard thing, lying to her son, with her whole life built on lies. And it still made her sick.

Tad wasn't afraid of storming into an office to face a man with a loaded gun. Didn't think twice about knocking down a door behind which men were waiting with weapons. He'd faced off against an assailant who had a bomb.

And he put off calling Miranda's father until Thursday afternoon. A lot could happen between Tuesday and Thursday. No point in borrowing trouble.

A couple of hours before he was supposed to show up for dinner, he was looking forward to the evening so much he knew trouble had arrived.

Pacing between the sock drawer in his bedroom and the living area of his small quarters, he gazed out at the ocean in the distance, listening to the ring on the other end of the line. Two and then three rings, although the chief always picked up on the first.

On Fridays, he expected Tad's call.

Figuring he was going to voice mail, knowing he couldn't leave a message, Tad shoved a hand into the pocket of his jeans—the black ones again—and repeatedly flexed his injured thigh muscle. Focusing on the exercise. Counting the squeezes.

"Is there a problem?"

To date the man had always answered his phone "Chief O'Connor." Every time.

"No."

"I was in a meeting."

"I'm sorry, sir." He didn't like feeling chastised and considered hanging up.

Let the chief wait until the next day to hear from him at their usual time.

"No. No, I'm the one who's sorry. I apologize. When I saw the number come up I got a bit tense. It's difficult not being able to handle this myself. To be there if there's an emergency. Please, forgive me."

Defenses immediately lowered, replaced by the respect the chief had earned from Tad, he walked out to his balcony, feeling a chill in the April air. The sun would be warm. It wasn't shining on his side of the building. He got the morning sun.

"I apologize for the unplanned contact," he said now. "I have a situation I need to run by you. Probably should've done that before now. I have a…meeting tonight and if you'd rather I didn't go, I need you to tell me."

"I told you before—you have free rein there. Whatever it takes to keep them in sight. To keep me apprised of their activities. To keep them safe."

"Your daughter and her son are befriending me."

"Good! Better than good. That's great. I couldn't have hoped for better." At his superior's enthusiasm, Tad squirmed. "The more inside you can get with them, the better you'll be able to protect them on the off chance that some of her ex's family is a danger to us. Or if she gets spooked and runs again."

"About that, sir. Have you actually found his family? Do we know if they pose a danger?"

"Some of them have been located. Others haven't. At least one, a brother, could pose a potential danger. We need to keep things status quo for now."

"If you give me the man's name, I can do some checking from here. It's what I do best. Investigate. Find clues. Put pieces together. Track down what others can't find. I've got the time."

"I appreciate your willingness, Newberry. I've got someone else, equally capable, working on this."

Yeah, the chief's eggs-in-different-baskets philosophy was frustrating the hell out of him.

And would be, even if he wasn't dangerously close to getting personally involved in this one.

"The thing is, sir, Miranda… Dana…has given some indication that there could be interest in a liaison between the two of us. I need you to know that I'm… I care about her. She's everything you'd want her to be and more."

A lot like the chief in terms of selflessly offering help to others. The way, for instance, she'd given Marie her phone number, telling the struggling woman to call day or night…

"Fine. That's fine, Detective. Your honesty serves you well. I've been following your IA review, and your integrity has come through loud and clear. Whether you resume your position with your current department or not, the state of North Carolina will definitely have a place for you at the end of your sabbatical."

But this wasn't about him. About his future. Though, maybe for some, it would be.

"They've invited me to have dinner in their home tonight." *In their home.* Just the three of them.

"I couldn't be more pleased. I knew you were the right man for the job. Just…treat her well, okay? If you feel something for her, then that's good, go with it. If not, don't let it go so far she gets hurt. I'll be looking forward to a more complete report on my grandson during our call tomorrow."

Had the chief just given him the go-ahead to sleep with his daughter? As long as he cared about her? It sure sounded that way to Tad. He'd been about to clarify when the chief was interrupted and ended the call.

Tad wasn't going to have sex with Miranda. Didn't think it was a good plan. But getting closer to her, maybe even close enough to hold her…

Shaking his head, he returned the burner phone to the sock in the drawer, grabbed the button-down shirt he usually wore with the black jeans, lined up the hanger with the others and shut his closet door.

He'd never done undercover work, but had a pretty good idea of what it felt like. And figured he'd been right to steer clear of that option in his career. *Complicated* was all in a day's work for him. Mixing life with the job, though… not his thing.

He could quit. He'd found the chief's daughter. Could tell him to hire another man to watch over her.

That possibility had merit. He hated it, but it had merit.

The cell phone in his back pocket sounded an incoming text from the woman who was never far from his thoughts these days. So much so that he'd given Miranda her own ringtones—separate ones for text and calls.

Everything okay with Danny and Marie?

Had Marie called her? His adrenaline sped up. Devon Williams had been spotted near Marie's house that afternoon by a police patrol. Not close enough to disobey the restraining order, but enough that a notice had been sent out.

Had he violated his order, after all? Approached Marie?

As far as I know, they're fine. Why?

Get the facts, then act.

Ethan saw you with Danny at school today.

He quickly explained that he'd been asked to make visual contact with Danny just as a precaution and had waved at the boy, who'd actually come over to ask him a question about running with a hurt leg.

Guess you were right, the visit to your office went well, he finished. It felt good, sharing a victory with her, small as it might be.

A heads-up. Ethan's feelings were hurt. Thinks you chose Danny over him.

So much for feeling good.

What did you say to him? he texted back.

He paced back to the living area, to the balcony, as he awaited her response. The job wasn't supposed to be this emotional roller coaster he'd been on for the past couple of weeks. It was supposed to be his head fully engaged, not his heart.

After his sister's death, Tad had made it that way. He was going to be a positive influence on the world. A help, not a hindrance.

And he was never, ever going to love anyone again as much as he'd loved Steffie.

Told him to ask you. Sorry. I passed the buck, came the eventual response. And then, I drew a blank. Can't tell him who Danny is or why you know him.

He read her response twice.

Why not?

Seemed to him that telling her son about Danny might be smart. If the boy knew that sometimes kids were in danger from family members, it would give him an awareness he might need if any of his father's family came looking for him.

Chief O'Connor had mentioned one family member of Ethan's father who could pose a risk, and that had been on the edge of his consciousness since the second he'd heard it. Made him anxious to get to dinner and have a closer look at Miranda's house. To make sure she had dead bolts, the windows were all securely latched. That…

He'd look at it all. He'd add more watch time, too. He'd been loitering around enough to be familiar with the neighborhood, to recognize her neighbors as they came and went.

He's only six. He doesn't need to know about the seedier side of life yet.

He disagreed. Completely. Given her circumstances— about which he supposedly knew nothing.

But he got her message. He wasn't supposed to say anything about Danny's situation to Ethan.

Telling himself he'd find a discreet way to approach the topic with her, Tad settled for, Got it. And thanks for the heads-up.

Her response was almost immediate. Thanks. Complete with a smile emoji.

Chapter 9

She had to do this. Not only for herself and Ethan, but for all those who came after her. For Marie and the Maries yet to come.

She had to be proof that life existed after domestic violence—even when the threat was so severe you had to run for your life. Others might not know her circumstances, but by living a happy, fulfilled life, she could teach others to do the same. She could teach with confidence.

Sometimes confidence was as much a factor in helping someone as facts were.

And someday, with life following a natural progression, her father and the threat he posed would be gone. Then she could use her story as an example to others.

Thoughts firmly stationed, she watched the clock, her stomach filled with butterflies as Tad's arrival drew close.

She'd originally planned for them to spend the majority of the early-evening get-together out on the patio, but the wind had kicked up, chilling the air, so she'd had to give up on that option.

Inside the cottage it was. She'd set the table in the small-ish eating area off the kitchen. Ethan and Tad could play *Zoo Attack* from the game box controller attached to the living room TV. She'd cleaned the bathroom in the hall. And shut both bedroom doors. For privacy, not because they weren't equally spotless.

In skinny jeans, a dark blue tank and a white, mostly see-through top with three-quarter-length sleeves, she examined her appearance one more time as she did a last check on the bathroom. She'd left her hair down, happy with the natural waves for once, and the rest… She'd never been a heavy makeup kind of girl. Basic foundation, a hint of eyeliner and that was it.

A thrill of anticipation swept through her as she caught her eye in the mirror. She was hoping that Tad really was attracted to her.

As much as that scared her, considering her secrets, it also felt good. Damned good. Her escape from hell wasn't a success unless she and Ethan lived a normal life. Anything less made her remain a victim trapped by the fear of further abuse.

Back out in the living room, she noticed that her son hadn't budged from his cross-legged position in front of the TV, where he was cleaning up his zoo, when the doorbell sounded.

"Remember, if you want to have a friend, you have to be a friend," she told him quietly as she passed, bending down to kiss the top of his head, hoping he'd lighten up and let the whole Danny thing go.

Either way, she knew that Tad wasn't going to tell her son about Danny's abuse. She hadn't run three thousand miles, given up everything she'd had, everything she'd known, to have her young son exposed to domestic violence. In time, when he was older and his psyche had been formed with loving family values…then she'd tell him.

Ethan didn't lighten up. On the contrary, he was pretty much a brat. A child Miranda didn't recognize as he insinuated himself between Tad and her, interrupting any time the two of them started a conversation, and refusing to answer Tad when he spoke to him directly.

Tad had been in their home less than ten minutes, and the evening was a disaster.

"Maybe I should go," he said to her, standing up from the couch several yards behind where Ethan sat on the floor. Setting the glass of red wine she'd brought him on the table, Tad pulled out his keys.

"I don't think a six-year-old has the right to determine our evening," Miranda said, surprising herself with the firmness of her tone. She didn't get demanding with her son, ever. He was a good kid. Rarely needed discipline, just guidance.

And she was not going to be like her father. Her son would never have reason to fear her. She'd promised herself, and him, too, when he'd been a baby on the run with her.

She stood, hands on her hips. "Ethan, turn around please."

At first, the boy didn't move, then, very slowly, he turned, looking up at her through his Clark Kent glasses. Her heart melted, as it always did, when he showed her the emotions he wasn't old enough to hide.

"Do you really want Tad to leave?" she asked him, praying he'd be honest with her. And with himself.

"I dunno."

"That's not good enough, Ethan. We have a guest in our home and you're being rude."

Not that she could totally fault him on his manners. If she'd ever had visitors, he might have been better equipped to be a proper host.

"I'm sorry." He sounded more petulant than contrite.

"The other day you asked me to come over," Tad said, dropping down to sit on the floor beside him.

The boy, his game controller in hand, stared at the television.

"You worried I'm going to win our next battle?" he asked, glancing at the screen.

Ethan shrugged.

While she didn't love video games, Miranda played them with her son. He'd never been a sore loser. Nervous, but also kind of fascinated, she got her glass of wine, had a seat on the couch and sipped.

"So…let me play, too," Tad suggested, picking up the unused game controller. He couldn't do much unless Ethan changed to a two-player version. She waited.

And let out a long breath when her son did just that.

Fifteen minutes into a silent but competitive game, she slipped out to the kitchen to put the finishing touches on dinner, telling herself not to make too much of Tad's advent into their lives.

Warning herself.

He was only with them for a short time. She could enjoy herself, *needed* to enjoy herself for her own and Ethan's health. Needed to introduce him to others.

And would continue to do so after Tad was gone.

He was just the first step on this next stage of her survivor journey. She'd start to open her home, their lives, more. Thanks to Tad.

The feelings he'd raised in her, maybe simply because she was ready and he was there, had forced her to confront her fear of inviting others in.

Ethan had forced it a bit, too, latching onto Tad as immediately as he had. Hearing their voices from the other room, she left the dressed salad in the glass bowl on the counter and went in to tell them dinner was ready.

"Why's it rude for me to ignore you when you ignored me?" she heard.

Oh, Lordy. Her son was not giving up. She wondered which one had broken the silence between them, and suspected it had been Ethan. Tad, with his honed self-control or discipline or whatever it was, probably could have waited it out for days.

"I didn't ignore you," Tad said calmly, his avatar racing around a checkerboard-looking thing, just ahead of the blockages that kept appearing on the path. "I didn't know you were there. But you know I'm here. That's the difference." Ethan, a full lane ahead of Tad in his own version of the same puzzle, was also two squares ahead of the blockages. And he had a hefty collection of blockage obliterators in the spare feeding trough in his zoo barn, meaning her son was winning soundly. "You knew Danny was there. Why didn't you look for me, too?"

"I was there to see Danny."

Wiping her hands on the towel she'd brought in, Miranda stopped. Stared at the back of Tad's head.

Should she put an end to the conversation? Call them in for dinner? Pull Tad aside to warn him, remind him, whatever?

"Who's Danny?" she asked, sensing she was overreacting even before the words were out of her mouth.

Tad's quick glance in her direction readily confirmed her suspicion.

Ethan, still looking at Tad, didn't seem to hear her. "Why were you there to see *him*? You know his mom, too?"

The question wasn't as friendly-sounding as it might have been. More accusation than curiosity.

Clearly she had work to do where her son was concerned. He wasn't just her little boy anymore. It wasn't just the two of them against the world. She'd known the time would come. Had to give herself a second to swallow the sadness.

And endure the instant shard of fear that followed.

"I do know his mom," Tad said. "So does your mom."

No! She stepped closer to them, but before she could get words out, Tad gave her another look. Not condemning. Not a warning.

More like a promise of some kind.

"She can't tell you about him because he's a patient and it's against the law for medical personnel to talk about their patients, but he's not my patient and while his stuff isn't my business, I can tell you that he knows I got hurt. Your mom knew I got hurt and brought me in to meet Danny."

Ethan's gaze had been locked with Tad's through the entire explanation. Miranda was close to tears.

"But why?"

"He just had a question to ask me about my injury."

Which didn't explain, at all, why Tad had been at the elementary school. She waited for Ethan to ask.

"I got a scar on my leg, and got burned on my back, too, see?" Turning, Tad pulled up his shirt, exposing the scars on the lower part of his back. She'd seen them higher up, too, that day in her examining room with Danny.

"Wow. Did it hurt?" Ethan asked, eyes wide behind his glasses as he talked to Tad.

"Yep. A lot. More than anything else. Ever. Except maybe…you thinking I'm not your friend."

"How'd it happen? Did you get shot?" Ethan knew Tad was a police detective.

"Nope. It was an explosion."

"With some bad guys?"

"One bad guy."

"Did anybody die?"

"Just the bad guy."

"Cool."

She didn't think it was cool.

"So...are we friends again?" Tad moved right in.

"I guess." Ethan turned back to the TV and started to laugh. "Hey! I won even when we weren't playing!"

Their time had run out and he'd been ahead when they stopped, but Miranda had a feeling her son had also won for real, having a man like Tad to look up to for a little while.

She had a feeling she'd won, too.

Chapter 10

He didn't get a look at all the window latches Thursday night. When he'd excused himself to visit the bathroom, he'd planned to check the bedrooms, but he'd found both doors firmly shut and couldn't risk getting caught inside the rooms.

He'd tried to get her to talk about the windows, noticing that the French door leading out the patio was sparkling, which only led to a conversation about cleaning windows and how she was good at dealing with the inside, but never got around to the outside. They'd only get dirty again next time it rained. He'd moved on to asking if she ever opened her windows to let the breeze in, and she'd said there was no need, since the place was small and she could open the front door, with the metal security screen locked, and get all the cool they needed.

So Friday, when he knew Miranda was at work and Ethan at school, he made a stop by the cottage to do a thorough check on the windows from the outside. To find out how hard it would be to break in. He brought along a squeegee, a spray bottle and a roll of paper towels as his cover, and washed the outsides of all her windows while he was at it. Which meant he'd have to tell her he'd done it, because she was bound to notice and get freaked out.

When he'd thought that Miranda's ex was her only threat, and had been confident—if not 100 percent certain—that the man was deceased, he'd contented himself with watching out for her as her father had asked.

Now that he knew there was a family member who could pose a threat, he was buckling down on his procedures. He was not going to lose a woman or child in his care. He wasn't going to let Ethan or Miranda get hurt, period.

And when he called her father for their regularly scheduled weekly chat later that afternoon, he was determined to get more information out of him.

"How'd it go last night?" Chief O'Connor asked as soon as he picked up.

"It went really well." Tad stood out on his balcony, needing the ocean view to keep things in perspective. To get away from his own interests and out into the world where he could help save lives.

"Tell me about Jeffrey. Is he a good eater? I'm sure he's smart, like his mama." The man's eagerness pulled at Tad, making him a bit sad for all of them. Jeffrey, whose name had been changed to Ethan, and who had no idea he'd ever been anyone else. Or that he had a wonderful grandfather. Miranda who'd lost the support of her family and friends. Chief O'Connor, with his unending well of unconditional love for his family which left him with such horrendous loneliness, and himself, too, because he'd never experience the depths of that kind of love again.

And then, with the next breath he took, reminded himself that he was alone by choice.

"She made his favorite dinner, so I don't know if the way he cleaned his plate is typical of his usual habits or not. And yes, he's a smart little guy. You'd be proud of him, Chief." He could have said so much more. Was probably being paid to say more…

And reporting details of his time with Miranda and Ethan, taking things he learned about them during the time he spent with them, seemed duplicitous. Or worse.

"What's his favorite dinner?"

See, that was one of those intimacies, those privileged pieces of information you got when you were invited into someone's inner circle.

"Spaghetti." Sort of.

"Baked spaghetti? In one of those long metal pans? Sauce and noodles mixed together with cheese?"

Tad half smiled as he leaned against the ceiling-high cement wall he shared with the vacant balcony next door. "Yeah," he said. "Clearly you've had it before."

"It was her favorite, too," O'Connor said, his voice growing soft. He paused, as though restraining emotion, and added, "It was one of her mother's specialties. She taught Dana how to make it, and other things, too, when we found out she was sick."

Tad might not want family of his own, but he knew, in that moment, that he had to get this one back together. Somehow, someway, he had to help them.

"How old was she then?" He had a feeling the older man never talked about his own pain. He was always too busy tending to others.

"Ten."

"And when her mother died?"

"Eleven."

He'd been fourteen when his sister was murdered.

Chin tight, he straightened, hating that Miranda, who gave so much, who truly cared about others, had suffered so much. And had to handle it all alone.

He had to right this wrong.

"I'm concerned about this family member of Jeffrey's father that you mentioned yesterday," he said. "I'm uncomfortable not knowing more. I can't do my job that way. I could have exposed her just by being here. She and Ethan could be sitting ducks..."

Surely the chief knew that.

"You think I'd risk the safety of my only child, my only grandchild?" The chilling tone came at him.

And he took the point. "Of course not."

"I appreciate your concern and I count on it, Tad." The chief softened his next words again. "And I respect that I've put you in a difficult position. You can understand, I'm sure, that I don't trust easily at this stage. Which is why I only give out information on a need-to-know basis."

Another point taken.

"I'm trusting you with their lives. You're the only one who knows I've hired you to find her. The only one who knows you've done so. If you're also poking around in things here in town, someone might be able to trace you to her. I need to make certain there's no danger to them."

Tad was on forced medical and professional leave. With no family. It hadn't been hard for people to believe he'd gone off by himself to heal.

And Chief O'Connor was on the money on every point—even to the point of not paying him directly, but rather funneling the money through a special police fund used for undercover work. As Tad would have expected.

"I'll watch them closely," he said, still uncomfortable with what he didn't know.

"How'd it go with Dana? She can be a little defensive, understandably. I'd like to think she has you for a friend."

His discomfort intensified—on a whole different front.

"Fine. She's accepted me as a colleague and a friend." He had to tread carefully, balancing on a fine line between allegiances.

But their goal—Miranda, Dana, safe and free, with familial support and love—was the same.

"Well, if it goes beyond that, I want you to know you have my blessing. Assuming it's what she wants, what makes her happy. I couldn't pick anyone better to see with my daughter…"

"I said good-night to her and Ethan—Jeffrey—together, as soon as the dishes were done," he inserted, not willing to have that conversation with his boss. He'd come clean with the chief about "caring" for his daughter for ethical reasons. And it stopped there.

He'd heard of mothers being matchmakers. The chief was both mother and father to his daughter. Still…the whole thing left him feeling like he needed a shower.

He was friends with Miranda and Ethan. He wasn't going to let it go "beyond that," no matter how tempted he might be.

For so many reasons.

One was that he had no intention of getting into a committed emotional involvement and Miranda deserved no less.

"I realize you feel I've left you somewhat vulnerable out there, but I can tell you that the family member of whom I spoke yesterday is no longer a concern," Chief O'Connor said, getting Tad's full attention.

He turned back to his apartment, went inside and shut the door.

"This same one who, yesterday, posed a threat?" he asked.

"Yes. The older brother. He's got a record, drugs and assault among other things, but he's been incarcerated for attempted murder for the past year."

"How long's he in for?"

"Twenty, with possible parole at seven."

Dropping onto his sofa, he wiped a hand down his face. God, relief felt good.

Miranda had just tucked Ethan into bed and kissed him good-night when her phone rang Friday night.

"Danny's leg is itching and he's lying in bed crying, saying it hurts," Marie said, after apologizing for making the call. "I gave him the acetaminophen you said I could, but it doesn't seem to be helping. Are we absolutely sure there's nothing wrong there? Some infection we can't see?"

"What did Dr. Bennet tell you on Monday?"

"That everything was fine, but that was four days ago."

"Is he running a fever?"

"No."

She went down the list of other possible symptoms that would indicate a problem, all with no signs of any concern. When they got to the end of the list, she suggested that Marie have Danny soak in a warm bath for a while and eat a healthy snack before going back to bed.

"Devon's been watching us," Marie said then. "The police caught him just far enough away so they couldn't arrest him yesterday."

As a member of Danny's medical team, she wouldn't have received the alert, just an update at their High Risk Team meeting on Tuesday, but Tad would have known.

Which was why he'd been out in the open, making it easy for Danny to find him during recess the day before.

"Have you seen or heard from him?"

"No."

"And your sister and brother-in-law are there with you?"

"Yes."

"So…our plan is working then," Miranda said, wishing she could climb into the other woman's psyche and help her with her battle, knowing that only Marie could do this part. "The police, they saw him, warned him, and he's staying away."

"I guess."

Marie was scared. She had reason to be. And she had to fight that fear, or it would consume her and the rest of her life, too.

"If the bath doesn't do the trick, it's okay to give him a little more acetaminophen," she said, in her most medical-professional-nurturing-a-patient voice. And then, speaking as a woman, she added, "If you get worried, call me back. I mean it, Marie. You're in the middle of the toughest part of this and I agreed to be a member of the team helping you because it's what I want to do. Your job is not to give in to feeling guilty, or apologetic. Just pick up the phone and call me. Or someone else who can help. You're not alone. I can't stress that enough."

Marie thanked her. A couple of times. Sounding more in control than she had at the beginning of their conversation. Miranda hung up, not sure she'd been able to do enough.

Five minutes later, when the phone rang again, she expected it to be Marie calling back. It was Tad.

Curling up on her couch next to the book she'd been intending to read, a feel-good paperback novel about two female best friends and how the friendship survived the different paths their lives took, she told him about Marie's call.

And received his assurance that there'd been no further notice of Devon's activity since the day before.

"I was wondering how you'd feel about me taking Ethan to the gym tomorrow?" he asked. "I offered to take Danny last week when I was in your office, and while Marie hasn't set anything up yet, she might. It would be good for me to do a test run with Ethan. And…good for Ethan to go there, too. The boys attend the same school. Ethan knows who Danny is now. They might talk at some point."

She didn't think so. More likely, Ethan would steer clear of the other boy.

That wasn't the reason for her hesitation.

"I take him to basketball camp when I work on Saturday mornings." Since January. Prior to that, she'd had him at the office with her, during the first year she'd been Dr. Bennet's PA. And before that, at a day care in the building where Dr. Bennet had his practice.

Ethan had declared, when he'd started first grade, that he was too old for the after-school day care, although it accepted kids up to the age of eight. She let him make the decision, because it was one she could allow.

"I can go anytime," Tad said.

Basketball camp hadn't been the cause of her hesitation, either.

"I'm worried about him spending too much time with you." She finally just came out with it. "I've told him you're only here for a while, that you have your life in Michigan, a police force that needs you. He says he gets it, but after the way he was when he saw you with Danny, like he's taking ownership of you—I don't want him to get hurt…"

"My life in Michigan?"

Embarrassed that she'd remembered so many details about him, she admitted, "You told us, on your first day with the team, that you were from Michigan."

"Are you saying that you don't want me around him?" he asked next. She wasn't sure whether she was relieved or not, that they were getting back to the point. "You said on Tuesday that you were open to friendship."

"I know." She understood his confusion. "I do want that. I just don't want him getting the wrong idea."

"People are going to come and go from your lives."

He was right, of course.

"And maybe when I'm ready to go back to work, I'll look for something here."

Her heart rate escalated abruptly. Grabbing her attention.

"I...told you, I'm not interested in a long-term...anything. At least until he's older," she got out, wondering how much of her breathlessness he picked up on.

Figuring all of it.

Hoping none.

"Friendship," he said. "Just friends."

But she wanted so much more than that from him. The night before, after he'd left, she'd ended up taking a long soak in the tub, thinking about him.

About how he'd dealt with Ethan's jealousy over Danny. About the way he engaged in her son's video game as if it mattered as much to him as it did to Ethan. His views on the state of the world, which they'd discussed over coffee after the past six team meetings. His awareness and compassion. His willingness to risk his life to help others.

His patience.

And his body. Oh, that body. What it did to hers. How could she have lived twenty-eight years inside her own skin and never known that she could feel like this?

"I know you've been through a lot, Miranda. Losing Ethan's dad. Having to raise him on your own with no family to help you..."

She'd told him she'd grown up in foster care—back during their first personal conversation. He'd apparently remembered things, too.

"All I'm suggesting here is that I hang out with you and Ethan for a bit."

He was new to town. Not there for long—if you discounted his what-if, and she was going to—and knew very few people. He was unselfishly and willingly volunteering a lot of time to help Danny and Marie.

"But if you'd rather I didn't, I understand..."

"No!" She couldn't just let him go. "I'd rather you did," she said quickly, trying to gather her thoughts.

Maybe she should stop now. End the friendship before any of them got hurt.

Go back to being who she was seven weeks ago, before she met him...

Even as she had that thought, she knew she was asking the impossible. Tad was changing her, *had* changed her. He'd awakened something—an awareness of herself, her needs—that she hadn't had before.

He'd brought Ethan's needs more acutely to her attention, as well.

She had so many silent battles to fight. Had been an army of one for so long. She wasn't sure she had it in her to fight her own yearnings for some good feelings in her life. Even if they only lasted for a while.

"Surely in the six years you've had Ethan, another man has shown interest in you. Asked you out, or hinted at a desire to," Tad said, causing another surge of desire.

What was wrong with her?

"Yeah, there've been a few." Most recently, one of the volunteer coaches at the city-based basketball camp she'd enrolled Ethan in. "And I wasn't the least bit tempted."

Let him make of that what he would.

"You think Ethan's dad would want it this way?"

If he knew why, probably. But… "No."

"Ethan's dad. I feel kind of ridiculous saying that every time. I assume the guy has a name?"

Yep, and there was why she didn't do *intimate* with anyone. Or get close enough for *intimate* to be a risk.

She hated to lie.

And the more lies she told, the more chance she'd make a critical mistake. Counseling had pounded that one into her.

"Ethan's named after him," she said. It was the truth. His birth name just wasn't Ethan.

"Ethan what?"

Why? Why did he need to know a last name?

If she came across like a crazy woman, she'd raise more suspicion than if she answered.

"Grossman," she said, blurting the name of one of her mother's doctors. Colleen had contracted hepatitis C while on vacation with Miranda and her father down in Punta Cana. They'd thought for a while that she was doing better. That she'd be okay.

She wasn't.

"I'm not going to hurt you or Ethan." Tad's soft voice came over the line. She couldn't remember wanting to believe a man so badly in her life.

But she couldn't.

Chapter 11

Tad didn't take Ethan to the gym Saturday. He'd decided not to broach the subject again during his Friday-night conversation with Miranda. He'd almost made a critical mistake, pushing too hard, with his request in the first place. Had teetered on the edge of losing her friendship altogether.

And he'd learned a valuable lesson about survivors. They were as vulnerable as they were strong.

Or maybe the lesson had been about Miranda in particular. As strong as she was, she was vulnerable, too.

He thought about her all day Saturday. Wanting to call her. To see her and Ethan. And settled for a couple of drive-bys. Now that he knew the possible threat against her was in jail, he wasn't as worried about her immediate safety.

He'd looked up Ethan Grossman the second they'd been off the phone Friday night. He'd found no one of that name in North Carolina who'd been in college six years before.

Or anyone close to college-age. Even using databases he still had access to, he'd only been able to find one listing. A man closer to her father's age than her own.

She'd lied to him about her husband's name. Not surprising. Smart.

Disappointing, too, on a strictly personal level. Which was at the bottom of his priority list.

Lying in bed Saturday night, thinking about her, he suddenly sat upright in the dark.

Ethan's named after him. She hadn't said the man's name was Ethan; she'd only confirmed the conclusion he'd drawn.

Ethan's named after him.

Ethan's birth name was Jeffrey.

He spent the next hour on his laptop, searching for Jeffrey Grossman in or around North Carolina.

And came up empty.

Frustrated, he pulled out his burner phone and texted the chief. I know the father's name. She told me.

It wasn't technically true. But he had to have answers. If leading the chief to believe he already had, by other means, the information that he wanted the chief to discuss with him, and the chief would then open up more to him, give him more complete information, then the end justified the means.

Miranda passed Tad on the road Sunday, on her way home from the grocery store. She waved. He waved. Ethan turned around, as much as the belt would let him, and kept waving.

She couldn't even pretend not to be thinking about him after that, and when her son was in his room, doing his weekly cleaning chores, she texted Tad, asking him if he

felt like grilling a steak. The man was alone. Healing.
Helping Marie.

It wasn't until after he'd said a steak sounded good that
she told him it would have to be at the play park on the
beach. She didn't own a grill.

Didn't have steak, either, but a grilled steak did sound
wonderful. And it was something she never had because
Ethan hated steak. On her trip back to the grocery store
for a couple of thick T-bones, she bought her son the hot
dogs he wanted as his dinner on the grill. She'd planned
to meet Tad at the park, which was really just playground
equipment, some grills and picnic tables cordoned off in
the sand of one of Santa Raquel's tourist beaches. But when
he'd offered to pick her and Ethan up, she wasn't quick
enough to invent a reason to refuse and said yes.

She told herself she wasn't going to make a big deal
of her appearance. The meal wasn't a date. She and Tad
weren't dating.

She wore leggings because they'd be comfortable to sit in
on the beach. And the thigh-length off-white figure-hugging
short-sleeved sweater was the only thing warm enough to
wear with leggings on the beach in April. Running a brush
through her hair was just polite, and she reapplied her minimal makeup because she'd rushed through it that morning.

The ride over could have been intimate, sitting next to
him in the front seat of his SUV, but Ethan, strapped in
the back in his shorts, long-sleeved shirt and tennis shoes,
took over the space and didn't let go during the five-minute
drive to the park. As soon as Tad answered his first question—had Tad ever been to the beach park?—in the negative,
the six-year-old regaled him with all the things he could
do there. How the slide was higher than the one at school,
there were a lot more swings for big people, and if you got

high up and wanted to jump out, it was cool because you landed on the sand.

The barrage went on. She was happy to listen. Her son sounded normal. Happy. Eager to face what was ahead of him.

She'd done some good as his only parent.

Ethan wanted to go down to the water first thing, so they left the cooler in the car and, after taking off their shoes, walked across the sand, down to the shore. The beach wasn't crowded, but it wasn't deserted, either, that Sunday afternoon. Seventy degrees and breezy was too cold to swim, but a couple of kids were wading, bending over, picking things up off the ocean floor. Another kid was building a sandcastle in sand wet from the surf. Three teenage girls walked past them, chattering and laughing. A few couples were scattered about.

Ethan liked to look for anything living on the shoreline.

"You're giving him a great childhood," Tad said, standing beside her just out of reach of the waves lapping at the shore.

"I do my best." The breeze was harsher down by the water, but she welcomed the coolness on her heated skin. Being around Tad, who needed central heat? Or warmth from the sun?

"I went to the beach once, as a little kid. In a town called South Haven on the shores of Lake Michigan across from Chicago. Mom rented a cottage there for the long weekend over the Fourth of July."

It was the first mention he'd ever made of his personal life. Avid for more, for a real picture of the man who compelled her to want to be around him, she asked, "Was your dad there, too?"

"Nope. He took off when I was a baby. Met someone

else, divorced my mom and moved to North Dakota. It was always only Mom, my older sister, Steffie, and me."

"Did you ever see him?" Fathers were a tough subject. No matter what they did to you, you loved them. Felt like you needed them.

Until you had a child of your own to protect.

"Not that I remember. He left that woman, too, luckily for her before they had kids. Last I heard, he was in Florida, working as a casino dealer. As far as I know he never remarried or had other kids."

"Have you tried to get in touch with him?"

"Not in a long time."

The way he said the words had her looking up at him, and she was shocked to see the bitter sadness in his expression. Ethan was talking to the kids who'd been in the water, picking up things from the ocean shore, seemed to be comparing finds. He was a friendly kid. Outgoing. She'd been worrying too much that week about the way she'd secluded him.

"How about your sister? Is she in touch?" She wanted desperately to know. But didn't want to push.

She didn't want to be pushed, either.

"Steffie's dead."

Her heart dropped, and the breath caught in her throat. "What happened?" She turned to him and when he met her gaze…it was like his soul and hers…knew each other. Connected as friends, not strangers.

"She and I were home alone one night. I was a freshman in high school. She was a freshman in college, going to a local university. Mom was at work. She was a nurse at the children's hospital in Detroit."

"Your mom was in the medical field?" He'd never said. And at a children's hospital… Her entire being tensed with the need to help him—because she was a nurse, too? Or had been. Before she'd left herself behind, invented a new life and become a pediatric PA.

She liked being a PA. As much as she'd liked being a nurse. Maybe even a little more. She so badly wanted to share that with Tad.

"Yeah. My father was an X-ray technician when they met. From what I can tell, he's had a lot of different jobs since then."

"Where's your mother now?"

She wanted to know about his sister. Had to get back to that. But it felt like they needed a moment. Or at least he did.

"She's gone, too. After Steffie died, she fell into a deep depression that she never really came out of. She died of an accidental overdose of prescription medications when I was in college."

Miranda knew how horrible that felt—losing your mother. Couldn't tell him that, either.

"Oh my God," she said, watching as the children moved a few feet farther down the sand. Ethan wasn't allowed in the water without her. So far, he was remembering that. A breeze blew against them, lifting tufts of Tad's short brown hair. The ocean sounds could have taken his words, their conversation, away.

Instead, they seemed to be enclosed by it all.

"I'm so sorry."

He shrugged. "It was a long time ago."

And yet…right there with them. Life had a way of doing that to you. No matter how many years passed, some things remained. Hurting you still.

"Tell me about the night your sister died." He'd brought it up. As though he wanted her to know.

"She was watching a movie the last time I saw her. Eating popcorn. I went to my room, had my headphones on, listening to music. When I went out to tell her good-night, she was gone."

"Gone?"

"From what they pieced together based on forensic evidence at the scene, and later a confession from the guy, the perp knocked at the door. A guy she knew from college. He'd had a crush on her, thought she returned his feelings. He said his car broke down and his cell was dead. Asked to use our phone. She went back to the couch. When he got off the phone, she offered him some popcorn. Apparently he made a move, she rejected him. Popcorn flew all over. Then he dragged her out of the house. Turned out his car was just fine, and parked at the curb. He'd just been looking for an excuse to spend time with her. But after her rejection, he lost it. He shoved her inside his car, drove her to a field, raped her, beat her to death and left her lying there. The neighbors heard her scream, called 911. I'd already discovered she was gone and had called, too, but by the time they found her it was too late."

Oh. Just oh, God. He'd been in his room with head-phones on. A fourteen-year-old man of the house. Coming out to see popcorn all over the living room.

There were no words. No way to fix this.

Sliding her hand into his, Miranda held on to him, hoping he'd know she was sharing his pain.

Hoping it helped.

"Look, I got three at once!" Ethan came running up from the wet sand, his hand outstretched, extricating Tad from an excruciating moment—and ripping him from a warmth he'd never experienced.

Miranda quickly pulled her hand from his and he tried to ignore the sense of loss as he bent to see the three sand crabs her son had in his hand.

"You want 'em?" Ethan asked him. "They don't hurt people, do they, Mom?"

"Nope." She shook her head, acting as though she'd just woken up from a nap. A little out of it, not completely with them.

Tad could relate. What in the hell had possessed him to tell her about Steffie? People knew, of course. And that his mother had died during the first year of his criminal justice degree studies. He'd moved from Michigan to complete his studies in North Carolina—choosing the state because he'd never been there and was offered an academic scholarship with work-study opportunity. Background checks told the facts.

They didn't reveal the details he'd given Miranda.

He'd known he was getting in deep. That things were complicated. Nothing had prepared him for the jolt he'd felt when she slid her hand into his.

It was that feeling that prompted him to make another unscheduled call Sunday night after the picnic on the beach.

He and Miranda hadn't had any more time alone after Ethan shared his sand crabs. The little guy had announced that he was hungry. They'd traipsed up the beach, cooked, played some three-way kickball in the sand, then headed home early because it was a school night and Ethan had to have a bath before bed.

Miranda had invited him in. He'd read more invitation than just the glass of tea or cup of coffee she'd offered, and despite all the desire flowing through him, he'd politely declined.

And then called her an hour later to apologize. He needed to stay on her good side. Wanted to believe it was for her father's sake and for her own ultimate good, which she'd see when she learned the truth. But he had to admit that the phone call was mostly for himself.

Being vulnerable with someone was new to him. He didn't like it. Didn't know how to get out of it.

And was mesmerized by it, too.

"I felt a little awkward, unloading on you like I did," he said by way of apology for his abrupt departure earlier. "I should have handled it better."

"You were fine," she assured him, a little more distant than she'd been when she'd called earlier in the day to invite him to dinner.

He was glad he wasn't the only one who recognized that they had to maintain established boundaries, but he was disappointed, too. Perversely filled with a need to get them right back where they'd been on the beach before Ethan had interrupted them.

It was as though unfinished business lay between them. Something that hadn't been there before.

Maybe it was time to get back to work. To occupy his mind before it flew off permanently.

"I unburdened myself. Now it's your turn," he said, pushed from within to move on from the standstill he felt trapped in. Maybe if she talked to him about her father, indicated that she missed him, he could convince the chief that she was ready for the truth. That would get him out of this mess.

"Excuse me?"

"I told you about my family and I know nothing about yours."

If silence could be heard, he heard it then.

"I don't have a lot to say," she told him after a lengthy pause. "You already know I grew up in foster care."

"Like Ethan Sr.?"

Maybe he was egging her on. Maybe he needed her to trust him.

A selfish need at best. Miranda believed her safety lay in her silence. And her lies.

"Yes," she said. "Except that I stayed in one place, and he was shifted around among different families."

"And your foster parents, were they good to you?"

"Yes."

"Are you still in touch with them?" Frustration motivated him. He was aware of it.

"No. They took in a lot of kids. I, um, didn't actually go into the system until I was eleven."

The year her mother died.

"So you were with your parents until then?"

"My mom. I never knew my dad." Something in her tone touched him.

More than mere sadness. Much more. What was he doing? Forcing a woman to talk about her father, the person she'd loved and adored, a man who'd been a true hero, who'd not only kept her safe but been all the family she had. Of course, she'd have to wall herself off from any admission that he even existed.

Tad's excess energy started to seep slowly away, bringing back the calm with which he did his best thinking.

He wasn't happy to be on the phone with Miranda in the middle of their current conversation.

He needed to be able to tell her that her husband really was dead. That the story she'd made up about Ethan's father's death was now reality. That she could see her father again. That the chief knew where she was and was watching out for her.

But it wasn't his truth to tell.

And how could he know, really, the nuances between

a daughter on the run and a father left behind? He'd never been either.

"See you for coffee after the meeting on Tuesday?" he asked her.

"Of course."

Tad hung up, completely dissatisfied, and yet relieved, too. They'd taken a step back.

And they were still friends.

Chapter 12

On Monday, Miranda took her lunch hour to visit The Lemonade Stand. She'd called first, found out that Sara Havens Edwin, lead counselor and the woman who'd counseled her when she'd first landed in Santa Raquel, had half an hour between appointments, and Miranda offered to bring lunch.

With her complete security clearance, she could park in the employee lot and did so, still wary enough not to want anyone to see her entering the Stand and assuming she was a victim. No one could know she'd been one, except the few who'd worked with her, those who'd initially helped her.

New identities had to be just that—brand-new. Zero ties to the old.

And yet her very existence was a tie to herself, to her own history, that would never be broken.

Placing two veggie pitas on the table between them in

the little conference room Sara had booked, she sat, sipping from one of the two glasses of tea Sara had come in carrying.

"We haven't had a meeting like this in well over a year," the counselor said, her blue eyes piercing. "What's up?"

"I've met someone."

"Ahh." The woman smiled, and her dark blond hair seemed to halo her expression.

"No…it's not like that," she said. "It's not…we're just friends. It's Tad Newberry. He's visiting, as you know, but we've been spending some time together."

"I'm glad."

Yeah, well, she didn't need a go-ahead on that score, although she could understand why Sara thought she'd come for encouragement. Sara knew she hadn't had a close personal relationship since Jeff.

"I keep having to bite my tongue not to tell him about my past," she said in a rush, feeling like a criminal for even having the thought. "I mean, you know him. You know we can trust him. Yesterday we took Ethan to the beach and got to talking, and he told me some things about his past and I just… His mother was a nurse like I was. I lost his sister—and then lost his mom young like I did. I understood and I needed so badly to tell him that. And I couldn't." The words came pouring out of her. "I felt like I was shortchanging him. And me, too."

Putting down the pita she'd unwrapped, but not yet bitten into, Sara placed her hands on the table. The counselor was familiar with trauma. She'd lived through some devastating stuff of her own. Which was part of what made her so supremely good at her job. She was also a natural calming influence.

Miranda didn't feel at all calm. A little more so when

Sara met her gaze, her tone dead serious as she started to speak.

"I want to be able to tell you what you need to hear," she said. "But I can't, Miranda." Miranda, not Dana. Always. Sara knew her birth name. She'd never used it. Not once.

"For your own safety, and Ethan's, there can be no ties. None. Particularly with law enforcement. When you left, your father had the entire state of North Carolina convinced he was to be revered, giving him a greater ability to find you than most abusers ever have. We've got no idea how far he's risen now and no one here is going to risk looking him up, either, in case a search shows up somewhere and an IP address is traced…"

"Tad's from Michigan."

"It doesn't matter. And I think you know that. You just needed *me* to know that you're tempted, didn't you?"

With tears in her eyes, Miranda nodded. She was fighting her battle.

And Sara was her arsenal.

Tad's biggest takeaway from coffee on Tuesday was relief that he and Miranda were okay. Her eyes had met his a couple of times over the conference table during the High Risk meeting. She'd smiled at him once, as though they were sharing a private joke. And afterward, at the coffee shop, she stayed for an extra half hour after everyone else left—as had become their tradition.

On Wednesday all hell broke loose. As it had been told to Tad, Marie had called Miranda to ask about swelling and pain in Danny's leg, asking for a doctor's excuse to keep him out of school. Danny had missed so many days over the past year that they'd reached the limit legally allowed before authorities got involved.

She'd needed to see Danny before she could write such

a letter, and told Marie to head straight to the office, and either she or Dr. Bennet would see Danny as quickly as possible. When an hour passed and she hadn't shown up, Max Bennet called the police, who'd already been contacted by Ruby, Marie's sister.

Tad was pulled into the loop when Detective Chantel Fairbanks called to find out if he'd seen Danny that morning. He'd already been by the school twice, but hadn't seen the boy—not all that unusual, since Danny would've been in class. He also hadn't seen anyone lurking nearby, which was what he was there to watch for.

Miranda called him a few minutes later, while he was still driving around the area, filling him in on the situation as she currently knew it. Apparently a friend of Devon's had seen Marie at a gas station where she'd been gassing up her car before taking Danny to school and then going on to work. The friend begged her to call to keep Danny out of school, so no red flags would be raised. And then to go home and call him. The friend just wanted to Face-Time with Danny, and would be at a restaurant, where Devon could look on from another booth and see his son.

Danny, overhearing the request, begged Marie to agree. She couldn't tell whether that was because he loved his dad and missed him, in spite of his rages, or because he was afraid of what his father would do if his mother didn't comply. Maybe they were both intimidated by Devon's friend, which was Tad's personal opinion, and he further suspected that Devon had intended them to be.

Regardless of the reason, Marie had agreed to wait half an hour and then do as the friend asked. She called her sister, who was already at work, to tell her she was taking Danny home to make the call. And then she'd called Miranda to get a doctor clearance to keep Danny out of school. Neither of them had been seen since, and Marie wasn't answering her phone. They were running a location trace, but so far had nothing. She could have turned her cell off.

Ruby had gone home immediately, hoping to talk her sister out of going along with wishes that had clearly come from Devon, and found the house empty. She'd called the police immediately.

No one had been able to locate Devon, either, but he wasn't due at work until later that afternoon, so it wasn't as if they could be certain he was involved in foul play.

"I'm finished with my morning patients," Miranda told Tad, "and I'm just sitting here, worried sick about her. I wish there was something I could do." He could hear the fear in her voice.

"Have you tried calling her? Maybe if she saw your number, she'd take your call."

"Twice," Miranda said. "It went straight to voice mail." She was sounding less and less like herself. Like the Miranda he knew.

And more like a woman who feared forces that were stronger than she was. Could be she was putting herself in Marie's shoes. Could be she was firmly planted in her own and living with the demons her ex had left her with.

He had to help her.

And to pretend he didn't know how much she'd suffered...and why.

"You want to go to lunch? We can wait together."

Expecting a refusal, he was surprised when she agreed immediately, asking him if he'd like to meet someplace or pick her up at the office. She mentioned a diner not far from the clinic and he headed that way, telling her he'd pick her up.

The fact that she'd even asked was a "tell" to him.

She was waiting for him at the door of the clinic and

came out when he pulled into the lot. "I've got an hour," she told him, settling her purse on the floor. In her cartoon character scrubs, with tennis shoes and her hair tied back, she looked as she did every Tuesday when she came from work to attend meetings, but there was something different about her, too.

A tightness in her face, lines near her mouth. She was definitely tense. Her hand was shaking as she buckled her seat belt. Or was he looking too hard? He didn't think so.

He wanted to reach over to take her hand in his, much as she'd done for him a few days before on the beach. She gave and gave and gave.

He wanted to give back.

Wanted her to know how great it felt to receive.

He asked her directions to the restaurant; she gave them and then said, "I just feel we should be doing something. At least be out there searching for her…"

As a detective, he'd been out searching more times than he could count. "Do you have any idea where she might go? Where Danny likes to go? Anyplace she might hide?"

He didn't think Marie was hiding. She'd have called for help.

Unless she'd been prevented from doing so.

"Danny likes to climb that little mountain on the south side. Out by the new housing development. Seer's Point? He told me that's when he'd know his leg was better. When he could get to the top again. Apparently Devon had been taking him there before he was old enough to walk. It seemed like a good memory for him."

And something for them to do that felt more useful than sitting in a booth at a diner. "How about we go to a drive-through for some take-out food and head over that way?"

Gratitude filled her eyes, and she nodded.

Tad put the car in gear.

* * *

She could feel herself slipping. Knew that panic was close. She'd called the school to confirm that Ethan was in class and okay before she'd called Tad, recognizing the ludicrousness of her actions even as she did it.

Devon Williams didn't know Ethan, and wouldn't have reason to hurt him if he did. Unless he found out that she'd given Marie her number in case she needed help. He could be after anyone who was trying to take his wife away from him.

She knew how the abusive mind worked.

Maybe he'd somehow come across her number on Marie's phone, or learned that she'd been involved in bringing Danny's case to the High Risk Team. Maybe he knew Tad was involved, too, and had seen the three of them together.

"What sounds good for lunch?" Tad's voice felt so close, while she felt so far away.

Eating in general sounded unappealing at the moment. But it was time to eat. She'd been hungry an hour ago. Acting normal was the way to beat the panic.

She felt anything but normal.

"Salad," she said, naming a new organic drive-through salad place on the way out of the downtown area, trying to think about what she'd order.

Ethan was fine. He'd been at lunch the first time she'd called. At recess the second. If she called a third time she was going to look like a lunatic.

She knew he was okay. But she was scared to death for Marie, afraid her sister in victimhood hadn't been as lucky as she herself had.

And Danny… At least Ethan had been spared violence in his young life.

She'd done the right thing. And she'd done it well. Her son was safe. Jeff would be proud of her.

Thinking of her best friend, of how incredible she'd felt the first time she made a comment about her father and, instead of doubting her, he'd asked some very serious questions and then sat and cried with her as she found a way to answer them.

She'd been lucky. So lucky.

Devon Williams had been a victim of domestic violence, too. By his father. It happened that way so often, the abused growing up to abuse.

But not with her. She'd never even come close to experiencing the white-hot rage she'd seen seething from her father.

Jeff hadn't turned into an abuser, either. He'd been gentle. Kind. Funny and emotionally strong.

"Ethan's dad was abused as a kid," she told Tad. She couldn't give him the facts of her life, but there were some things she *could* say. Things her father had never known. Things he'd never associate with her so things he'd never mention as an identifier if he was looking for her. "In his first foster home," she added, when her gut clenched anyway.

It had actually been his birth home. And his birth mother. She'd been a single mom. An addict. She'd already been at her wit's end with his older brother, and then Jeff had come along…the son of her pimp, he'd always believed.

Ethan would be back in class by now. She couldn't call to verify. Had no legitimate reason to call.

They'd phone her if there was a problem. Reaching into the pocket of her scrub top, she checked her cell. Just to be sure she hadn't missed a call.

And tried Marie again, closing her eyes as she waited for a ring, willing the woman to pick up.

"Voice mail," she said, dropping her phone back in her pocket.

"You mentioned Ethan's dad being like Devon—"

"No!" she interrupted him, horrified at where his thoughts were taking him. Where her stilted conversation had led him. "He was nothing like Devon," she said now, scrambling for safe words. "He was my best friend. The one you went to when the rest of the world was crashing in on you. He always made things seem a little less intense. I could tell him stuff I never told anyone else."

All true. All untraceable.

And talking about Jeff, with Tad, calmed her in a whole new way.

"How'd he die?" She should've expected Tad's question, especially after he'd told her how his mother and sister died. It still caught her off guard.

"He was in a car accident," she improvised quickly. In reality, he'd been playing intramural football with a group of fraternity brothers. Had taken a slam to his left kidney. When they got him to the hospital, they found he only had one working kidney. And it had been ruptured.

He'd recovered. Was on dialysis, and waiting for a kidney to become available, but there was one complication after another. Six months later, they'd told him he wouldn't survive a transplant, although he'd seemed fine at first, other than being tired a lot…

He'd already talked to her about his last wish. And they'd conceived Ethan while there was still hope that he'd live to hold his child in his arms.

"What would you like?" Tad had pulled into the salad place. She had to think a minute. Asked for the turmeric with rice and cranberry because she saw it on the menu board. She wasn't fond of cranberries. But as she and Tad sat in his SUV at the foot of the mountain ten minutes later, she ate as much of the salad as she could.

"I'm worried sick about what he might be doing to her," she finally admitted when the silence was rotting her mind again.

"I know."

She put the lid on her bowl, noticing that he'd only eaten half of his roasted vegetable salad. "I can't eat any more."

"You want to walk?"

They'd already perused the small dirt parking lot at the foot of the trail. Not only was Marie's car nowhere in sight, there were no other vehicles, either.

"Can you?" she asked him, looking down at the thigh she'd seen in an examining room without jeans covering it. She'd never seen him limp, but he'd told Danny that he still hurt sometimes, when he pushed things.

"I can climb the mountain," he told her, looking up at the top of the peak. "I'll probably have to limp down."

Miranda couldn't go far, had to get back to work and was in her scrubs, but she got out of the car. She figured they could walk until the trail started upward.

And when he reached out, offering her his hand, she took it.

Chapter 13

It took more emotional strength than he'd ever have guessed for Tad to do nothing other than hold Miranda's hand that Wednesday afternoon. They walked the trail for about ten minutes, then sat on a cement bench. It was in the sun and Miranda had said she wanted to soak up some of the warmth.

What she'd done was look over at him, sitting shoulder to shoulder with her out in a deserted patch of nature, with trees and brush and the mountain ahead of them obscuring them from view. She met his gaze and then stared at his lips.

He could tell she'd wanted a kiss. Maybe as a distraction. Maybe to assure herself that she wasn't Marie. That she was well and healthy and perfectly safe.

Or maybe because sexual tension had been buzzing between them since the day they met.

He wasn't a guy who was good at figuring out all those

nuances. He didn't usually get himself in situations where he'd need to be good at it.

But he was a guy who knew that, even tempted as he was, hard as he was growing sitting there beside her, he couldn't act on the desire pulsing inside him.

Not with the secrets standing between them.

She hadn't pushed it. Hadn't actually leaned over and kissed him. But she'd reached for his hand as they walked back to the car a few minutes later.

As though they were…a couple. Not just friends.

An alert was sent out to the High Risk Team late Wednesday afternoon that Marie Williams was safe and at home. Whether or not she'd let Danny make the phone call, seen her husband or just skipped town for the day, Tad didn't know, but assumed he'd hear the details at the next High Risk meeting, if not before. He was asked to resume watch duty at Danny's school, and sent a text to Marie reminding her that he was happy to help out in any other situations, as well, if she needed him.

He got a "thank you" in return, and nothing else.

Miranda also texted—to thank him for lunch. He called, wanting to see how she was doing, but she didn't pick up.

Friday's phone call couldn't arrive soon enough as far as Tad was concerned. He wasn't going to break protocol again and phone the chief unexpectedly. He respected the man's position, the difficulty of his circumstances. And pissing him off or making him uncomfortable would be counterproductive to the goal he had in mind.

It was time to get Miranda and her father back together. To end a very long and difficult chapter in both their lives.

Where that would leave him remained to be seen. He'd be lying to himself if he didn't admit he was entertaining thoughts about some kind of future in which he knew

Miranda. Dana. Whether it would be back home in North Carolina or here in California, he didn't know. He was open to various possibilities.

Once he had the older man on the line Friday afternoon, he got right to the point. "We were involved in an incident with another victim this week," Tad told the chief. "Nothing notable with that case, except that for a while there, it looked like the woman and possibly her young son were in immediate danger. I was with Miranda. She was beyond frightened, Chief. It was difficult to watch. More so because she doesn't have to live this way. I'm recommending that we tell her the truth. She deserves to know that she doesn't have to live in fear. That her ordeal is done."

"Was she afraid for herself on Wednesday?"

"No."

"Then her knowing the truth wouldn't have changed anything. I imagine she's suffering from some form of PTSD. Or at least memory-related stress. Wednesday's incident was a trigger, and there's no guarantee that will ever end for her."

Tad let the anger surging inside him burn silently for a few seconds. And saw the reason in what the chief was saying.

But did he have to be so…cold, so scientific about the whole thing? This was his daughter they were talking about. If he'd seen Miranda, seen his own daughter teetering in a hell of her own and yet managing to stay afloat, to tend to others…it would break his heart.

Which was why the chief had to approach the situation from a cerebral place. Understanding dawned on Tad as he stood there in his bedroom, looking at the open sock drawer from which he'd pulled the burner phone.

Brian O'Connor might be a hero, might seem larger than life, but he was just a man, too. One who'd lost his wife to illness and then his only child to a fiend who'd beaten her to the point of fearing for her life. Running for her life.

Like his daughter, the chief might grieve, but no matter how intense his personal pain, he managed to stay afloat. To tend to others.

"You two need each other," he told his superior.

"I'm not at all sure she'd agree with you on that." O'Connor's tone was less robust than Tad had ever heard. "I haven't been completely forthright with you, Detective."

Heading out to his balcony, Tad counted the black bars across the front of the space by rote. There were twenty-four of them, mounted on top of a four-foot-high stucco wall. Spaced four inches apart.

Do not tell me her husband's still alive. Not trusting himself to speak, knowing he had to learn the facts before he acted, Tad waited.

"The truth is, finding out that I know where she is could trigger Dana to disappear again," he said. "I don't *think* it would. If she's as far along in her healing as you've reported, then she almost certainly wouldn't. Trouble is, I'm not ready to take even that minute chance of losing her again."

Tad was trying to keep pace with him. And to understand what was being said behind and inside the words, too.

"You think that anyone from her past life finding her could trigger the fight-or-flight reaction?" he guessed. Miranda in no way seemed to him to be so vulnerable that she'd run without first seeking assistance. Her whole world was filled with professionals trained to help those in her situation.

That was no mistake, he realized. Even the doctor she worked for was dedicated to the fight against domestic

violence; not only that, he was a donor to The Lemonade Stand.

And the man she'd befriended, with the clear indication
that she'd be open to more, the first man she'd, by her own
admission, been interested in since her ex's death, was a
detective on leave volunteering on the High Risk Team.

As far as he knew, none of them had any idea about her
past—except him, and she didn't realize that—but she'd
planted herself in the middle of a fortress.

A surge of emotion flooded him—like nothing he'd felt
in many, many years. Deeply warm. And fiercely protec-
tive. The woman impressed the hell out of him over and
over again.

"I think my daughter could still be hugely angry with
me."

Not at all the words he'd been expecting. Or any version thereof.

"Excuse me?"

"We didn't part on good terms," the chief said, giving
Tad a feeling he didn't like at all. Like when an investigation took a bad turn. A really bad turn.

"Mind explaining that one?" He didn't consider himself
subordinate at the moment. Or the receiver of a paycheck.
This was news to him and he didn't like being misled.

"I was trying to get her to leave the bastard," O'Connor
said. "She said I didn't understand, that she loved him and
he loved her…"

Lips pressed firmly together, Tad waited.

"The truth is, he turned her against me, Tad. I couldn't
believe it was happening at first. *Didn't* believe it. I thought
she was just having a hard day or was taking it all out on
me. She said she could handle him. That I was making
things much worse. Said she wanted her space, so I did my
best to give it to her. And she'd go longer and longer be-

tween phone calls. Too late I realized he was isolating her from me, the one person who could protect her. She had few friends, had been a quiet child ever since her mother died. Didn't date in high school or go out much. She was ripe for him and no matter what I tried to do to help her, it was always the wrong thing."

Tad slumped into one of the two chairs on the balcony, elbows on his knees as he stared at the artificial-grass-covered floor. Having spent close to four months studying the insidious hell of domestic violence from all sides, he could hear the truth in every single unbelievable word O'Connor was saying.

His heart went out to the guy.

"I'm sorry, sir."

"No. No. Don't you be sorry," he said in return. "You being there, what you're doing, you'll never know how much it means. I just need you to be patient, Detective. Give me insights into her current situation. Give me a little time to get to know her again, through you. To figure out a way to approach this. But if she finds out I've got you looking out for her, it could ruin everything. Unless she understands that in the past, I wasn't butting in or trying to control her, but to save her life. And that now, I just want to give her life back to her. To see her again. To love her and Jeffrey and do everything I can to help them be happy. Keep doing what you're doing. When the time is right, I'll know."

"Okay."

The last thing he wanted was to screw up Miranda's life further. He'd read a ton, witnessed a small fraction firsthand, but he had no real experience with how either Miranda or her father would be feeling.

He was superimposing his own feelings onto theirs, colored by his own experiences.

He didn't like feeling he was spying on her. But there

was no way he was leaving her, either. Whether he worked for her father or not. He had to know for certain that her ex was dead. That all the danger from her past was gone. That she had a chance to know real freedom, and to have her father in her life again.

He could quit working for the chief. But then O'Connor would find someone else. Someone who might not care about Ethan and Miranda as much as Tad did. Be as respectful of them. Someone who might tip her off and send her running again as her father feared.

He hadn't learned enough yet. So he was trapped.

"She told me Jeffrey's father was killed in a car accident," he said aloud. "Do you have any idea if that's true? Do you know how the guy really died?"

She'd also told him she'd never been married.

"He died of an overdose," O'Connor said. "And I'm not sure anymore that they were ever legally married. She told me they were. That they'd flown to Vegas, did it at one of those wedding chapels."

He could never, in a million years, see Miranda doing that.

But he'd never known Dana.

"Problem is, I haven't been able to find any record of the marriage."

Even in Vegas you had to apply for a marriage license.

Clearly there was more investigating to do. And he wasn't in a position to do it. O'Connor had been right on that score. If by chance a search was noted, if it was somehow traced back to Santa Raquel, someone could come looking. He'd done a lot more reading on identity change over the past week—including the risks.

And if Miranda and Ethan's father really *hadn't* been married, did it mean other things weren't the way they seemed, either? Like the man's death?

"Another concern has been brought to my attention," O'Connor said. "There could be others, besides the brother in prison, who know that Dana's the mother of this guy's son, and who aren't the most upstanding citizens, if you get my drift. Maybe this guy owed someone drug money. Anyone could be out there, knowing that she's my daughter, knowing the position I've reached, that I've amassed a substantial amount of money, and try to get to that money through her or Jeffrey. We just don't know enough yet."

O'Connor clearly had someone good on the case. Looking at every angle. Out to protect Miranda and Ethan, Dana and Jeffrey. And the money—Chief O'Connor had been left a huge inheritance by a man whose family O'Connor had once saved. It had been all over the news. Anyone who knew Miranda was his daughter would know he'd be able to pay a tidy sum for her return...

The chief might not have told Tad the full details of his and Dana's personal situation, but he hadn't lied to Tad, either. Tad had understood all along that he got information on a need-to-know basis. Chief O'Connor was absolutely certain his daughter's ex was dead. Tad had to go with that. Deal with feeling uneasy.

O'Connor didn't get where he was without having to prove himself, again and again. He'd climbed the ranks based on his deeds, not on who he happened to know. He was a fireman, a lifesaver. He wasn't going to risk his own daughter's life or that of his grandson. On the contrary, he'd do everything possible to protect them.

"I've got your back, sir."

He made the promise before ringing off.

"And your daughter's, too," he added after he disconnected the call.

Chapter 14

Ethan had a surprising request for Miranda when he came out of school on Friday. She'd spent the past two days, since hearing that Marie and Danny were home and fine, alternating between wanting to hold her son, never letting go—and needing to push both of them out into the world to live. Fear and paranoia versus strength and mental health.

"Can I spend the night at Jimmy's tomorrow?" her son asked as he climbed into the car, shoving his backpack on the floor at his feet.

Spend the night away from her?

It was as if the universe was testing her. Ethan with Jimmy.

And her with Tad.

Could she be a normal mom? Give her kid a normal life?

And a normal woman? Surrender to the intense attraction she had for Tad Newberry?

"It's his birthday and his mom said he could invite one

friend and that's me," Ethan continued, taking an envelope out of the front pocket of his pack and handing it to her.

Wanting to put the car in gear and drive away, she took the envelope and pulled onto the street.

She'd met Jimmy Randolph's parents a few times. The boys had participated in T-ball together the previous summer and James Randolph, Jimmy's father, had helped coach the team.

The boys had never played together outside of school and sports, though. Ethan had never even been to Jimmy's house.

"You've never spent the night away from home," she said, still holding the sealed envelope with, she assumed, a birthday invitation inside, as she drove them toward home.

What did she do with this? Stay safe? Or take a chance?

"So?" Ethan's defensive tone told her clearly what her son wanted her to do. She could coddle him, but only so much. He was growing into his own person. Would fight for the chance to live his life.

He was six and had no idea of the reality of their lives.

What should she do? She signaled a turn and made it around the corner.

"You'd have to follow Jimmy's parents' rules. Go to bed when they say. Get up when they say, even if it's different from how we do it at home."

"I *know*, Mom, I'm not dense." The blue eyes peering over at her from behind those dark frames just took her breath away. God, how she loved him.

What should she do? There was a car slowing in front of her. She slowed, too.

"And if it sucks, I can call you and you can come get me," he added. Practical. What she should have been.

"Don't say *sucks*. You know I don't like it."

What should she do? What should she do?

Stop it, she told herself.

"I want to go, Mom."

She knew what she had to do. What the rational part of her wanted to be able to do. "I'll call Jimmy's mom and work out the details," she told her son. But she wasn't thinking about Barbara Randolph as she turned into the driveway at home a few minutes later. She was thinking about Tad Newberry.

And wondering if, maybe, he'd be free to go on a date the next night.

She'd need some pretty stupendous distraction if she was going to survive this one—her first night ever without her son.

Tad stepped out of the shower Friday evening, having just come home from an extra workout at the gym—his third visit that day—to hear his phone ding an incoming text. Still dripping, he dried his hands, threw his towel around his neck and grabbed the phone. Very few people texted him anymore.

Recently, only one.

Miranda's icon showed on his screen.

You free tomorrow night?

Funny how in an instant you could go from sore and irritable to...

Sure, he texted back. He wondered what she had in mind. Maybe invite him to the movies with her and Ethan? He would've been glad to go with them the previous weekend.

Or another picnic on the beach.

Maybe Ethan was bugging her about another round of *Zoo Attack.*

Hell, he'd be willing to sit in a puddle with them on the back porch. His, hers or someone else's.

Feel like going out to dinner?

Sounds good. Uncle Bob's again, probably. Or somewhere he hadn't been that was equally pleasing to kids. Some pizza place where he and Ethan could play Skee-Ball or shoot hoops. Rubbing his hair while the rest of him drip-dried, Tad waited for more details.

And maybe a club or something? Adult time.

He read the screen while the phone lay on the bathroom counter, then pulled the towel from his head and wrapped it around his growing midsection.

At the word *adult*?

He stared at his phone, as though touching it would make it explode.

Unless you don't want to.

The sudden hesitation struck him. He knew what it would have taken for Miranda to issue that invitation.

Picking up his phone, he typed, Of course I want to. Sorry, just getting out of the shower, went to the gym for supper tonight.

They were going out for "adult" time. Just the two of them. He felt like a randy teenager. And a fool. He was on a job.

With permission for fringe benefits.

But Miranda didn't know that. Any of it.

Still, his feelings for her were as genuine as he could get…

If he pulled back now, she'd be hurt.

Ethan's spending the night with a friend, she texted.

When should I pick you up?

I drop him off at five. How about six? Let's dress nicely. My first time out in six years.

Images of Miranda in a form-fitting dress that showed some cleavage and shoulder immediately overwhelmed him.

Got it.

Got that they'd have all night, too. That she could very well be expecting the kiss he'd managed to avoid on the trail on Wednesday. And more.

Fully erect now, he noticed the bulge of his towel in the mirror's reflection and knew he was in serious trouble.

Miranda's Saturday off meant cleaning day, and she hit it like a maniac. Ethan went along with her plans to clean out his closet until he realized that meant getting rid of things he hadn't worn or played with in at least a year.

He agreed to dust the living room and bedrooms. And to empty all the trash cans. He started to grumble when she suggested he sort through his video games and choose some of them to donate—the ones he hadn't played in quite a while.

She'd been spraying down the back patio, cleaning the table and chairs, and came back in to find him playing video games. Every one he hadn't touched in what he figured was the past year.

Errands were next, and leaving a completely spotless

house that now smelled like cleaning solution mixed with lavender, she got them through six stores, including the toy store where Ethan dawdled as they chose Jimmy's present—an educational race car building kit. They were still back home with a couple of hours to spare before she had to drop him off.

She'd meant to shop for something to wear that night. Had glanced at some outfits as she breezed through the mall, but nothing had grabbed her.

Worried about shoes—mostly that she wasn't sure she had any that wouldn't make her look like a frumpy old mom—she tackled her own closet, rearranging, organizing, filling another bag of things to donate to The Lemonade Stand. What the women there couldn't use, they could sell in their thrift shop.

And why the hell had she said that about dressing nicely?

Or—she cringed—used the word *adult*?

Why was she going at all?

With the beginnings of a panic attack tightening her chest, she walked out to find Ethan and conjured up another job for him. He could rearrange the cupboard so all the cereal labels faced out, and the boxed dinners were all stacked together.

But her son was sound asleep on the floor in front of the couch, his glasses skewed and pressed against the bridge of his nose.

She'd worn him out.

Too bad her energy crisis was stemming from nerves and wouldn't give in to fatigue.

Back in her bedroom, she got practical. She had a dress, one she'd purchased to wear to a fund-raiser for The Lemonade Stand—a fancy wine tasting and auction put on by Hunter Rafferty's company, A Time of Your Life.

Hunter's wife, Julie, was the sister of Colin Fairbanks, millionaire husband to Detective Chantel Harris of the High Risk Team. The event had been held the previous Christmas at the Fairbanks mansion, hosted by Julie and Chantel together, with wine from Tanner Malone's local winery. Tanner's then-fifteen-year-old sister Tatum had been a resident at The Lemonade Stand for a while.

Tatum, now twenty and going to college to study public relations with a plan to work for her brother's growing winery, had organized a play night for the children of attendees in a different wing of the mansion, with popcorn and other treats, and a host of games for them all to play with prizes for everyone.

And the dress…

It was black, tight down to midthigh and then split on the sides to just above her knees. She'd still been on an extremely tight student's budget when she'd purchased it, and it had been the only thing at the overrun store that had been classy enough for the event, in her size, and with a price tag that wouldn't deprive her and Ethan of lunches for a week.

The top part of the low-cut dress consisted of satin shoulder straps. Had she been smaller-busted, there would've been no cleavage showing. That evening she'd worn a short red satin jacket she'd found on the clearance rack at the overrun store. It was Christmastime, so it looked as if she'd picked the perfect outfit for the occasion.

Tonight, mid-April, on a date…no way was she wearing the red jacket.

But she had a black sweater, short and a blend of Lycra and wool. She'd bought it to go with the crop top she'd worn for working out in college, but who had to know that?

Which brought her back to shoes. She'd never be able to dance in the high heels she'd settled for…

She tried them on, studying herself in shorts and a T-shirt in the full-length mirror attached to the back of her bedroom door. Too sexy. Definitely.

Walking back and forth in front of the mirror, forward and backward, turning to see herself from behind, she bit her lip.

Her calves looked…attractive.

But when she walked in those shoes, her hips swayed back and forth.

Tad might notice. In fact, he might like the whole ensemble. Might want to partake of…

She shook her head. Kicked off the shoes. She'd had an erotic dream with him as the star two nights before. Probably because although they'd talked about their attraction, about being together, he'd still never even kissed her.

And she wanted him to. Badly.

It was a matter of wanting what you didn't have, she told herself.

Great way to get a woman to want you—lead her on and then do nothing.

Tad wasn't the type of guy who'd lead a woman on, though. Or do nothing about it if he did.

Other than Wednesday out on the trail, when would he have had a chance to kiss her? Ethan was always with them.

What if he kissed her and she messed up kissing him back? It wasn't like she'd ever had hot sex in her life. Or been all that good at kissing. Always too closed in on herself. Feeling like a loser because she'd let her father's issues do that to her.

She'd never been a raving beauty. And when you felt ugly, it was hard to imagine someone else finding you desirable.

With that thought, she lifted up her shirt, turning to see herself from different angles. Slender at the waist. Smooth skin, if a little too white in a state where tanned blondes were the norm. Her breasts looked good. She'd always thought they were her best feature.

Her thighs did, too, she decided, dropping her shirt as she put the shoes back on and paraded again.

Until she caught her gaze in the mirror. What was she *doing*?

She was a twenty-eight-year-old medical professional. A mother.

If he liked her enough to kiss her, then fine.

If she liked his kisses, she'd kiss him back. If he didn't like her kisses, they'd take it from there.

She needed to get Jimmy's present wrapped. And talk her son into taking a shower because he was sleeping in someone else's sheets that night. She checked the battery on the watch she'd bought him for Christmas. A kid version of a smartwatch, designed to keep kids safe when they were apart from their parents. They could make and receive calls with up to four people.

Hers was the only number programmed in it.

Might not be a bad idea to have Tad's there, too. Just in case. With something practical to do, she warded off the panic for another few minutes.

Chapter 15

Tad was going to keep his hands off her. Or die trying. From the second she opened her door to him that evening, he'd been salivating. Wanting her like he'd never wanted a woman in his life.

Even more than the first time he'd had sex. He'd been eighteen, the summer before he'd started college. She'd been five years older than him—working at the same restaurant he had. He'd had women since, a fair share, but only those who were happy to keep things casual.

He'd done some research that afternoon, and took Miranda to a five-star restaurant with a renowned chef, but not because of the stars or the chef. The place was situated on a cliff overlooking the Pacific and had a wall of windows on the ocean side. He'd been lucky enough to get a reservation for a window table for two, and was glad he had when they were seated and he looked across the candlelit space to see the glow in her eyes.

"This is wonderful," she said, her voice caressing him like a warm massage. "I've never been to a place like this in my life."

Her hair, down as usual, was shining and curled around her shoulders. She leaned forward and, not expecting the move, he found that his gaze was trapped by her cleavage. Something he'd purposely been avoiding. He could see the swell of her breasts, right there, naked, in front of him, and got instantly hard.

Then her words registered. "Never?" he asked. Although the chief hadn't always been a millionaire, he'd done well for himself, making six figures by the time Dana would have been old enough to be taken out to fancy places.

"Nope," she said, still glancing around. And then, sobering, looked at him. "I...grew up in foster care, remember?"

Right. He knew better. And yet...when she'd first made the statement, he could have sworn she was telling the truth. Not just Miranda's truth, but Dana's, too. The whole truth.

Surely, even if it was only for her high school graduation, the chief would have treated her to an elegant dinner. Tad had been out with him twice, and that had just been for informal job interview conversations.

Brian O'Connor liked fine food.

So did Miranda, as it turned out. She enjoyed a good glass of wine, too, although they limited themselves to one apiece since he was driving.

"I have a bottle at home," she said as they were waiting for their check after dinner. They'd talked about innocuous things, like books they'd read, movies they'd seen, which ones they'd liked. They'd found several in common, and a couple not so much. She went for the more emotionally intense. He liked action. "The wine at my place won't be as good as this was, but it's in the fridge chilling…"

She was inviting him in.

He wanted to go in.

Miranda called Barb Randolph as she waited for Tad to get the valet to bring the car around. She didn't feel like herself, was tingling with awareness and anticipation, but she was still a woman who knew she was solely responsible for the little boy she'd taken on the run with her.

To save their lives from a madman who should've been the one person in the world who'd protect her.

The man was famous for saving lives. Revered for it.

The irony wasn't lost on her.

And she wasn't going to let it taint this night, either. As soon as she heard that Ethan was doing well, had eaten three pieces of pizza and was with Jimmy and his dad in their workshop—where James was making both of the boys little cars out of wood—she was just a woman with the most gorgeous man on earth.

At least, that was how Tad seemed to her as he came strolling toward her, his long legs and firm body filling out that fitted black suit with the red satin tie. She could have worn her jacket, after all.

She could pretend he wasn't as hot as he seemed, except that she'd seen those legs. Knew how muscular and firm they were. Had seen the boxers, too…

Were they blue tonight?

Shivering with the need to know, she took the hand he held out to her and walked with him to his SUV, not caring that the slit in her dress rode up to the silken line of her black panties as she climbed inside.

She caught him looking. And smiled. Noticing how he pulled the corner of his jacket closed.

Being with a man, being in want, being wanted, was delicious. If this was healthy living, she was all for it.

After he started the engine, it was quiet inside, dark and intimate. He reached for the radio controls, finding a streaming station that played soft music with no commercials.

"Dinner was delicious, thank you," she said as a love song that had come out a couple of years before filled the car.

She'd heard the song a hundred times. Knew the words. It had never meant a darn thing to her.

Suddenly every word was etching itself on her body.

And she got nervous.

She wasn't in love. Couldn't be in love.

But she was in a whole lot of like. Infatuation, even. Respect and a ton of lust...

And didn't know squat about casual sex. Not personally.

"You want to stop at the beach? We could take off our shoes and walk in the sand," he suggested as they drew closer to her part of town.

A reprieve. And romantic, too.

"We could stop at my place, pour some wine into plastic cups and walk over." She'd have to change shoes. Or go barefoot.

"You want more wine?"

Not as badly as she wanted him.

She nodded.

He stopped at her house. And poured the wine while she changed into flip-flops. He got a pair of his own out of the back of his SUV as they passed it on their way down the driveway.

"From my gym bag," he told her. "I don't go barefoot in the sauna."

Neither did she...when she'd gone to the sauna back in

college. Her roommate at the time, a girl she'd only lived with for one semester, had teased her about it. That was the first time she'd gone to college. She silently took his hand as they started down the street.

Tad was about ready to explode. He'd clearly been without sex for too long, and he was having a hard time thinking about anything else. Found his thoughts thinning as though the synapses in his brain had gone numb. His penis had not. Darkness hid the evidence, for which he was thankful.

But he had to keep his wits about him or risk making a huge mistake. He couldn't afford another one of those. Which was why he was carrying a cup of wine but not drinking from it.

He didn't want to lose his closeness with her. And not because of her father. But because she'd come to mean more to him in eight short weeks than he could fathom. His life, a life that had been like a spinning top, had finally settled in a little beach town in California, thanks to the woman walking beside him in the dark, holding his hand.

And yet staying in Santa Raquel wasn't a reality he could seriously consider. More and more he knew that he needed to get back to work. That quitting what he did—putting himself on the line to save lives—would destroy part of who he was. He needed his work.

And he needed her happy, too. Such an odd concept, to care so much about a person that his or her happiness made you feel…satisfied.

The air was cool and although she was wearing a sweater, she shivered. Removing his jacket, he put it around her shoulders and then took her hand again.

"You'll need this," she said, turning as though to shrug out of it and give it back to him.

He knew he wouldn't need it. Not for the warmth. He was burning up.

And darkness was his cover.

She hesitated, but let the jacket stay where it was. Let herself accept the gift. And he could feel her struggle. Like she had to fight, constantly, to accept anything from anyone.

"I washed your windows." The asinine comment blew out of him.

"What?"

"The day after you were talking about not getting to the outside windows. I came over and washed them for you."

What the hell was he doing? Trying to piss her off?

Or ingratiate himself? No, not that. Definitely not that.

"Oh." She didn't miss a step. Didn't drop his hand. But she was quiet for a minute or two and he couldn't gauge her mood or come up with any guess as to what she was thinking.

"I didn't notice," she finally said. "I'm sorry. And thank you."

All appropriate responses. But he wanted the truths she held inside.

"I shouldn't have been on your property without letting you know. Shouldn't have touched your house without letting you know." One more block to the beach. They couldn't get there soon enough. Maybe he'd take a head-long dive into the ocean.

"So why did you?"

"Because I wanted to help you and had a pretty strong suspicion that if I offered, you'd refuse."

She chuckled. "You're probably right." Then, shaking her head, "I know you're right."

He didn't want her agreeing with him. He wanted her writhing beneath him.

"I took away your choice about making that decision," he said, feeling as cantankerous as he ever got. Playing to the victim in her, even though he was taking advantage of his private knowledge about her. His secret knowledge.

It was all to remind himself that their playing field wasn't level. To make her less into him because he wasn't sure he could trust himself to say no to anything she offered.

But one less secret felt pretty damned good, as it turned out.

"Being a friend means having someone's back enough to know when that person needs help," she said.

Oh. God, what was he going to do with this woman? The minute he felt he had it all under control, she surprised him again.

In ways that captivated him.

They'd reached the sand. Kicked off their flip-flops, leaving them on the edge of the sidewalk. No one else was out, but the beach, reserved for homeowners in the neighborhood, which included Miranda's cottage, seemed to beckon them.

Not only were the waves rushing in to shore, but lights shone out on the ocean from some kind of vessel, and the shoreline in the distance was dotted with lights from houses and establishments. The sand was cold between his toes, in direct contrast to the heat of her hand in his.

"You need your coat back," she said as a breeze lifted the hair on his head.

"I need the fresh air," he told her. And then said, "You ever listen to older rock bands? You know, the classics?"

"Like the Eagles?"

"Yeah, or Kansas. They have this song, 'Dust in the Wind.' You ever hear it?"

"Dah, dah, dah…" she hummed the tuned. And then

recited a couple of stanzas about dust and wind and how small each person really was.

"Sometimes I think about that, how we're all little more than a grain of sand," he said, talking in a way he never talked aloud. Sharing thoughts that embarrassed him somewhat. "And I take comfort in that." He glanced over at her. Her hair was blowing back from her face, the moon shining on her cheeks. He moved in, not thinking, just moving, taking his lips to hers and then, in the last second, pulled back.

"It's good to know I don't always have to carry the weight of the world on my shoulders," he told her, hoping she'd see that she could feel the same way. That he could somehow find a way to truly lighten her load. Other than by washing a few windows. "Sometimes, I can just be one grain of sand blowing in the breeze, and the world won't even know I'm not doing anything."

"I heard a wise woman speaking once." Her voice was louder. They had to speak up to hear each other over the waves. "I can't remember the occasion or what exactly she was talking about. But at one point she said, 'All shall be well,' and the words stuck with me. Sometimes, late at night, if I wake up and the world seems too heavy for me to carry, I tell myself, all shall be well. In the long run, no matter what I do or don't do, no matter what does or doesn't happen, all shall be well. Usually, remembering that, I can let go long enough to fall back asleep."

Just like a grain of sand, able to lie on the beach and not matter, for a minute or two. A moment to lay down your burden and rest.

She got it. And he was glad.

Chapter 16

It was way too chilly to sit on the beach. Or even think about getting naked there. When Tad suggested heading back, she readily agreed, although she'd only had about three sips of her wine. She dropped the cup into the trash can as they passed it, and he did, too.

There was more at home, chilled. Mostly she just wanted to get there. To be alone with him.

The whole day had been building to this point and the walk on the beach had made it completely clear to her. She wanted this.

And all would be well.

The universe had sent her a man when she was ready to meet him, and yet, if he'd offered to wash her windows, she'd have turned him down.

For no good or rational reason.

She wasn't going to turn him down that night. She was

ready to start living again. Being a woman, a person, not just a mom and a PA.

While she loved being both of those things, she needed more.

It was time.

And she'd met a man, developed feelings for him, and was ready to take this first step. To get on with her life.

It helped that he was only in town temporarily. She didn't have to worry about long-term consequences. About the secrets she couldn't ever share.

There'd be no need. He was going to be a lover—she hoped—not a life partner. Or even a lifelong friend.

And if, in the throes of passion, she let something slip from her old self—like she'd admitted that night that she'd never eaten out in such a nice place—then she had to trust herself to find a way out of it. To explain. To cover.

Just as she'd been doing since she'd signed Dana O'Connor out of existence. She knew how to do it.

Had become quite adept.

She could be a grain of sand. A speck of dust in the wind. For a little while. Her son was safe. For the first time since she'd run with him, she had an entire night ahead of her, a night without having to listen for him, to know that it was up to her to keep him safe if anyone broke in...

Tad walked her to the door and hesitated behind her, almost as though he wasn't going to follow her in.

"You want a fresh glass of wine?" she asked him. "You want to come in?" would probably have been better. She wasn't going to drink much more. An occasional glass of wine was it for her.

Her father had never raised a hand to her until he started drinking after her mother died.

Not on the job, though. No, he only drank at home. On his days off. When Miranda was trapped there with him, taking the brunt of his anger. All the bitterness at the death of his wife…and for years Miranda had been the recipient of that rage.

Tad nodded and followed her inside. She didn't ask about the wine again. She just poured some for both of them. But didn't drink.

She watched him take a sip, knowing, somehow, that he didn't really want the alcohol any more than she did.

They could sit on the couch. Or go to her room. She had nightstands. They could set their wine down…

She wasn't all that up on seduction technique.

"It's nice here," Tad said, walking barefoot in his suit to the living room, taking a seat on the couch. "You've made it comfortable. Peaceful."

Smiling, she hesitated a second before sitting next to him, curling her feet up on the couch as she turned to him. If she acted all virginal, she might give him the wrong impression.

"My goal is for Ethan to grow up in a healthy happy space. Apart from the rest of the world. Which is why I have so few visitors."

As soon as the words were out, she knew they were wrong. Gave away too much. Freezing, she started to slide backward in her thinking. To…

"You've only been here for what, a year? Since you finished school?"

She'd told him during one of their coffee shop visits that she'd been a PA for a year. That she and Ethan had lived in an apartment building close to his school during the time she'd been in PA school, moving into their current home in Santa Raquel last year. All her hands-on clinical work had been done at the new children's hospital in Santa Raquel. The story that she'd had help creating for herself, and that she'd given to Tad early on, was that she'd gone to high school in Portland, Oregon—a place she'd visited, so she could speak of it believably—and that she'd dropped out of school to have Ethan. After that, she'd told him, she'd moved to Santa Raquel because of the study program that allowed her to do much of her work online, since the Santa Raquel children's hospital worked in coordination with an online PA degree program.

The truth was, she'd chosen to become a PA because she'd been in Santa Raquel due to The Lemonade Stand, though she'd never been a resident at the shelter. Then she'd heard of the PA program. With a nursing degree she couldn't use, needing a new career, the situation had been ideal for her.

That was another time the universe had provided for her after she'd done all she could.

"Yeah we moved in last year during spring break, and most of the stuff is secondhand," she admitted. "I'm slowly buying new as I can afford it."

She made good money now. More than she'd ever have made as a nurse. But she put a lot of it away. Some in a bank. Some not.

If she ever had to run again, she wouldn't be doing it destitute. She'd make it an adventure for Ethan. Taking him someplace decent. Telling him they were on vacation.

Maybe it wouldn't ever happen. She hoped… Maybe she worried for nothing. But with her father, a man who never gave up, she had to be on alert.

"It doesn't look secondhand…" He was holding his glass, watching her, not studying her belongings.

His gaze, so warm and intimate, fired her blood, made her wet with wanting, and…he didn't move. Didn't lean in as he had at the beach. They weren't even touching.

He took a sip of wine, breaking eye contact. She sipped,

too, a little taste, and when she saw how much her hand was shaking, put her glass down.

"Is there something wrong with me?" she asked. It was late. They were alone with wine. Wearing sexy clothes.

"What?" His wide-eyed glance might have been comical if she hadn't been starting to panic. In a way that was wholly new to her. "Something wrong with you? No! Of course not." And then, in that soft voice of his that made her feel…wanted all over again, he murmured, "Why do you ask?"

"You said you wanted to ask me out. Or you were hinting that you did. We're…you're…you and I, you and Ethan. You said you wanted all three of us."

"I do." He set his glass down, too. And somehow managed to move a little farther away as he turned toward her and took her hand. "I really do."

"So? Why is nothing…happening?"

He didn't say anything. Just studied her. Like he was reading a book or something.

"Ethan's usually around." His answer, when it came, was a huge disappointment. And a relief, too.

Only because he was confirming an excuse she'd already come up with. A reality she'd already created.

"But he isn't here tonight."

Her father had not taught her to be a woman who threw herself at men. On the contrary, he'd beaten her bloody the first time a boy had kissed her on her front step after a summer dance hosted by their high school—and the great chief had witnessed the unremarkable occurrence.

Buzzkill. Maybe this evening wasn't a good idea, after all.

"I'm afraid that if I touch you, I won't stop."

Tad's words brought her head up. She saw the truth

in the light in his eyes. In the way his jaw clenched. And when she dared to glance lower.

"Who says you have to stop?" she whispered, aware only of him again. Sand. Dust. All would be well.

"Sex complicates things. I don't want to lose you."

I don't want to lose you. She'd dreamed those words. Back when she used to fantasize about meeting a good man, having a husband who'd cherish her as much as she did him.

I don't want to lose you, she'd cried in Jeff's arms when she'd finally accepted what he'd known—that he wouldn't live long enough to see the birth of their son.

"You aren't going to be around forever," she reminded Tad.

"Like I said, it's complicated."

But not impossible.

He wanted her. And she needed him. To help her get to that normal life she was supposed to live.

She was a woman who didn't trust, but she trusted Tad. Enough to have him in her home. To give him time with Ethan. To want to share her body with him.

She was horny as hell and maybe she wasn't thinking straight, but it felt so…good. So right.

"I've never felt anything like this before. Been turned on like this." She couldn't keep it to herself anymore. "It's making me crazy. I think about you all the time, about how you looked that day in the examining room with your pants down around your ankles…"

Just saying the words made her heat up. She reached for her wine, took another sip. So yeah, usually one glass was her limit, but there was nothing usual about this night.

"Surely you must've been attracted to Ethan Sr.," Tad said. He had a look in his eye, a wanting, that reached right inside her.

She didn't want the wine anymore. She wanted Tad. For real. Needing him to know her in ways no one else had.

"I...wasn't attracted to him," she said slowly. "Not sexually, at any rate." She was attracted to his heart. To his friendship.

And could tell this part of the story. There'd be no way to trace what had happened between her and Jeff.

They'd never dated. No one had suspected.

"You had a child with a man you weren't sexually attracted to?" His frown showed concern, but the edge in his voice sounded suspicious, and he seemed more like a detective sensing something criminal. "Did he rape you?"

She might have seen that coming if she'd been herself.

"No!" Oh, God, no. While the lie might be a good cover, she couldn't let it stand. "I'd just...never..." She faltered. "He was a friend. A close friend. I wasn't into partying and drinking, and sometimes he'd stay back and hang out with me. Mostly we talked. Trusted each other with things we never told anyone else. We'd both grown up in foster homes and it bonded us." Her father's abuse, his birth mother and then foster father's abuse, that was what had bonded them.

"The car accident I told you about, that killed him..." The football game. She'd been there, standing on the sidelines, cheering for his fraternity. "He didn't die immediately." He'd had long enough to find his long-lost brother, contact him. The guy had offered insincere commiseration, asked for money and then moved on.

"But he knew he was going to die," she went on. "The one thing he wanted was to have a child, a legacy, part of himself to continue on in the world. He wanted that with me. And he wanted his child to be connected to me. Someone who would give me unconditional love. When he first talked to me about it, I didn't think he was serious. But he wouldn't let go of the idea. And the more he talked about it, the more I saw that if I did as he asked, he'd be able to die peacefully. I had to give that to him. I knew I wanted children someday, and if that day came sooner..."

Her biggest concern had been her father. He'd gone nuts when she'd just kissed a guy. The second she'd come in the house and shut the door. As far as she knew, he'd only taken it out on her, not the boy she'd gone out with. The date had been during the summer between her junior and senior years of high school, and she'd stayed home until she healed. But the guy had never called her again—not that their date, or the kiss, had been that great. And not one guy had asked her out in her senior year, either.

If that kind of reaction had happened after just a kiss, no telling what he'd do to her, or Jeff, if she turned up pregnant without a husband or full-time job. She'd been going home less and less since leaving for college and hadn't gone at all during the months her pregnancy was showing. She'd been petrified of what he'd do.

And had known that eventually she'd have to tell him. He was her father. He still insisted on birthdays and holidays together.

"You're saying Ethan was conceived on purpose with someone with whom you'd had no sexual relationship?"

She nodded. "And it wasn't all that terrific for either of us," she admitted. "The sex, I mean." Jeff had struggled to even make it happen. They were so close emotionally, and physically it had been so awkward...

"Was he your first?"

She'd hoped he wouldn't ask that. But nodded.

"And since Ethan...there's been no one?"

More to the point, "I haven't felt even a hint of wanting someone." She'd never been fully turned on in her life, until him.

Having endured beatings that escalated over time from

a man she'd loved and trusted sometimes did that to a girl. Squelched her ability to feel attractive to men. To be turned on by them. Or so she'd been told in counseling. She'd only been eleven the first time he'd hit her. He'd apologized almost immediately and then gently explained how it had been her fault for clinging to him and crying, for reaching for him over and over, after her mother's funeral. With it being her fault, she'd been loath to mention her bad, clingy, needy behavior to anyone else.

He'd been smart, too. Always hitting her where it wouldn't show.

"And you weren't molested?" His gaze was intent.

"No." From what she'd learned since she'd reinvented herself, she was lucky on that score. She looked him straight in the eye as she answered him.

After a long moment of studying her, he asked, "So, why me?"

His question was fair.

"I have absolutely no idea." It was the truth. "I just know that if you don't kiss me, I'm going to cry myself to sleep tonight." Being honest was one thing; too much information was another. It felt as if once she'd opened her well of secrets, anything that could slip out by chance did so.

"Well, we can't have that…" His voice had dropped to almost a whisper, a guttural one, as he moved slowly forward, sliding his arm behind her, and pulled her closer to him. She ended up with her breasts against his chest. The contact sent immediate electric shards of warmth down to her crotch.

His lips touched hers and all thought fled. There was only sensation. Incredible, delicious, delightful sensation. She opened her mouth at his probing, eager for whatever he had to give her. To show her.

Eager to learn. To do.

To know what being with him would be like.

He moved lower, kissing her jaw, her neck. He smelled like some kind of musky man something and as his day's growth of stubble rubbed against her sensitive skin, she shivered with a need for more.

Her hands moved over him, exploring the muscles in his chest, his arms. Exploring his back. Noticing the differences between his body and hers. Getting turned on by those differences.

And from knowing those were Tad's hands on her. That it was *him* she was touching.

"Are you okay?" he asked, drawing her attention to the fact that she'd stopped moving.

"Better than okay," she told him. She could stare into his brown eyes all night. She ran her fingers through his hair. "I just like having the privilege of touching you."

Maybe she was odd. And no good at love talk. But she had to be herself. Her deep-down true self. The one without a name who lived both lives within her.

"I hereby grant you that privilege anytime you want it," he said, groaning as he drew her even closer, lying down on the couch with her mostly on top of him.

"We could go to my bedroom," she offered, playing with a button on his shirt, wanting to unfasten it. To feel his skin against her fingers.

His hands were still touching her back but not holding on.

"I know," she added, "it's complicated. No strings attached, Tad. Just come to bed with me. Please?"

She'd probably die remembering these moments in the morning, but she was a woman who'd awakened from a hellacious nightmare and had this opportunity. He'd be gone soon, back to his own life.

She would come to her senses; she already knew she

couldn't be part of a long-term, committed relationship because she couldn't lie to her partner, even by omission.

"Things aren't always what they seem," he told her.

She might have laughed at the irony of that statement, but was too far gone, desperate to get naked next to him while she could. Moving her pelvis against his rigid penis, she said, "It seems like you want this as much as I do."

It didn't take a lot of experience to know some things.

He kissed her. Long and deep. Then looked her in the eye again. "I've never wanted a woman more than I want you right now."

That was all she needed to know. Standing, she held out a hand to him. He took it. Stood up and then, when she would've walked down the hall with him, he scooped her up and carried her.

Chapter 17

Tad was pretty sure he wasn't thinking straight—or thinking with his brain at all—as he fell down onto Miranda's double bed with her still in his arms. He just knew there was no way he was sending this woman off to cry herself to sleep. To believe she wasn't enough. Or desired.

This whole situation was beyond rationalizing, in a sphere where right and wrong didn't exist. The need was devastating. And mutual. It had to happen.

So he quit fighting the inevitable.

"Tell me what you want," he said as he pulled his lips from hers and saw her looking up at him, those big blue eyes wide. Her blinds were closed, but she had some kind of night-light in the adjoining bathroom and it spread soft, subtle light over portions of the bed.

"I want to unbutton your shirt."

Slipping off his jacket and tie, he tossed them toward the end of the bed, then lay back against the pillows. She had them stacked two deep and he sank into them with pleasure. "Have at it," he said, smiling at her.

Slowly, she tended to his shirt. With each button, he could feel the soft brush of her fingers against his skin, first his chest and then lower. He could feel the passion fueling his body's need for release growing more and more intense, too. Her movements were mind-blowingly hot and excruciating, but he didn't stop her. When she finally reached the bottom of his shirt, he waited—partially to give himself time to recover enough so he could continue without ending things prematurely, and partially out of curiosity.

What would she do next, this glorious feminine mixture of knowing and innocence? Of strength and vulnerability. The cleavage that had been teasing him all night was above him, a temptation he was savoring. But he willed himself enough control to be able to uncover her gifts slowly, to touch and taste and know them thoroughly.

Pulling wide the edges of his shirt, she put both hands on his lower belly, and his hips thrust upward with the force of his reaction. Seeming not to notice, she slowly moved both palms upward, fingers splayed, covering every inch of skin on his abdomen, his ribs, then his chest. She rubbed her face in the hair and flicked her tongue against his nipples before taking them between her fingers, touching softly.

She might be personally innocent, but she knew erogenous places, knew how to tantalize them, and it dawned on him—she was a medical professional. Had to have studied all the major nuances of the human body. She'd probably had a course in human sexuality.

He wanted to know every little thing she'd learned on that subject. Wanted her to show him. To do things to him.

He wasn't sure he had the time. Not on this first go-round. He groaned and she straddled him, settling her weight against his bulging fly. Not moving, just weighing him down.

"You're going to get more than you bargained for down there, missy," he told her, and she smiled.

"How do you know what I'm bargaining for?"

"How do *you* know so much about tantalizing a man?"

Her grin didn't change as she continued to tease his nipples. "I'm actually playing out my own fantasy here, but I'm glad it's good for you, too."

Not sure whether she was messing with him or not, Tad rolled to his side, and then, with another quarter turn had her underneath him. One tug and he had her dress up over her hips and his hand down her panties. She was as wet as he was going to be in a couple of seconds.

He yanked at those panties and got them down low enough. By the time he'd tossed them, her legs were spread and she had his belt undone and was working on the clasp of his pants. He helped with the zipper, pulled himself free of his boxers, then took a condom out of his back pocket and opened it with his teeth and slid it on with one hand.

"I'm sorry," he told her. "I wanted to take all night."

"We've got all night," she squealed as she thrust herself upward and over him. He moved as slowly as he could, wanting to remember every single sensation along the way, the tightness of her. The welcoming.

She wasn't as gentle as he was trying to be as she answered his thrusts, and within a few seconds it was all over.

Remarkably, for both of them.

Blissfully sore, Miranda still wasn't ready for sleep an hour later. She and Tad had made love twice more, taking more time, exploring.

"If I'd had any idea it could be like this…" Her sentence trailed off because she couldn't finish it. Even if she'd had an idea, there hadn't been a man in her life who could arouse these feelings in her.

Physical satisfaction came from more than just body parts. At least for her.

"I hope that means you'll consider repeat opportunities as soon and as often as we can arrange?" Tad half growled as he curved into her, his arm around her waist, his face snuggled between her breasts.

"I was hoping you'd be amenable to the possibility," she told him, grinning. Her hands, running lightly along his back, moved over the raised skin of his scars as they had several times during the past hour. This time they stopped there, tracing the lines. She sat up and climbed over him and then, lying behind him, began to kiss those scars. Lightly, one by one. Needing to know…

He turned, maybe uncomfortable that she was delving so completely into a different aspect of his life, but she couldn't let him disappear—back into their world of secrets. She sat up. "How'd it happen?" she asked. "For real," she added, letting him know she wasn't going to be satisfied with the generic answer he'd given Danny and Marie at the clinic.

Sighing, Tad rolled onto his back, put his arm over his eyes, and she wondered if he'd fallen asleep. Then he pulled himself up against the pillows and met her gaze.

"It started with a report of stolen property. A series of home invasions in an upscale neighborhood. A single perp. He didn't take electronics. Just jewelry, silver, some collections, an artifact. He'd hit eight homes that I knew of, in at least three neighborhoods, and at the last one, an old man was home and got hurt. There was no obvious point of entry, but the thief didn't seem familiar with the homes. You could tell he spent time in each place, looking for things. He always hit when the owners were on vacation. In the last case, a grandfather was cat-sitting for the family while they were out of town. He ended up in the hospital with—fortunately—minor injuries. Could've been a lot worse. There were never any prints at these sites. No sign as to how the guy was getting into gated communities, which told me he had to have access to them.

"I checked all the maintenance people they used, down to cleaning crews and pool companies. Nothing. Until I was questioning the old guy in the hospital and he said something about getting up to have a snack and all he could find were the pastry puff things the caterer had left after the party his son had the night before they left town. Turned out that the caterer had been to many homes in each of the neighborhoods, though not all the homes he hit were his clients'. He knew how to get in the neighborhood gates, though, without alerting anyone."

Listening to him was like watching an episode of a cop show on television. Miranda almost forgot why he was telling the story. Almost.

"The caterer denied everything, of course, but his wife said she'd seen some receipts from an antiques dealer that she'd questioned him about. They didn't have any antiques. She was able to find one of the receipts, which she gave to me. I showed up at the address on the receipt—an upscale antique store—early one morning, on a tip from a neighboring business that the owner usually came in an hour or so before he opened. As I get there, a woman's walking out and I held the door for her and went on in. I had a black-and-white backing me up, two officers, on the street. I was thinking I'd just question the guy, but the second he saw my badge it all went south. Fast. There was this little girl behind the counter and the man grabbed her, put a gun to her head and started backing toward this door, telling me that if I came any closer he'd shoot the kid."

He looked so…sorry. Like it was his fault. Miranda's heart pumped heavily. She knew this story wasn't going to end well. She'd seen his scars.

And remembered that he'd told Danny that only the bad guy had died. Of course, what else would you tell a seven-year-old who'd just narrowly escaped a beating from his father and ended up with a serious leg wound?

"I radioed outside, and then called for hostage negotiators. I was told to stand down, to wait for backup, but I could hear the little girl crying in there. Something crashed and the girl screamed. Like she'd been hurt. I tried to get the guy to talk to me, thinking that he couldn't hurt her if I kept him engaged in conversation. It worked for a minute or two. He told me he wasn't going to jail. No way was he letting his wife give his daughter another father. I figured I was getting him to trust me and I motioned for the two officers to come in and back me up. Others were arriving, coming in through the rear entrance, but the negotiators weren't there yet. I was standing right outside the door by then. I could hear a toilet flush. The guy said something about taking the girl with him, and then she screamed, 'No, Daddy, no!' and I burst through the door. I couldn't just stand there and let that little girl die.

"Turns out he'd rigged a bomb to go off when the door was opened. What he told me was that if anyone came in, he and his daughter would die. I saw the wires as I was pushing through. It was too late to stop the explosion, but I dived for the girl, pushing her out of the way and landing on top of her. The guy had been going through a divorce and didn't want his ex and her new man to have full custody of his daughter. He knew that if he was charged with a criminal offense, he'd lose her for sure. Apparently, he was dealing drugs out of the shop, too. Probably thought that's why I was there. Up until a few months before he'd been a law-abiding citizen. Ostensibly he was doing it all to have the money to pay alimony, child support and legal bills, according to a source who worked for him."

"Did the bomb really kill him?" He'd told Danny it had.

"It just knocked him unconscious. He killed himself in the hospital."

Miranda smiled, a sad smile, but still… "So you saved the little girl's life and all was well—other than your own need to heal, of course."

Tad shook his head. "I'm not just on leave," he told her. "I'm under an IA investigation. I tried to quit outright, but the department didn't accept my resignation. They want me back. They just have to work out how to get my fellow officers to believe I've got their backs."

"I don't understand."

"The bomb didn't completely detonate when I pushed through the door. It was still active and there I was, in there with a little girl who was going to die in my arms if someone didn't figure out a way to get us out of there. The shop owner was unconscious, dead for all anyone knew, but that girl was very much alive and aware.

"If I'd waited for the hostage team, chances are they either would've known there was a bomb and taken proper precautions or, best-case scenario, they'd have been able to talk the owner down. Get him to release the girl, at least."

"Sounds like he wouldn't have done that. Not if he knew he'd be releasing her to her mom and this other man."

"Hostage negotiators are trained to find out what they're facing. If they'd had no luck, they could have rigged a small camera under the door, seen the bomb. People specially trained in volatile situations would have been on hand. As it was, there were two other officers and me, and a ticking bomb."

Mouth dry, she tried not to imagine the scene in the detail he was giving.

"So what happened?"

"Help arrived. Someone who recognized the type of bomb, the particular chemicals used, and knew how to disarm it in a way that curtailed the blast."

And all that time he'd been lying there, in excruciating pain based on his scars, with the little girl. Probably telling her that everything was going to be fine.

She'd seen his patience with Ethan.

"It was clear after further investigation that the shop owner was uncomfortable with his illegal activity and had been getting more and more paranoid. He'd been planning his way out for weeks. The theory was that he intended to blow up the office to hide his illegal activity. They think the flush I heard was him getting rid of cocaine. I don't know if he'd meant all along to take his daughter with him, though. I do know she wasn't even supposed to have been there that day. Her mother had been called into work on her day off. She's the woman who'd been leaving as I'd come in."

"And the girl? Is she okay? With her mother?"

"As far as I know. She was treated and released the same day."

Reaching underneath him, Miranda placed her hand on the scars. "You saved her life," she said. "If her father was as unhinged as he sounds, chances are he wasn't going to wait for the hostage negotiating team. He knew there was no way out for him and had already decided he'd rather die than be caught."

"Maybe. That was my take."

"I'd wear these scars as a badge of honor," she told him.

"Life is complicated," she echoed his earlier words. "It's a messy situation and definitely doesn't follow the rules."

His raised eyebrow made her want to start kissing him again. Life got so unexpectedly ugly sometimes, you needed to lose yourself in exquisite sensation just to survive.

"Think about it," she continued. "Look at Danny and Devon." Look at an eleven-year-old girl whose mother had just died and whose father got drunk the day of the funeral and backhanded her for coming to him crying—begging him for solace.

He hadn't been able to handle his own grief, let alone hers. She'd understood. Which was why it had been so much easier for him to get her to believe that *she* was the problem. That *she* made him lose his temper. He'd never once hit her mother. Or her either, until that day.

"Rules and protocol are great for most situations," she said, overtired suddenly. "But when they don't work, you have to go with your gut. That's why we're given instincts as well as intellect."

It was a lesson she was still learning. To trust her instincts.

"Come here." Tad held out his arms to her. Miranda hesitated, afraid now to seek her own comfort.

She should be allowed to be happy. She had that right.

Just as she should've been able to seek comfort from her father the day her mother was buried. Just as Tad should've been celebrated for saving a life, not put under investigation because he hadn't followed protocol. She should never have had to take her child and run, leaving her father to grow old all alone.

Tad's arms slid under hers and he lifted her up against

him, sliding the covers they'd pulled down earlier over both of them.

Life wasn't fair. It was filled with tough choices.

And sometimes…miraculous moments, too.

Chapter 18

The sun was shining all that next week. Tad had to make a conscious effort not to get lulled into a sense of laid-back, carefree California life. Marie and Danny were living their lives, going about their normal routines for the most part. Danny was in rehab, working hard and showing progress already.

They found out at Tuesday's High Risk Team meeting that Marie had taken Danny to make the phone call to her ex, but at the last minute, she'd felt herself being sucked in again and refused to go through with it. Danny had been upset with her and she'd just started driving. Afraid to go home. Not wanting to call the police for fear of getting Devon in trouble and having Danny hate her more. In the end, they'd driven up the coast, had lunch and talked, just mom and son. They were both undergoing counseling, but Danny was only seven; he'd witnessed a lot in his young life and the mom-and-son time had been good for both of them. When they returned home, he was no longer mad at his mom, and Marie was readier than ever to divorce Devon and get on with her life.

They'd also heard at Tuesday's meeting that Devon had gone to a couple of job interviews. And he'd been sober for them.

Tad had difficulty keeping his hands to himself when Miranda stayed for coffee with him after the others who'd joined them had left. The two of them had been texting back and forth since they'd shared breakfast in bed Sunday morning before saying goodbye.

He'd been hoping for a dinner invitation, but hadn't received one.

"I need to kiss you," he told her as they sat, looking into each other's eyes like a couple of lovesick kids.

"I know."

"I could come over tonight." He'd sworn he wasn't going to push himself on her. That he'd wait for her to set whatever pace she felt comfortable with.

Disappointment hit when she shook her head, but he quickly deflected it. He'd known, going in, that they weren't building to something more. They couldn't, not with the secrets that stood between them.

He shouldn't have slept with her at all. He'd known that, too. Had been determined not to. And then she'd bared her sexual self to him, told him she'd cry herself to sleep...

From anyone else that might have been a come-on, a tease. He'd been completely certain Miranda had been giving him the truth.

"I don't want Ethan to get the wrong impression." The intimate way she was looking at him wasn't at all disappointing. In fact, the opposite was true.

He had to be careful. And he cared so much, he couldn't

snub her advances. "You don't want him to know we're anything but friends," he surmised.

"Right. You can't touch me or be anywhere near my bedroom when he's around. The way he's suddenly look-ing for more relationship contact in his life... I've told him you're only here for a while longer, but he's only six. Knowing that isn't going to stop him from making more of it than there is."

He understood completely. Knew she was right. "So, coffee and wanting to kiss you is it," he said.

He smiled. Remembered what it felt like to touch his lips to hers.

And remembered a whole lot more when she smiled back.

It was one thing to know what was best. And another entirely not to want what wasn't. When she'd had sex with Tad, she'd been in that one moment. With a need so intense it had to be assuaged.

She would never have believed that when it was done, she'd need him even more. That wasn't generally how life worked. You built up to an event like that, had all these expectations, and even if it lived up to your expectations, when it was over, some of that anticipation was gone.

Nothing was as good as the first time, right?

That was what she told herself for days after spending all night in Tad's arms. She couldn't get into bed without smelling the clean, sexy scent of his body—although she'd washed her sheets Sunday after he'd gone.

It was what she was telling herself Thursday when she left the clinic at noon. It was her half day because she had to work Saturday morning, and she had errands to run. Things she liked to do while her son was still in school and she didn't have to make him tag along.

Like checking out clothes. Buying new underwear.

Stopping at a jewelry counter just to look. Girlie stuff that bored Ethan to tears.

Sometimes she did the grocery shopping so he wasn't constantly bugging her to buy junk food that wasn't good for him.

The current bottle of disinfectant was almost empty, which meant she'd be opening the spare that weekend. She didn't like to be without a spare.

She thought about getting her hair trimmed. Her usual place took walk-ins. Or maybe she'd see if she could get in for a massage. Or a pedicure.

With her current salary she could afford either. Or both.

They weren't things she normally considered. She didn't need them. And the more money she could stash away, the more secure she and Ethan would be. No matter what happened...

She hadn't even reached her car yet when she had her phone to her ear.

"You feel like lunch?" she asked as soon as the call was answered. Before she could talk herself out of it.

"Of course. When? Where?" His deep voice made her feel like liquid gold.

"My house."

"I'm on my way."

"I can't believe it was even better than last time." Miranda let the words fall out as she lay, replete, in Tad's arms an hour and a half later. They'd been very careful about condom use, and then, when things had started up again, she'd used her hands to please him.

Her face on his chest moved with his chuckle. She ran her fingers through the hair close to her cheek.

So this was what got people to do crazy things to be together.

But she couldn't be like them.

Couldn't be crazy. Not completely.

"It's only for a little while," she told him, loving his leg between her thighs. She'd straddled him, was holding him down—sort of. He could move anytime he wanted to. He didn't.

"I know." He was playing with a strand of her hair.

"No touching around Ethan," she reiterated. "We aren't a family and can't give him the idea we might be. It's not fair to him."

"I know." He didn't sound any happier about that than she did. But he wasn't arguing, either. Had she wished he would?

She'd have had to say no if he'd offered any chance at anything more permanent. She had secrets she could never share. But he didn't realize that.

He had a job to get back to.

And a house.

He had a life to get back to, she reminded herself, back in Michigan. He wasn't married, didn't have family, but he had colleagues he'd known and worked with for years. He had people going to bat for him. Friends.

"So when can we do this again?" she asked.

His finger was drawing circles on her shoulder. "Tad going to Jimmy's again anytime soon?"

"No."

"Then give me a little time to recoup, say half an hour from now?"

She laughed, as she supposed he meant her to do.

And the subject was dropped.

Tad couldn't get anything about that afternoon out of his mind. From the sight of her heart-covered scrubs on the floor, the bottoms, half inside out, trailing from the bedpost, to the ray of sun that had shone through the closed blinds. From the way she'd sounded when she'd come, like a fierce feminine warrior who'd found bliss, to the hint of emotion in her voice when she'd kissed him goodbye at the door twenty minutes before she had to go pick up her son.

He seemed to be smelling the lavender that pervaded her home in every room of his own place now. Even after he showered her scent from his skin.

He'd had lovers. Enjoyed his time with them. He'd never known anything like this…thing…he had going on with his client's daughter.

What was wrong with him?

Or had he found something very, very right? He made his trips to the gym on Friday, with drive-bys to the elementary school, Marie's house and Miranda's, with one scenario playing over and over in his mind.

He's with Miranda, alone, but they're dressed. On a balcony. His. He tells her who he is. Why he was initially in town. Tells her that her abusive ex really is dead—not from some imagined car accident, but from a drug overdose. That his criminal brother is behind bars. He tells her that her father loves her so much he sent Tad to find her, just to make sure she's safe.

She'd be shocked. It would take her a few minutes to assimilate it all. To come to terms with his duplicity. But she was so mature and wise, she'd see his heart. Her father's. Ethan's. And her own. She'd know that the way they'd become involved was meant to be. She'd be grateful to him.

It could happen.

When he stood on his balcony with his burner phone on Friday, calling Brian, he was determined to get things moving forward.

"Tad? You're a minute late."

Taken aback by the greeting, he apologized and didn't feel he should've had to. Really? A minute?

"Something wrong, sir?" he asked. The chief was a fair man. Reasonable.

"Damn straight there's something wrong! My grandson's across the country from me, that's what's wrong."

O'Connor's tone, the way he said his words, didn't seem quite right. He was slurring. Didn't sound tired, but…

"So let's bring him home." Tad jumped on the opening. "I'm ready anytime you are." *Now. I'm ready now.*

"Not time yet," the chief said, sounding almost petulant for a second. And it occurred to Tad—the irritation, impatience, petulance…

"Have you been drinking, sir?" He'd never heard of the man having so much as a beer at a dinner function, but it wasn't a crime. As long as he wasn't driving. Or working.

"Yes. I apologize." He sighed. "Today is the anniversary of my wife's death and I came home with a six-pack of beer. I'm afraid I nearly polished the thing off. I don't normally touch the stuff," he said.

"It's okay, sir," Tad quickly assured him. He'd had his own share of six-packs over the years. Usually after a tough case.

"No. No, it's not okay. I know better and should hold myself to higher standards."

Shouldn't they all?

"So…tell me about your week. Their week. How's Jeffrey?"

He told the older man about his grandson's first sleepover. About the friend's father building a wooden car in his workshop.

"I'd like to have been there," O'Connor said, not quite sounding maudlin, again, but not himself, either. "There's so much I could be teaching him."

Tad didn't doubt that. He could barely imagine how hard it must have been, missing the first six years of his only grandchild's life.

Missing his only child.

"She told me that Jeffrey's father—Jeff, right?"

"Yes, Jeff, that's right."

"She told me they were friends, not a couple. That he didn't die immediately in the car accident. That he'd been injured and the injury led to his death months later. And it was only after he'd known he was going to die that they'd conceived Jeff."

He felt like scum, sharing Miranda's secrets behind her back, but this was her father. They were two men whose goal was to help her, protect her, give her back her life. He was doing what Miranda would do herself, if she could, telling her father whatever he needed to know to help her.

"Lies. All lies." Brian O'Connor sounded sad as he said the words. "That Jeff guy got hold of Dana good. Got her to lie about all kinds of things." His tone held definite tones of irritation now and a hint of bitterness, even as he said his daughter's name.

Tad's own anger rose with that one. This wasn't her fault. None of it was her fault.

The chief clearly wasn't used to drinking. He didn't seem to hold his alcohol well.

"I need more, sir," he said. He wasn't just the chief's employee now. He was Miranda's lover. That came with responsibilities.

"I can't keep doing this job for you without knowing certain things. I need proof that her ex is dead. That I'm not somehow putting her in further danger, having found her, having ties to you and to her former life."

He'd tried his damnedest to get beyond an almost ir-rational need to overcome his inability to trust anyone or anything on a gut level. He'd come to terms with the fact that perhaps he'd thrown protocol to the wind on that last case because he hadn't trusted the system or his peers. He'd somehow seen himself as the only one capable of saving that little girl.

But he'd made love to Miranda. Trust in the chief aside, job aside, he had to know. Her father could fire him, but Tad wasn't going to leave Miranda now. He was going to finish what he'd started.

"I need to know for sure, or I'm done."

"You're falling for her."

"I need proof that her ex is really dead. That she's out of danger."

"Proof coming your way," Chief O'Connor said, and there was a beep on the line signifying an incoming text.

He wasn't ready to climb off his high horse yet. Which had probably led to the wrong decision in that antiques shop, too.

"I need one more thing," he said. "A list of car accidents in and around Asheville—" the North Carolina town where Dana had gone to college "—for the eighteen months before Jeff was born."

"Since my beer binge has trapped me at home with nothing to do, I'll get to work on it and have it to you before day's end."

Tad slid back down to reality. To being just a guy on a private payroll because he'd screwed up his job.

"Thank you for understanding, sir."

"Back at you, Detective. Not one of my best days."

Tad hung up feeling he'd gotten to know the man he'd long admired more in five minutes than in all the years he'd been hearing about him. Sitting there all alone, mourning his wife.

And his daughter and grandson, too. Having risked his

life so many times to save others, only to have everything he cared most about stripped from him. It had to be emasculating to someone like the chief to sit back and let others tend to his family. To know there was nothing immediate he could do to help them.

Kind of like Tad's need to do more for Miranda, to end this. The chief's need, by comparison, would be that much greater.

You couldn't blame a guy for drinking on that one. Or for irritability and rudeness.

Chapter 19

Tad had been expecting a death certificate. Really, really needed one. The text that he opened as soon as he ended his call was not a death certificate.

It was a coroner's report. A confirmation of the deceased's identity and the manner and cause of death. Not a matter of public record.

More than a death certificate.

Jeffrey Muldoon Patrick. Aged 23. Death by opiate ingestion.

It didn't get much more official than that.

Or more convincing, either. He'd had Dana's birth certificate from the beginning, but got Ethan's now, too. He knew that Ethan's real name, his birth name, was Jeffrey Patrick O'Connor.

Named after his father, just as Miranda had said.

Thank God. She was in no danger. Miranda and Ethan really were safe. The giddy feeling of relief carried him to dinner at a place not far from his apartment. And to the grocery store to restock some essentials afterward.

If only he could tell her, be honest with her. This was good news. She should be the one buoyed by it.

But he couldn't break the chief's faith in him, break his word to a man of honor.

No matter how much he wanted Miranda to be happy.

This mission belonged to Chief O'Connor. He had a right to determine how he reintroduced himself to his daughter. He knew Dana. Tad only knew Miranda.

But if Tad could somehow get Miranda to tell him the truth about her husband—take the huge risk of exposing her past to him… No, he still couldn't break his word to the chief. If he acted too soon, if Miranda was angry with her father, as the chief believed, and he didn't give O'Connor a chance to mend fences, she could very well cut him off again.

He couldn't be responsible for a hero losing his family for the second time. Or for Miranda and Ethan—Dana and Jeffrey—losing their chance to be reunited with the man who adored them both, even though he and Jeffrey, aka Ethan, had never met.

In other words, it was none of his business. Shit.

When the list of car accidents came over his burner phone later that evening, Tad perused it carefully, but wasn't surprised to find there'd been no fatal or near-fatal crash involving anyone named Jeff, or any other man in his early twenties, in or near Asheville around the time of Ethan's conception.

As he'd suspected, Miranda's story had been a lie.

Living a lie had never been harder for Miranda than after she'd started sleeping with Tad. So many times she'd wanted to call him and tell him the truth about herself. She could trust him with the truth.

She knew she could.

And yet something held her back.

Sara Edwin's advice, for one. And the fact that Tad exhibited signs of a tendency she knew all too well from her father—one of the things she'd admired about him, actually. An inability to let injustice just lie there. Tad was a detective. A damned good one based on what he'd told her. He'd been willing to risk his life without hesitation to save a little girl.

There was no way he'd sit idly by, letting her and Ethan live in constant danger of having her father find them. He'd take on the man the state of North Carolina revered. He'd want her to prosecute her father.

He'd probably believe she could win.

What she knew was that there wasn't enough evidence. She'd never told anyone about the years of beatings. At first, because she'd felt responsible. And because she'd loved him. Because he was her only security and support. Her only family. If she didn't have her father, who did she have? There were no grandparents in her life. No aunts and uncles. Her mom's parents were both gone. Her father's dad had beaten him for much of his life. She'd never met her paternal grandmother, either.

Her father had an older brother whom she'd never met.

If she'd lost her father, she'd have been a ward of the state, and the one or two times she'd told him she'd rather be that than live with him, he'd not only punished her for the words, but had brought home reports of some of the things that happened to wards of the state. Of course, now she knew that most children in foster care were lovingly and well cared for. But back then...

Didn't matter. There was no way she'd be able to prosecute her father without evidence. No charges to file against him. Just like the courts couldn't file anything against Devon on Marie's behalf. Not yet, anyway.

You had to wait for the abuser to abuse in a big way in order to get away from him, and then you'd have a chance.

So many times, in situations like hers, the victim died first. She wasn't going to let that happen. To her or her son.

Ethan was an unknowing victim.

The train of thought led her right back to where she'd started. She absolutely could not tell Tad about her past.

And so she tried not to think about the things she couldn't change, things she could do nothing about. She had a really easy way to do that, too, and found herself sinking into a world where she worked, took care of her son and then let her thoughts be consumed by Tad—and her body governed by sexual adrenaline.

The weekend following her Thursday tryst with him, if she wasn't working or watching out for her son, she was thinking about ways to be alone with Tad. Finding times in her schedule where there might be a possibility.

Barring anything else, they could squeeze in an hour on Tuesday morning, if they didn't go for coffee with the group after the High Risk Team meeting. And if she skipped lunch.

On Monday, she proposed as much in a text to him. And got his immediate affirmative response. Hell, yes.

Then she walked around hot for him the rest of that day, dreaming about him that night, as she anticipated being with him.

She shaved her legs with extra care on Tuesday morning and left the conditioner in her hair a little longer than usual. Chose her newest scrubs—a lavender pair with rainbows and bears—and used a touch of rose-scented essential oil on her wrists.

Buzzing with need, she walked into the police station for the meeting Tuesday morning, trying to look nothing but professional as she approached the conference room. Smiled and said hello to everyone before she let her gaze home in specifically on the chair Tad always occupied.

Trying not to falter when she saw it was empty. He always got to the meetings early because he was also in domestic violence training sessions at the station and in meetings with other detectives, listening in on discussions about other domestic violence–related crimes.

He didn't show up at all that day. Neither did Chantel Fairbanks, their High Risk Team detective.

Five minutes into the meeting, she knew why.

Tad had seen Devon Williams lurking outside a business near the elementary school that morning. He'd been wearing a janitorial jumpsuit and a hat. He'd turned to a dumpster, reaching inside as though looking for something when Tad first drove past. A dumpster-diving janitor had alerted Tad enough that he'd parked and taken a walk around the building. Devon hadn't seen him, but Tad made a positive ID and called Chantel, who'd asked him to keep Devon in sight until they could get to him.

Miranda was back at the clinic, seeing patients, before she got word that he'd been apprehended—and then let go. It turned out that Devon had been just far enough away from school property to be within his allowed limits.

All team members had been put on high alert. Devon was biding his time. Chantel—and everyone else involved—was sure of it.

Suddenly sex was the last thing on Miranda's mind. Leaving work as soon as she'd charted her last patient, she drove straight to Ethan's school. Didn't matter to her that she was half an hour early. She'd rather sit in her car and wait than have him come out a second early and her not be there.

She wanted him close.

Needed him close.

He was her life.

This was her life.

She was thankful for that reminder.

Tad hated feeling uneasy. He went to the gym Tuesday night after texting with Miranda. On Wednesday he was at the police station for a while. There'd been another domestic call while he was there, regarding a first-time abuser, and he'd been asked to ride along. He stayed by the car, watching, and still got an eyeful and an earful. The man came out of the house brandishing a gun, clearly out of his mind with rage.

From what he'd heard on the way over, the guy was a high school teacher and coach. A good guy who'd come home from school sick to find his wife in bed with another man.

The officer who'd gone to the door knew the man. Talked him down. Got him to come to the station with them.

In the end, no charges were filed. He hadn't hurt anyone, only threatened. His wife wouldn't testify against him.

The next day, he'd filed for divorce.

And Tad was still uneasy.

Why, if Chief O'Connor missed his family so much—and it was clear he did—and if he knew for sure that Miranda's ex was dead—which he did—did he insist they wait longer before telling her?

Why postpone the reunion that would be so good for everyone?

Another thing was bugging him, too. The chief was

known to have nerves of steel. A man who could think clearly under the most severe pressure.

And now for the second time he'd gone off on Tad. The day he'd called a day early, and then, much worse, when he was drinking. Yeah, they were dealing with an emotionally intense situation, but wasn't that what he excelled at?

Granted, it was different when it was your own family. He of all people knew that.

But something felt off.

Could it be that Jeff Patrick was still alive? Maybe under an assumed identity? That idea was far-fetched. But Miranda wasn't Miranda, either.

So what if this Patrick guy had somehow gotten to the chief? What if O'Connor was being blackmailed, forced to find his daughter? That could explain why he'd put Tad onto her without anyone's knowing—and forcing him to remain silent now that he'd found her. Could also be why the chief was so adamant that Tad not do any checking that could lead anyone to California.

Had his original search already set things in motion? Did Jeff Patrick have a way of monitoring searches? Had he allowed the search with the understanding that when Tad found something O'Connor would turn it over?

Was O'Connor putting the guy off? Saying Tad hadn't found anything?

Yeah, right. The state fire chief of North Carolina was going to sit back and let a criminal abuser blackmail him.

But the chief had to be protecting his daughter and grandson from *something*.

Maybe, just as he said, he was waiting for the right time, the right piece of information from Tad that would give him a way in with Miranda. That would soften her heart toward him.

Didn't make sense to Tad. She might once have been

under the control of a man who'd turned her against her father, but no one was brainwashing her now.

He couldn't do any checking into Miranda or her past life, couldn't risk leading anyone to her, but he could call a former colleague of his, using his burner phone, without saying where he was, and have her do a covert check on the chief for him. It would come from North Carolina. And had nothing to do with Miranda.

The idea had niggled at him all day Wednesday, and by Thursday, with no further invitation from Miranda, he made the call.

Gail Winton, a woman who'd been a partner of his on their force, knew him better than just about anyone. They'd had a brief, very brief, sexual encounter early on in their relationship. She was now married to an army veteran–turned–refuse company owner she adored. They had two young kids.

And had Tad over for dinner most holidays, too.

After getting up in his grill for not calling sooner, not letting her know he was okay, and after he'd assured her he was indeed following doctor's orders, eating right, resting and doing all his workouts, he got to the point. She agreed to help him, no questions asked, warning that it might take a few days since he didn't want anyone to know they were looking. She didn't ask why he wanted the information, either. Didn't know what information he might suspect she'd find. That was how they'd always worked. Let the facts speak for themselves, then come up with theories to further investigate.

"And, hey," she said when he was about to ring off.

"What?"

"I'm glad you're working on something. A year off, no way that could be good for you."

She knew him too well.

Chapter 20

Someone was watching her. In line at the grocery store Thursday afternoon, Miranda had the distinct sensation of prickles on the back of her neck.

"Are you mad at me?" Ethan, at her side, looked up, his eyes wide behind those Clark Kent glasses.

"No, but I do want you to remember to tell me when you need something special for school." Someone was definitely back there. In another line. Or down an aisle. Watching her. She'd seen the same gray baseball cap three times in two days, most recently over in the produce section.

"I thought we already had potatoes."

"Usually we do." And she was glad he'd volunteered to bring them. They were doing a group science project, putting potatoes in water to see the roots grow, and he was being an active participant.

"Jimmy hasta bring jars." He looked around. "Maybe he and his mom are here, too. He didn't tell her, either."

"Turn around." Her tone of voice, her whole demeanor, was off. She knew it. And couldn't relax.

Not saying another word, probably thinking he really was in trouble over a stupid potato, Ethan stood silently beside her.

When his text dinged on Thursday night, Tad's first thought was that it was Gail, with information on the chief. Until he realized the sound had come from his regular cell phone—an entirely different notification tone. He had the burner phone out, though, on the table beside his regular phone, while he sat and tried to watch a wildlife documentary.

You want to have dinner tomorrow night?

His body leaped to immediate attention. Had Ethan been invited for another sleepover?

Of course.

He was typing in another text, telling her to name the time and place, eagerly anticipating the response of *my place*, when she texted back.

Ethan wants to know if you'll play Zoo Attack.

Of course. His response was just as quick. The rest of his bodily reaction took a bit longer to be agreeable to the plan.

She was being ridiculous. Miranda knew it. And yet, after Ethan was in bed Thursday night, she paced their small house, making certain multiple times that all the doors were dead-bolted. That the windows were latched. She kept her phone with her constantly. Placed her keys by the garage door.

In her closet, she checked inside the toe of a particular shoe, pulled out a roll of bills. Stuffed it in her bra. She was wearing it to bed that night.

And from under the bed, she dragged out a backpack, making sure she had underwear and jeans that were Ethan's current size. Added some extra granola bars to the nonperishable food stash in the front pocket.

The poor kid had a mother who was a paranoid mess. She saw it. And couldn't stop.

The only way not to be afraid was to act. So she was acting like a woman who could keep them safe. Preparing herself to calmly get them out of there if she had to. Grabbing her extra set of car keys, she carried them to bed with her. And then decided to sleep on the couch.

Routine was bad when someone was after you. It made you an easier target.

What she wanted to do was sleep in her son's room, on the floor between his bed and window. She went in there for a while.

And realized that if he woke up, there'd be no good way to explain what she was doing. Or why.

She had to get a grip. Live normally. After all, lots of people had baseball caps. Gray was a common color.

Thinking back over the past couple of days, she couldn't even be sure that whoever was wearing the cap—or caps—had been the same person all three times.

She hadn't gotten a good enough look on any of those occasions.

She'd turned away whenever she noticed him, so as not to draw his attention.

She couldn't describe his clothes. They'd been different, but baggy all three times.

That similarity sent a spark of fear shooting through her again. This was what being afraid did to you. What domestic violence in particular did to you. It made you feel unsafe in your own home.

Out in the living room, she picked up her phone. It was almost eleven. Too late to call anyone. She wasn't Marie, assigned to a High Risk Team with people on alert on her behalf.

She didn't want to call "anyone." She wanted to call Tad.

Or at least, text him.

Instead, she lay down with her phone in her hand and thought about being in his arms. Pictured her head on his chest, listening to his heart beat.

Her nerves started to settle. The constriction in her chest loosened. And eventually, she fell asleep.

Tad hadn't heard from Gail by the time he had to call the chief on Friday. After his week of high alert, frustration, theories and readiness, he was prepared for anything.

The call was as unalarming as it could be.

"I apologize for last week," the chief said on answering. "I knew you'd be calling and I was way out of line, allowing myself to get in that state."

"It's okay, sir. I know what it is to mourn a loved one." The chief, and everyone else looking into his suitability to resume his job, knew about Steffie. They figured he'd acted without thinking because he was responding to the possibility of another girl being hurt on his watch. That was partially why the chief had hired him to search for Dana.

Because he understood how it ripped a man up inside, losing one of his own, when he should've been able to protect her. Standing on his balcony in the jeans and T-shirt he'd be wearing to dinner, he felt for the guy.

"So what news do you have for me?"

He told the chief about dinner that night, without mentioning that he hadn't seen Miranda or her son all week—not counting the day before, when he'd been driving by to make sure Danny got into his aunt's car, instead of his mother's, after school. He'd been alerted to the change. Marie had a meeting at work that she really needed to attend. As a precaution, everyone wanted to confirm that the meeting wasn't a fabrication Devon had somehow forced so he could get to his son.

While Tad had been watching for Danny, he'd seen Ethan run out to Miranda's car in a line of parents waiting to pick up their kids.

"I've been thinking about what you said, about moving things along," the chief said, gaining Tad's full attention. "Maybe this week, when you talk to her, ask her something about her father. I know she's lying about her past, I understand she has to be the person she's created, lies and all, but maybe some truth will come out, too. A nuance. A word. A missing detail that would normally be there. You're trained to notice such things."

He was. Interrogating people, getting to various truths, was one of his fortes. Which was why it was going so much against the grain to live with the secrets between him and Miranda. They were consuming him. Every minute of every day.

Glad to hear that the chief was at least considering an end to this, Tad readily agreed to his request.

Miranda didn't see Gray Cap at all on Friday. And she looked. Everywhere. She had to get a good visual, just in case. Given how many people wore gray baseball caps, wasn't it odd that now there wasn't a single one anywhere in her vicinity?

Or maybe she'd been dreaming the whole thing up. Making something out of nothing. Or her head was playing tricks on her.

For instance, when she came out of work a few minutes later than usual, she was sure that the person in the black sedan in the corner of the parking lot was watching her.

Why wouldn't he be? If he was waiting for someone to come out of an appointment, he'd be watching everyone who came through the door. She was going to get this under control. It was because of Marie and Devon; she knew that.

Everyone on the High Risk Team was aware that Marie wasn't safe. They were doing everything they could to protect her.

Sometimes everything wasn't enough.

She couldn't get over the feeling that someday, someway, her father was going to use all the tools at his disposal—the police forces, the power, the access to confidential information, the reputation that let him go anywhere, do anything he wanted without question—to find her.

And when he did...that would be the end. There was no doubt in her mind about that. He didn't want or need her. She was nothing more than a reminder of her mother to him. When she'd been little, maybe not so much, but after puberty, when she'd matured, everyone had said she looked just like her mom.

It had taken Miranda a long time to realize that where her father was concerned, that was a bad thing.

What Brian O'Connor wanted wasn't his daughter. He wanted his wife—and his grandson. The son he'd never had.

She'd die before she'd let him spend five minutes alone with her boy.

And she wasn't going to think about any of it that night. Tad was coming over. It had been more than a week since she'd seen him. The longest it had been since they met. She wouldn't be able to touch him, to feel his lips on hers, but safe in her home with her son, she was going to soak up Tad's presence. Let him know, somehow, that he mattered, and let herself believe that all would be well.

She was going to be a grain of sand. Mere dust in the wind. Just for a few hours.

Tad played *Zoo Attack*. He ate two helpings of chicken-and-rice casserole. Helped with dishes. Kept his hands to himself where Miranda was concerned. But not his gaze. From the second he'd seen her, in skinny jeans and a sleeveless, gauzy, flowing tie-dyed tank thing, opening the door to him, he'd been obsessed with the sight of her.

She was like the sun and moon in one. A natural Madonna with the power to take him over completely.

They ate out on the back patio. After finishing his chocolate chip bar with ice cream, a treat for when the dishes were done, Ethan asked if he could go in and watch a movie, naming a popular kid's flick that had just come on the streaming service. Miranda let him go.

Tad had never been so glad to have a boy want to watch television.

He couldn't touch Miranda. Couldn't kiss her. But…

"Do you have any idea how badly I want to hold you right now?" he asked.

"Maybe about as badly as I want you to?" She smiled, but her lips were trembling.

He got it. He was dying, too.

And had a job to do so he could get them out of this misery and into the next part of wherever, whatever they'd be.

"You're incredible, you know?" he said, just because he wanted to talk about her, them, nothing else.

"I'm just me. Don't see more than what's there." She'd brought ice water to go with their dessert and took a sip of hers, then set her glass down next to Ethan's empty milk cup.

"I'm seeing what's there. You're both mother and father to your son, doing a remarkable job of raising a well-adjusted kid."

Her shrug seemed to be one of discomfort more than anything else, and he was acutely reminded that she was a woman forced to keep secrets. Trying to make her feel cherished, he was, instead, doing the opposite.

He asked her about her mom, about life before she was eleven. And spent the next half hour hearing wonderful things about a woman who'd clearly had spunk. Loved adventure. And her daughter.

"She never said anything to you about your father?"

"No. But I was only eleven when she died." She glanced toward the house, toward Ethan, for the first time in a while. He could see the boy. They could hear the television. But for some reason, mention of her father had her turning around.

The chief was right; Tad knew how to read nuances. He just wasn't sure what this particular one meant.

That she missed her father? That she hated seeing Ethan miss out on knowing him? And vice versa?

Probably blaming herself, he surmised, based on all of the literature he'd been reading.

"Have you ever tried to find out who he was?" he asked.

"No. Why would I? Clearly he wanted nothing to do with me."

Her lack of emotion struck him as odd. She didn't sound bitter, and she might have, given the circumstances as he knew them. If she was angry with her real father, some hint of that should come out in her talking about her fake father.

Unless she wasn't angry?

"Having no father isn't an issue for me." Again, her response seemed odd. As if she truly didn't care.

But she had to, didn't she? A young woman who'd lost her mother, been raised by a doting, heroic father—one who was beside himself with missing her? Who'd do anything to protect her and see her happy, even deny himself her presence? Growing old all alone.

Was she that good at hiding her feelings? Studying her, Tad felt off the mark for the first time since he'd met her. Unable to tune in. As though she was a complete stranger. Closed to him.

"What about for Ethan's sake?" He pushed where he would otherwise have dropped that line of questioning. He'd given the chief his word.

Her shrug, the expression on her face, held some regret. He paid eager attention. And then she said, "I hate that my son doesn't know his own father because he was such a great guy. Other than that, no. Our society gives us the idea that you need two parents to grow up happy and well-rounded, but I truly think that what it takes is unconditional love, continuity and security. That's why I won't let you stay here when Ethan's home. I won't let him grow up with a confusing message caused by different men staying in his home and then leaving. With different authority figures."

If they hadn't already established that he was only there for a period of time, he'd have been hit hard by that one. As though he was just one of a number. She'd put it right out there without her usual compassion. It wasn't like her to be harsh.

And then he understood. She was being practical, with her emotions shut off, because she had to be. How else could she have faced leaving her father? She'd had to ignore the demands of her heart when she left that life. It was the only thing that made sense.

It wasn't much to give the chief, but he was done fulfilling that request.

Chapter 21

It was getting too messy. Miranda saw everything closing in on her and knew that her time with Tad had to end. She'd known it all along.

Just as she'd known she couldn't have a long-term committed relationship—with anyone. The closer she and Tad got, the more he tried to know her, to discover exactly who she was. And there was only so much "her" to know. His questions weren't wrong. His curiosity was perfectly normal. By the same token, she wanted to find out everything there was to learn about him.

Still, she didn't ask much. She couldn't take what she couldn't give.

But she wasn't ready to lose him. Not yet. He had at least half a dozen more months in town. Maybe she wouldn't be able to handle the lies for that long. For now, for this day, and maybe the next week or two, maybe even a month, she had to try.

Just thinking about him had pulled her out of the dark realms of paranoia and panic, to a place where she'd actually been able to sleep the night before. She'd woken around three in the morning on the couch and had managed to get to her room, crawl into bed and fall back asleep.

She hoped she was helping him, too. He didn't want a long-lasting relationship with her, either. He was far from home while he healed—not just physically, but emotionally. He had to be somewhat on edge, waiting to hear about the Internal Affairs investigation and his job. His entire career. She and Ethan did seem to be helping him get through it.

They might be ships passing in the night, but were meant to anchor together for this brief time. She had it all worked out.

She just had to quiet the clamoring of her mind and live in the moment. The day. The next week or two. A month…

She had to get through this stage of whatever step she'd reached on her life's journey. Ethan was branching out. She was branching out. They were getting through the changes.

And it was understandable that she'd be uneasy. That a bit of paranoia would present itself. It always would during moments of vulnerability. The trick was knowing how to deal with it. To beat it back rather than give in to it.

"Time for bed, little man," she said as she and Tad came in from the back porch just as Ethan's movie was ending. "Say good-night to Tad and then put your jammies on and brush your teeth."

Ethan got up from his place on the floor, his glasses bobbing on his face as he rubbed his eyes. "Night," he said to Tad, and headed down the hall.

A signal to her that it was Tad's time to go.

"He doesn't ever argue about going to bed," Tad marveled, after telling Ethan to "sleep well."

"Never has," she said, loving her boy so much. "When he's tired, he wants his bed." She didn't invite him to sit. To hang around. She stood there, listening while Ethan brushed his teeth.

"Mind if I use the restroom before I go?" Tad asked. "I thought I'd drive by Marie's place before I go home."

Of course she didn't mind. She told him to use her bathroom, since Ethan was in his. And then stood there wishing she could join him in his car, in the dark, driving slowly through town. Wished she could help him more than she did.

Perhaps they could go to the beach again on Sunday. The three of them.

Ethan crossed the hall to his room and she went to tuck him in, reveling in the small arms that wrapped sleepily around her neck. "Night, Mommy, love you," he said, and her heart lurched. He was already half-asleep as he turned on his side and curled his hands under his pillow.

Mommy. He hadn't called her that in a while, other than when he was particularly sleepy.

"Love you, too, sweetie. Sleep tight," she whispered.

This was why she lived as she did. Why she'd gone through everything she had to get Ethan out of North Carolina. And continued to sacrifice to keep him safe. She and Jeff had created a life—their son's— purposefully. Jeff had trusted her, even knowing about her father's power over her. And she was going to do everything in *her* power to give Ethan the life she and Jeff hadn't had. A life free of violence, with a caring parent who was capable of unconditional love.

She heard her bathroom door open and instead of returning to the living room to show her guest to the door, she pulled Ethan's door partly closed and continued into her own room.

She just needed a minute. Something to sustain her as she spent the rest of the evening alone. The ghost in the black sedan that morning was starting to loom in her mind again, gray baseball cap and all. But she had it under control. Knew it for what it was. Now those memories were simply reminders that she'd never have a man in her life full-time—at least until Ethan was grown. She'd never know what it felt like to say good-night to her child and crawl into bed with his father.

Meeting Tad halfway between her bathroom and her bedroom door, she wrapped her arms around his waist, shivering as his arms came around her.

"I wish you could stay," she whispered.

His answer was to press his pelvis against hers, letting her feel how ready he was to crawl into her bed.

Conscious of the hallway, of her son's door just feet away, she pulled Tad into her bathroom, closing that door.

It was the one door Ethan was used to seeing closed. She'd decided when he was four, and getting curious about physical differences, to answer his questions as they came, and to shut that door so they didn't come too soon or too often.

She'd opened her mouth to tell Tad that she just needed a kiss before he left, but his mouth covered hers before she got the words out. She eagerly met his tongue with hers. He broke the kiss, breathing heavily, and trailed his lips across her jaw to her neck, sending tingles all through her.

Weak-kneed, she fell back against the counter, leaning there as her hands touched the bulging fly of his jeans. She rubbed it, wanting more access, but when he reached for the button on the fly, she stopped him.

"Not like this," she said. And not with Ethan in the next room. "But…how about Tuesday? After the meeting."

He laid his forehead against hers. "You're killing me, you know," he said, but he was grinning.

"So that's a yes?"

"That's a *hell, yes*! Of course."

With that he kissed her, hard, one more time, then let her go.

Tad hit the gym first thing Saturday morning, intending to be home, showered and ready to get to the baseball diamond where Danny Williams would be playing T-ball. Not running the bases yet, but practicing fielding and batting. Marie had texted the night before to say she was scared someone had told Devon she'd signed their son up for the intramural spring league, but she didn't want the police involved. She thought Devon was finally doing better, that they could part amicably, and she didn't want to raise his ire.

Tad had responded immediately, telling her he'd be happy to hang out and watch the practice.

Miranda, as she'd stood at the door the previous night, watching him walk to his car, had called out an invitation to go to the beach for another cookout on Sunday. He'd been happy to accept that invitation, as well. For entirely different reasons.

Everything felt like it was coming together. He didn't know how things would end up, but he was tentatively hopeful that his future would somehow include Dana O'Connor and her son. Probably at his job in North Carolina. More and more it felt like he needed to get back to what he was trained to do. What he did best. Didn't have to be in North Carolina, but if he had a job there…he really would like to pursue the idea of starting a High Risk Team in the area.

And figured, once she'd reconnected with her father, Miranda would want to head home, to be closer to him.

Tad didn't kid himself—there was a chance she was going to hate him, or at the very least feel unable to trust him, when she found out he'd been duplicitous with her from day one. Who wanted to hear that your lover was on your father's payroll to spy on you? But as bad as that sounded…when she heard the truth, when she knew why, surely she'd understand…

Just as he fully understood why she was still keeping her secrets from him. Hell, her whole life was a lie. But one that had to be told to save her life.

Because he was waiting to hear from Gail, he checked his burner phone before jumping in the shower. While he was eager to get out of his sweat-soaked T-shirt and gym shorts, they weren't the priority.

He had a text.

Not much yet. Looked at all finances that were filed as part of his campaign for office. Seem to be perfect. Tax records, the same. I've got a couple of people looking into how he spends any spare time. Will be following up with his public calendar. He's on vacation right now. Left a couple of days ago to go fishing.

That was it. Innocuous. Nothing at all, really, which was what he'd hoped he'd find. Not that any blackmailers, if they were any good at it, would likely show up in the first go-round. But if it was someone connected to her ex, chances were it wouldn't be a professional. Still, on the surface things were as they should be. Nothing obvious.

And yet… He stood there, reading the message again. *On vacation?*

He'd just talked to the chief the night before and he hadn't given any indication that he was vacationing. Out on a fishing boat, or at a lodge.

Not that the man owed him any explanations as to his whereabouts, but it seemed…odd. Under the circumstances.

They were talking about getting him and his daughter back together. About moving forward. If he were the chief, he'd have been waiting by the phone to see if Tad called with responses from the interrogation he'd agreed to do. A call Tad had planned for later that afternoon.

The news would be disappointing to the chief. But maybe not. If, as Tad was thinking, Miranda's lack of emotion, of any reaction at all, where her father was concerned was because she'd loved him so much, she'd had to block that love in order to leave him. To survive without him.

And he remembered the way she'd looked at Ethan at the first mention of her lack of a father, as though she regretted her son's not knowing him.

Just because the chief was on vacation didn't mean he wasn't waiting to hear from Tad. They hadn't specifically arranged a call outside their normal Friday ones, but the chief had said to keep him posted when they'd rung off the night before.

Deciding his shower was going to have to wait, Tad dialed the chief's private cell number.

He picked up on the first ring. Because he was on vacation? Or *had* he been waiting to hear from Tad? Hoping to hear from him?

He filled the older man in on his conversation with Miranda the night before, ending with, "It was my impression that she might be blaming herself for the fact that you aren't in their lives," he said. Could be his theories were based on what he thought, not on what actually was. He was getting too close to Miranda to be just a detective.

"You think she could be ready…" the chief began.

"I do, sir." With the man on vacation, the timing might

be right. "If you want to fly out here, I can meet you if you'd like. Tell me how you want this to play out." The man was on vacation. Now was the time to tell Tad, to let him know that he could fly out there that day. Tension filled him as he realized that he might not have any role in the reunion at all.

Or any chance to tell Miranda he hadn't just been seeing her at her father's behest. To tell her how his heart was open to her in a way it hadn't been open in a very long time.

He hadn't thought this part through well enough.

"I'm kind of involved at the moment," the chief said. "Business I can't leave unattended. And, frankly, I want to plan the reunion. So much is resting on it. I'll go through some of her mother's things. Take them to her. That way, even if she rejects me, she'll have them. I don't know when exactly I'll go out there, but it'll be soon. Very soon. For now, if you could continue as you are…"

There was nothing for him to say but, "Of course."

In the shower, Tad was feeling rather glad the chief wasn't rushing right out. Now that he'd realized he might not have a chance to explain himself to Miranda, he needed time to think about his own plan. To figure out if there was anything he could do, prior to her learning the truth. To let her know that his feelings for her were completely personal. And not likely to end.

Yes, he was glad, but a little uneasy, too.

The chief had said he was involved in business that couldn't be left unattended. A fishing trip?

Surely his daughter and grandson meant more to him than catching fish.

Unless the "business that I can't leave unattended" had to do with blackmail—someone trying to force him to provide large sums of money for Dana and Jeffrey's safety.

In which case, he couldn't afford to expose their whereabouts. Any traceable contact between the chief and Tad could do just that.

If that was the case, O'Connor should've told him. Eggs in different baskets or not. Tad understood the man was in an impossible position, but Tad couldn't do his own job if he didn't know what he was up against.

Not to disrespect the chief, but he wasn't liking the guy all that much at the moment.

He couldn't rest easy unless he knew for certain that Miranda and Ethan were safe.

Chapter 22

Miranda was cleaning bathrooms Saturday afternoon, with her son using the toilet brush to scrub his toilet and splashing water all over the rim and onto the floor, when the tone she'd set for High Risk Team notifications sounded.

Grabbing her phone out of the back pocket of her shorts, she clicked on the text.

Marie Williams and son Danny did not return home after T-ball practice and lunch as expected. Not answering cell. Devon not answering either. CF

CF. Chantel Fairbanks.

The notice went out to the full team, putting everyone on alert. And anyone who was available could join a search party to try to find them.

"Who's that?" Ethan asked, peering up at her from behind his glasses. The unusually solemn expression on his face alerted her to the fact that she must look concerned.

She didn't want him to know who it was. Didn't want domestic violence to be a part of his life.

She had to help. As many vehicles on the road as they could get, as many eyes looking, would increase Marie's chances that someone would spot something and be able to alert authorities in time to save her.

If indeed she was with Devon. They didn't know for sure.

Which was why there wouldn't be an Amber Alert.

It was up to them, the team and anyone the team could contact, to be the equivalent of Danny's Amber Alert.

"You remember Danny, the boy you saw with Tad that day?"

"Yeeahh…" Ethan drew the word out as though hesitant about wanting to know more.

"His mom's car is lost and she's hoping some of us can drive around and help her try to find it. She can't get to work without it." The words came to her as though inspired.

Her son scrunched up his nose. "Huh?" he asked, the toilet brush dripping on the floor as he held it suspended above the bowl. "How does a car get lost?"

Okay, not inspired. "I don't know. Maybe it was stolen," she said, taking the brush from him and wiping the floor with the towel in her hand. "But I think we can help, don't you? Just drive around for a while and see if we see it. I'd need you to do most of the looking, since I'll have to pay attention to the driving."

"Okay." Ethan shrugged. "Can I have a hamburger and french fries for lunch, then?"

"Of course." Maybe he was playing her. Bribing her. Maybe she should teach him that doing good deeds for others meant you didn't get paid for it. Teach him a lesson in self-lessness. At the moment, though, she'd be willing to buy him ice cream for dessert, too. She just had to get out on the road.

Tad knew for certain that Danny and Marie made it safely away from T-ball practice. There'd been no sign of Devon all morning, and no cars following Marie as she left the diamond. He'd been watching.

He hadn't followed them to lunch afterward. She'd texted, letting him know that Danny had asked for pizza and she was taking him to buy some at a place not far from home. That was the last he'd heard until he got a call from Chantel an hour later.

He was the last person to have seen the mother and son. He told Chantel that Marie had been wearing black capris and a ribbed white T-shirt, and Danny had still been in the jeans and T-shirt he'd worn to practice. He told her where they'd been headed.

She already knew both things and was just verifying what Marie's sister, Ruby, had told her. Marie had texted her after she'd texted Tad, to ask if Ruby and her husband wanted her to bring home any pizza.

She'd never made it to the pizza place. And she wasn't answering her phone.

He got the High Risk Team alert almost immediately after his call with Chantel. Was back out to his car and on the road immediately. She'd asked him to start from where he'd last seen Marie, to check around the ballpark, see if anyone remembered anything. And then to drive all the streets between the park and the pizza place.

Officers were going to be talking to neighbors along the route. And expanding the search farther out.

He reminded himself that they'd thought she'd gone missing once before, that she'd failed to answer her phone then, too, and that she'd eventually returned home, safe and sound.

He told Miranda the same thing when she called a few minutes later to let him know that she and Ethan were out looking for Marie's car and would call the police if they thought they saw any sign of it.

"Don't approach, no matter what," he told her, instantly alert. They needed eyes on the road. He just didn't want Miranda or Ethan out there.

But he couldn't stop her. And probably shouldn't. As long as she kept her distance, she was in no real danger. Devon would have no idea that a woman out driving with her son would be any threat to him. It wasn't like he'd be shooting at every car he passed as he drove wherever he might be taking them. That would be the quickest way to get himself arrested.

If he even had them.

Marie had been told, after the last incident, to let someone know if she was going to change her schedule, told to call before she took off again. She'd apologized for the time everyone had spent looking for, and worrying about, her.

"Maybe Danny changed his mind about which pizza place," he said now, conscious of the fact that Ethan was in the car with Miranda, making it difficult for her to speak freely.

He'd caught the "looking for Marie's car" remark. Took it to mean that Ethan didn't know Danny and Marie had been in it or were in any danger.

And maybe she was right to keep the news from her son. Earlier, Tad had figured Ethan would be better prepared in the event of danger in his own life if he knew. He'd since changed his mind about that. She was raising a happy, healthy, well-adjusted child.

"Could be they went to Charlie's." A pizza place with

gaming rooms. He'd driven by it but never been inside. "She might not have heard her phone ring, or isn't getting cell service in there," he finished.

He was at the ball field. Had to get going. Talk to some people. He didn't tell Miranda that, though. He just asked her to please keep in touch, assuring her he'd do the same.

"And be careful," he told her. "No risks."

"You, too," she said, and he wondered if she was thinking about the time he'd gone rogue. If she was worried he'd get hurt. He had a gun on him, not that she knew that. He never took it into her home, leaving it locked in the glove box of his SUV. But he was licensed to carry and always did.

Telling himself that Ethan was his assurance that Miranda wouldn't take risks, he exited his vehicle and headed into the park.

"There's a red car."

"But see how it only has two doors? We need a car that's bigger, like ours," Miranda told Ethan as they drove slowly through the streets of Santa Raquel. She'd tried Marie's phone, just in case the woman would pick up a call from her, but it went straight to voice mail.

As she drove, trying to see every single car within sight, she prayed that Marie and Danny were okay.

And that Tad would be, too. Knowing that he was out there, also looking, was a comfort to her. Strange how in her most frightening situations, thoughts of Tad were what brought her back to a sense of being okay.

The sexual attraction she got. The other, the comfort part, not so much. Maybe she just didn't *want* to get it. Knew that she couldn't take it any further, so she didn't want to think about it.

"There's one!" Ethan said, pointing at a car that was

the same size and basic shape as Marie's, but a different make and model. She'd shown her son a picture of the vehicle before they'd left their driveway, having checked it out on the internet on her phone.

"That's almost it, but remember that symbol on the back of the car I showed you? That's what we're looking for."

They'd been at it for half an hour, up one street and down another, just driving and watching, when Ethan saw a car that looked exactly like Marie's parked in a driveway. Devon was staying with a friend in the area, which was why she'd chosen to search there, but she didn't know which house.

Picking up her phone, she dialed Chantel, gave her the address and prayed again.

It took too much precious time for Tad to make it all the way around that park. Parents and kids were filling all three diamond areas as different T-ball and Little League teams held practices and scrimmage games. He talked to at least fifty people, showing them Devon Williams's picture, but no one had seen him.

Anxious to get back on the road, to get to the part where he was out there doing all he could to find the guy, he nonetheless stayed his course. Chantel had asked him to cover the park. He was going to do that.

Others were out on the roads, cops and volunteers like Miranda. He didn't always have to be on the front line.

His call with the chief still plagued him a little as he walked from the second to the third diamond area, completely on the other side of the park from where Danny had practiced. Why had O'Connor led him to believe he was tending to an important business matter if he was on vacation?

Could Gail's source have made a mistake?

The possibility was highly unlikely. Gail checked and double-checked everything, just like Tad did. Needing to know firsthand. It was one of the shared traits that had made them such good working partners.

Approaching a woman who was sitting alone on a bleacher, watching a group of little boys gathered around a man on the field, Tad said, "Excuse me. I'm looking for my brother. You didn't happen to see him around here, did you?" He showed the picture of Devon.

"He's not from around here, recently had surgery, and needs his medication…" He'd invented so many stories over the years, he always had one handy.

Expecting to hear the same "no, sorry," that he'd been hearing for the past half hour, he was surprised when the woman took a second glance.

"Yeah, actually, I did," she said, looking up at him. Her eyes were squinting against the sun, but she appeared to be about Miranda's age, late twenties. She was dressed like almost everyone else, in jeans and a T-shirt, had short brown hair, and wasn't wearing a wedding ring.

Something about her expression had Tad paying close attention.

"It was kind of sad," she said, "the way he missed his son's practice."

"You spoke to him." *Careful now, he's your missing brother needing medication at the moment. Not a potential suspect who might be hurting his wife and son.* He softened his features.

"No." She shook her head. "I just heard him talking to the coach, right before practice started. He seemed to think his little boy would be practicing at noon. He acted somewhat…off, though."

"He needs his medication."

"He was really mad, like he thought the coach was hiding his son from him."

An angry Devon. Things didn't look good for Marie.

"Did you see which way he went?"

"Yeah." She tilted her head to her left. "He got in a blue full-size pickup right over there. I'm sorry…he obviously shouldn't be driving, but no one knew."

"It's not your fault," Tad said, hurrying away. She'd understand his urgency and even if she didn't, he couldn't worry about it. Pulling out his cell phone as he ran, he got Chantel on the line.

The car Ethan had pointed out didn't belong to Marie. He and Miranda didn't find her car. The police did. Abandoned on the side of the coastal road leading out of town. There'd been signs of a struggle. Of another car coming off the road right behind her, possibly back-ending her to get her to stop.

An all-points bulletin was put out for Devon's truck, and a text went out to let volunteers know they were no longer needed. Finding Devon was up to the police now.

"Why are we stopping, Mom? Did they find the car?" Ethan asked as she pulled into the drive-through lane of his favorite fast-food place.

"Yes, they did," she told him, trying her best to sound upbeat about that. "Isn't that lucky?"

"I guess." He didn't sound all that glad. "I was hoping it would be me who'd see it first and then I could tell Tad."

She hadn't told Ethan that Tad was involved in the search, but he might have assumed it.

"Can we go in? Please?" Even though he was too big, Ethan still liked to play in the jungle gym set up for kids inside the restaurant.

She wasn't getting out of her car until it was safely

parked in her garage. "Nope. We've got cleaning to finish," she told him, which, of course, brought another groan.

She bought him a chocolate shake to go with his lunch to compensate for being a mom.

Tad wasn't on the scene when they found the Williams family. Chantel was, though, and called him personally to ask him to join them.

Devon was holding Marie hostage inside an abandoned shack. Whether it was one he'd known was there or one he'd just seen driving by was yet to be determined. He'd sent Danny out, unharmed, when the police arrived and now Danny was asking for Tad.

He made it to the scene, fifteen minutes outside town, in ten. It had taken another hour for negotiators to get Devon to let his wife go. But he didn't do it without first punishing Marie for making him miss his son's first T-ball practice. He'd roughed her up so badly her face was barely recognizable. And from the way she was holding her arm, Tad figured it was broken.

Tad wished he could wipe the vision from his mind. He was glad Marie was safe. Thankful that her husband was in custody. But all he kept seeing was Miranda in a similar state. Imagining her face behind Marie's bloody swollen bruises.

He called her as soon as he left the scene. Needing to say so much, to promise her she'd never suffer like that again, but unable to let any of it out.

"You're sure she's okay?" Miranda asked softly. "You saw her for yourself?"

"She was talking when they put her in the ambulance," he said. "Asking about Danny."

He'd let her know from the outset that the boy wasn't hurt. Physically. That he was with his aunt and uncle.

"Danny told me he was the one who called his father about the practice," Tad said. "He was afraid if he told the police he'd done that, they'd take him to jail, too."

"You assured him he's not in trouble, right?"

"Of course. He said he was scared to play without telling his dad because when he found out later he'd be in trouble. So he got hold of Marie's cell phone and called him. Somehow he messed up the time, or Devon would've been there this morning, I'd have seen him, and all of this could have been avoided."

"Poor little guy. No way he should be going through this."

She sounded angry.

And kind of frightened, too. He figured she was probably experiencing some of Marie's pain, her fear, vicariously. How could she not be? He remembered how frightened she'd been the last time Marie had gone missing.

She'd never ask for help, but...

"You mind if I stop by? A little *Zoo Attack* with Ethan sounds pretty good right now."

"Of course," she told him. "I'll thaw some hamburgers and we can have sloppy joes for dinner."

A community had come together and saved a life that day. And, for the moment, he had a place in Miranda's and Ethan's lives.

He started to feel a bit better.

Chapter 23

Someone was following her. There was no doubt in Miranda's mind as she drove from the big-box store to Jimmy's house on Sunday afternoon. She'd told Ethan he could invite his friend to the beach with them, thinking it would be good for Ethan not to have Tad all to himself. It would be a chance to repay Jimmy's family's hospitality, as well, without having the boy running around their home.

She wasn't ready for that yet. There was nothing for him to find there that would alert anyone to the fact that she wasn't who they thought she was. But the idea of him going home to tell his parents about her house, or their private lives, or anything he found different from his... Nope, she just wasn't ready.

Turning two blocks before Jimmy's street, she noticed the black sedan doing the same. She couldn't be positive it was the same car she'd seen in the clinic's parking lot on Friday. Couldn't tell, from surreptitious glances in the rearview mirror, if the driver was male or female.

Didn't see a gray baseball cap.

But she was definitely being followed.

Watched.

It wasn't her first time. Or even her tenth. She had no way of knowing when it had started. But she'd first been aware of it when she was only sixteen, and out after dark for the first time. Scared, but unwilling to admit that to her father, she'd been paying extreme attention to everything around her and had noticed the car turning whenever she turned.

Not knowing what to do, she'd hurried home, found her father there waiting for her. Sober for once, and in a good mood. She'd never told him that someone had been watching her.

She'd been afraid it was him. That he'd hired someone. And hadn't dared bring down his wrath by saying anything.

And now, heart pounding, she went over her car in her mind. Told herself to stay calm. Hyperventilating could get them killed. The roll of bills under the spare tire would last for at least a week. If she was careful. A duffel bag holding clothes and food rations was in the back, beneath the duffel that held her jumper cables and medical kit. She had an extra phone charger in her purse, and in the console, too, not that she'd use her phone if she ran. Too easy to trace.

"You know what? I'm not feeling very well," she told Ethan, turning again. And again, ending up on a main thoroughfare. A couple of seconds later, she saw the black sedan turn, too, far enough away that she couldn't make out a license plate. "I think I'm going to have to cancel today, sweetie. I'm sorry," she told Ethan.

"You sure?" His brow was creased. "Maybe you just have to go poop and then you'll feel better."

Because in his world, life was usually that simple. Thank God.

"Maybe, but we can't take that chance, not with other people involved." She glanced in the mirror again, not seeing the car. "Will you get my phone out of my purse and dial Jimmy for me?" she asked him. The car's Bluetooth system picked up when he'd done as she asked, and she spoke to Jimmy's mom, asking if they could do the beach trip another day.

The car was there, several vehicles back, when she got off the phone.

Heading slowly back to his place from the gym on Sunday, Tad tried to relax, still coming down from the weekend's events. But he couldn't lose the sense of unease that had been slowly building where Miranda and her dad were concerned.

He was falling in love with her. He saw that now. Didn't like it. But knew there was no way he could stop it, either.

And chances were good that when she heard he'd been on her father's payroll all along, she'd want nothing to do with him.

He'd still have it that way, though, if it meant she was happy and able to live free from fear.

He'd just pulled into his complex when his phone rang. Putting the SUV in Park, he grabbed it by the second ring.

"Would it be okay with you if we just stayed home tonight? I can cook the steaks under the broiler…"

"Of course." His standard answer with her these days. "Or you two could come here. We've got community grills at every building…"

She hesitated, and he thought she might accept the invitation, but in the end, she said, "It's probably better if we do it here," she said, sounding disappointed enough that he smiled. She'd wanted to come to his place. That was satisfactory for now. "Ethan's got all his things here, and that gives us time for adult conversation."

Even knowing that with her son at home, she just meant conversation, Tad was still wearing a full-on smile as he climbed the steps to his place. He was obviously growing on her as much as she was growing on him.

And that boded well for the possibility of a future.

Even after he dumped the big secret...

Her secrets were going to show. Miranda had debated canceling dinner with Tad altogether, but she'd needed the peace of mind being with him brought her, needed it too much to deny herself.

If she was being followed, she'd have to leave. To start over. Again. Lose not only her home, her life, but her career, too. She had enough saved to get her through school a third time. Maybe. But she wasn't sure she could do it. Just the thought of not having a solid way to support her and Ethan, the thought of losing her solid income, panicked her.

She needed to calm down. To think practically. Tad's presence helped her do that. And yet, when she jumped, hearing his car door in her driveway, she knew she was taking a huge chance seeing him when she was like this. The man was a good detective. Astute. He was going to notice if she was jittery.

He'd come at the time they'd originally designated for the beach, which meant they had an hour, at least, before dinner.

"You want to play *Zoo Attack* again?" Ethan asked before Tad was even fully in the door.

Wearing jeans and a black polo shirt, he looked so good to her. Way too good. She wanted to sleep with him, to lose herself in good feelings and then lie in his arms and rest, and didn't care—in that second—that she shouldn't.

"You got to play with him all last night," she said to her son. "Tonight's my turn." True to his word, Tad had come over the night before, played *Zoo Attack* for a while and then left. She hadn't invited him to eat with them. He hadn't suggested it, either.

"Can I watch a movie, then?" Her son was jumping up and down with the grin that told her he was being cute on purpose because he knew she usually gave him what he wanted when he did that.

"You may watch two episodes of *PAW Patrol* before dinner," she told him. He'd been watching the popular cartoon since he was a toddler, but he still liked it, so she allowed it when she could.

"You just didn't feel like the beach today?" Tad asked as he followed her through the living area toward the back-yard.

"She didn't feel good, but she pooped and now she's better," Ethan blurted, and Miranda wanted to sink her chin to her chest and cry in embarrassment.

"You know, some girls don't like to talk about bathroom stuff like a lot of boys do," Tad said. "To us it's gross and funny and kinda cool sometimes, but to girls it's often embarrassing."

His words were offered so easily, naturally, that they stopped her in her tracks. Everything about Tad Newberry arrested her attention.

"Oh. Sorry, Mom," Ethan said.

The truth hit her then, in her dining room, talking about poop.

She was in love with Tad.

As the realization hit, she did start to cry.

* * *

Tad saw the tears. Miranda turned away, and there was no sign of them by the time they got to the patio, but he couldn't get past the sight of them.

He'd only known her a couple of months, but from what he'd seen Miranda wasn't a crier.

Already worried about her because of the rough weekend, he was growing ever more frustrated by his inability to bring everything out in the open between them and deal with the facts together.

Including the fact that he could very well be falling permanently, completely, in love with her.

"How'd you sleep last night?" he asked, taking the bottle of water she handed him as she sat down with her own. He'd hated leaving right after his gaming session with Ethan. Had wanted a chance to have a conversation with Miranda after the day's events, to make sure she was okay.

She hadn't invited the intimacy and he'd felt that pushing her would be wrong. At least he'd been able to stop by. To be with her so she'd have some sense that she wasn't alone in the world.

"I slept okay," she told him. "I was thinking about Marie a lot, of course. How could I not? I called the hospital today and spoke with Ruby. Marie's expected to recover, though I expect she's going to need some facial reconstruction. Ruby will be bringing Danny to his next appointment with me. He's in counseling, too, of course."

"I talked to Chantel this morning, and then had a brief conversation with Ruby, as well. I told her to call me if she needed any help."

With Devon being held without bail, at least until a hearing to determine the extent of further danger if he were released, the physical danger was over. For the time being, anyway.

Maybe he'd get some help. There were programs for abusers. Some benefited.

The whole incident must have brought back memories for Miranda. Ones she couldn't share. But there was a key difference in her case.

Her abuser was dead. The danger was over forever. She just didn't know that.

A sound came from inside the house. "What was that?" She jumped up, going through the sliding screen door.

The bang, faint as was, had been obvious to Tad, but he stood behind her as Ethan came down the hall back to the living room.

"I put the toilet seat up and it fell," he said, his attention already back on the television recording he hadn't paused.

"Did you flush?" she asked, her tone kind.

"Yes, Mo-o-om."

Tad was seated again when Miranda turned and re-joined him.

"You're not quite yourself today," he said, studying her. Frustrated and unable to sit and calmly chat. He had her answers, the information she needed, right there in his mouth and they were about to choke him.

With a glance at the living room, she said, "I'm being followed."

Thinking he'd misheard her, Tad frowned. "What?"

"I'm being followed," she repeated, glancing toward the house again, as though making certain that Ethan couldn't hear them.

"What do you mean? Being followed." No need to fake relaxing chat now. Sitting up, he leaned forward. "Who's following you?"

"I don't know," she told him.

He didn't know, either. Her abuser was dead.

Although…could this be a manifestation of the paranoia she'd spoken about regarding Marie? The reason she'd given the woman her private number? So she could help Marie fight off the insidious effects of domestic violence–based fear?

"When were you followed? Where?" he asked, thinking that if he could talk her through it, she might see things differently.

"I first noticed a gray baseball cap. Earlier in the week. I saw it three times, three different places, the last one at the grocery store. But I'm not even sure it was the same person, or the same hat."

Okay, good. She was talking herself down.

"But then Friday, when I left work, I noticed this person sitting in a black sedan in the corner of the parking lot. I couldn't tell if it was a male or a female, but…he seemed male to me, based on shoulder width. There was no gray cap. The head was in shadows, and I couldn't make out hair length, but I think it was dark. And he could've just been watching the door, waiting for someone inside having a procedure or appointment."

He nodded, almost smiling as he listened. Miranda was impressive. He'd known her such a short time, but was so damned proud of her. Her strength. Her determination to be accountable for her life and make the best of it.

She didn't need him to help her beat any residual paranoia. She was doing fine on her own.

"Yesterday, I didn't see anyone, but since we were out looking for Marie, I wasn't paying as much attention, either."

"You were watching every single car on the road. I'm guessing you'd have at least noticed if a similar black sedan was anywhere nearby."

Meeting his gaze, she nodded, sitting upright in her chair—as though she were on the witness stand in court.

"Then today…he was back. Never close enough for me to make out facial features, but again, very clearly a male physique, based on shoulder and chest width. He was wearing dark, loose clothing, I think, so it was hard to tell anything for sure. He was clean-shaven. His hair's dark. And kind of long. Not like mine. It didn't cover his neck, but it wasn't short like yours."

All his emotions went on hold as Tad listened. She hadn't just superimposed the fact that someone was following her on a random person in her area. She was attributing it to one person. As though readying herself for a police report.

"Where were you when you saw him? Another parking lot?"

"Driving," she said. "I was on my way to Jimmy's. He was there for a couple of miles and two turns, so, instead of going straight to the Randolphs' house, I took some nonsensical turns, you know, going in a circle, and he was still there."

Yeah, and now he wasn't smiling. At all.

"That's why I canceled the beach. And Ethan's visit with Jimmy, too. No way would I involve an innocent little boy in anything that could potentially be dangerous."

She was serious.

And she hadn't called him. Or anyone.

Because…she wasn't going to. It was like the chief had said, Miranda's fight-or-flight mechanism went naturally to flight mode. She'd run if the danger warranted it.

Something had made her not trust anyone to help her. As though she didn't believe anyone *could* help her. That the danger would always be there. It was stronger than anyone's ability to stop it. He was reading her easily. On that, at least.

"Who do you think it was?" he asked, all detective now as he worked his way through the situation.

He waited. Was she going to tell him about her ex? Clearly that was who she thought was behind this.

She shook her head. "I don't know." She looked him right in the eye as she said the words.

She wasn't going to tell him.

So why was she still there? Why hadn't she run? Or called Chantel?

"It was weird. He followed me, and then he didn't. I got to Ocean Street and he was there, and then he turned off. I saw him go."

Ocean Street ran from one end of town to the other.

"How far were you from home?"

"Five miles. I wasn't going to bring him here!"

In about five seconds he'd head out to the street. To check her house, and every one within a two- or three-mile radius. Just in case.

"Have you seen any black sedans around here? Any that you don't recognize as belonging to a neighbor?"

"No. Again, I wouldn't be sitting here if I had."

He nodded. Whether she'd be at the police station, or on her way to becoming someone else, he didn't know.

But he understood one thing. She was still sitting there only because the threat hadn't become real enough.

So he had to make sure it never did. Even if it was imaginary, if she truly believed Ethan was in real and immediate danger, Miranda and Ethan Blake would cease to exist. Just like Dana and Jeffrey O'Connor had.

Chapter 24

Miranda considered not going into work and keeping Ethan home from school on Monday. Briefly. A few times. But she recognized that if she did, she'd be reacting to the negative stimulus, not acting in a rational manner.

She'd very knowingly put Tad on their detail, now that he no longer had any reason to watch Danny. Her belief that she had someone following her gave away no clues to her former identity, or even that she had one. So she'd chosen to tell him about the black sedan.

If not for him, for knowing that Ethan would be protected by a top-rate detective, they'd have gone already. Maybe they should be. Maybe they would be soon. And it would kill something vital in her to leave Tad without saying goodbye.

Before she gave in to instincts that could be tainted by the week's events with the Williamses, before she gave up a great career, a home in a town where both she and Ethan were happy, before she pulled her son away from school and the beginnings of friendships that could prove lifelong, she was going to be very sure there was legitimate cause.

Tad texted her three times on Monday while she was at work, to let her know that Ethan was at school, that there'd been no dark sedans hanging around—either near the elementary school or her clinic. She hadn't asked him to check or to keep her informed. But she'd known he would.

And thanked him profusely when he did.

Still, she looked around carefully before exiting work that afternoon, and then watched her rearview mirror as carefully as she watched the road in front of her when she drove to Ethan's school. If they were truly in imminent danger, keeping to her normal routine wasn't wise, which made her a nervous wreck by the time she arrived safely at the school with no sedan sightings. There'd been some black ones, but none that looked the same, with only a dark-haired male driver. None that had turned every time she had, or missed a turn and shown up behind her again.

She could be experiencing a particularly severe bout of paranoia. Because of Marie. The timing made the possibility rather obvious.

And still, she was certain she was being watched. A gray cap. A black car. Maybe it would be a bicycle in her neighborhood next.

If it was, Tad would see it.

Unless her father didn't want him to. There was nothing out of the realm of possibility where Brian O'Connor was concerned. She'd spent the first twenty years of her life watching him in action. Everyone she knew in her old life—other than a few people from college in Asheville—knew and loved her father. He'd lived an exemplary life, every place but in their home.

"How does going on vacation sound?" she asked Ethan as they drove home after school. Her scrubs, the bears with hearts, had a stain on the front from a can of orange drink she'd dropped while eating lunch in her office. It was bugging the crap out of her.

"Where to?"

"I don't know. We haven't been to Disneyland yet." A person could get lost there for a day or two. Mostly she needed him to be prepared for the fact that they might go on a trip soon. She'd work out the rest as it came.

"What about school?"

"Maybe it would just be for a weekend. Maybe we could go to Yellowstone National Park. You said you wanted to do that after you learned about it at the beginning of the year."

"Is Tad coming?"

"I haven't decided if we're going yet or not," she told him, trying to sound vague, a "talk about the weather" type of conversation. "But if we do, no, I was thinking just you and me. We've never gone on vacation."

"If we go, can I swim in a hotel pool?" Jimmy had talked to him about his family trip to a resort in Mexico over Christmas. According to him, the best part had been the pool.

"Yes."

"Cool!"

She'd stopped at a light. She turned to look at him. "If you had to pick your five favorite things, what would they be?"

"Why?" He looked at her, eyes wide behind his glasses. "You aren't going to make me give away more stuff, are you?"

"I have no plans to pack up your stuff," she said truthfully. "It's a game." For now. "I think I know what they are and I want to see if I'm right. Then you think of five of mine and see if you're right."

"That's a dumb kinda game."

Probably. But it was the best she could come up with at the moment.

"Tell me anyway," she said. Depending on what they were, she'd know to grab them if she had a chance in the event that they had to leave.

Not that he could keep them long-term. If they had to start new lives, everything would go. Or be buried somewhere, like her gold heart charm from Jeff.

But having them with him in the short run would help. She knew. Been there, done that.

"My blue teddy bear, but don't tell Jimmy. Or anyone," Ethan said, his small face serious. He was watching out the front of the car as if getting them home safely was his responsibility.

"This is our game, sweetie. I don't tell anyone our private stuff."

"Not even Tad?"

"Nope, not even Tad." Though that was getting increasingly more difficult. It was breaking her heart. "Okay, what else besides the teddy?"

"*Zoo Attack*, that award I got at Charlie's for winning Skee-Ball, my model car and the M&M's from Easter that are still in the 'frigerator."

Smiling, she said, "Ready for mine?"

"Wait." He frowned. A minute or so passed, and he said, "Okay, now I'm ready."

"The charm bracelet you gave me last Christmas, the picture you drew of us in preschool that's in my bedroom, the clay bowl you made last year, pictures of you when you were a baby…"

"You said only five things. Pictures are more than five in one thing."

Smart boy. "Okay, the one with you in the little blue

suit." Because baby pictures could never be replaced. She'd cried so hard, leaving his newborn photos behind. And one of the first things she'd done as Miranda Blake was get new photos done. He'd been three months then. "And for my last thiinngg…" The memory of making love with Tad Newberry. "My PA certificate."

"Oh, dang!" Ethan exclaimed, causing her heart to jump.

"What?"

"I got one wrong." Oh.

He was so damned cute she couldn't help adoring him. "Which one?"

"The certificate," he muttered, clearly disgusted with himself. "You hung it and everything."

She hadn't expected him to guess it. But she was curious. "What was your fifth guess?"

"Me. I thought you'd choose me."

She had, of course. A long time ago. Which was why they were playing the game in the first place.

He'd seen no black sedan. Though he'd left Miranda's right after dinner on Sunday night, after having already made a run around her neighborhood while she was preparing dinner, he'd stayed in the area half the night. And had spent all day Monday and a good part of Monday night cruising between Ethan's school and her office and then their neighborhood after he'd seen them get home safely.

If he'd somehow put her in danger by finding her, he was damn well going to keep her alive.

And if she was imagining that she was being followed… Well, it didn't hurt to keep the vigil. He missed going to the gym and his leg was a little stiff Tuesday morning as he rolled out of bed after only a few hours' sleep, but he felt better than he had in a long while.

It was preferable to be doing something, rather than just waiting. Miranda had unknowingly freed him to watch her closely without freaking her out.

The burner phone, which he was keeping out of the sock drawer and close to him whenever he was in his apartment, dinged a text from the nightstand beside his bed.

Nude except for his boxers, he practically dived for the thing. Brian or Gail. Either way, the message could be critical.

It was from Gail. And not at all what he'd expected.

Totally off the record… Brian O'Connor was diagnosed with terminal lung disease four months ago. Mesothelioma, is what I was unofficially told. Maybe the "vacation" is to get treatment?

Shit. The news hit him hard. Just…damn. Gail's point about the vacation made sense. O'Connor clearly didn't want Tad to know he was dying. Treatment would explain why he hadn't told him he was on vacation. And why he'd said he couldn't come immediately because he had "business that I can't leave unattended." It could also explain the apparently drunken state the man had been in. Chemo and other treatments, with heavy pain meds, could've had the same effect. Or he could have been drinking as he'd said. The medications could also explain the unusual irritation. The mood changes.

Dropping his phone on the bed, he walked to the living room, looked outside, entered the kitchen, then left again. Miranda and Ethan were going to get back with her father only to watch him die? She'd lost the last years with him?

Back at the sliding glass door leading out to the small balcony, he stared at the ocean in the distance. And…

God, no.

Had Brian contracted his services to find her, in spite of the danger to all of them, because he couldn't die without seeing them?

Had he fudged that coroner's report? Was that why he'd been so adamant about refusing to let Tad know any more about Miranda's ex, Jeff? Because the man really wasn't dead?

The string of words that came out of his mouth as he headed back to his bedroom weren't ones he normally used. They were profanities and referred to improbable sexual acts. And eased his anger not at all.

Forgoing a shower, he shoved his legs into jeans. Pulled a shirt off the hanger and let the clothes holder lie untouched on the floor where it landed after flying off the rod. He grabbed socks, leaving the drawer open, and, yanking on tennis shoes, left them untied as he collected his keys, wallet and both phones and hightailed it out of the apartment.

Miranda was pretty certain she was being followed. If Brian O'Connor had lied to him—and he had by omitting his illness as it would be at least part of the motive for Tad's employment—then there was every possibility that Jeff Patrick was still alive.

And, because of Tad, right there in Santa Raquel. Lying in wait.

Ethan's little tushy looked too darned cute as, in jeans and a T-shirt, he ran toward the school building wearing his backpack Tuesday morning. Watching from the car, as she always did, she saw him turn at the door and wave at her. She waved back, and he was gone. For another day.

And this afternoon she'd have some alone time with Tad. Right after the High Risk meeting they were going to her place. Pulling out into traffic after checking for black sedans, heading down the street toward work, she couldn't help the little thrill of anticipation that shot through her. In fact, she reveled in it. She could use a huge dose of naturally induced euphoria.

Her phone rang, and thinking it was work with some schedule adjustment—a patient cancellation or the addition of one who'd woken up too sick to go to school—she pushed the button on her steering wheel to answer.

"Hi, it's me," Tad said. "I'm a couple of cars behind you."

She glanced at the rearview mirror. Didn't immediately see Tad's SUV. And then she did.

Another thrill shot through her. He really had her back.

The only other time she'd felt like that since her mother died had been with Jeff.

"I've seen no black sedans, gray baseball caps or any other indication that anyone is watching or following you, but I need to talk to you, if I can. Is there any way you could skip going into work this morning? I realize it's a horrible thing to ask, but I hope you trust me enough to know I wouldn't ask if it wasn't important."

She could call Annabelle, the PA who was off on Tuesdays. There were three of them who worked for Dr. Bennet and they were permitted to exchange hours however they saw fit. She'd just never asked before.

But she'd exchanged shifts with Annabelle a couple of times when the other woman had requested it.

"I'll have to make a call… I'll see what I can do. I can't leave patients at the clinic unattended."

"I understand. Call me back as soon as you know."

Looking in the rearview mirror again, she saw that he was still only two cars behind her and nodded. "You're scaring me."

"I'm sorry. I don't mean to. I just have something to tell you that I think you'd want to know."

"Are you leaving Santa Raquel?"

"Make the call, Miranda. Please?"

Less than a minute later, she had him back on the phone. "All set. You want to go to my place?"

"No. And not mine, either. You know that car dealership out by the freeway?" He named a cash-for-your-car type of lot. One that didn't ask many questions if you had enough money, which made her even more uneasy.

"Yeah."

What was he doing? What could he possibly have to say?

Unless he'd found out who was watching her...

"Head over there," he told her. "I'll be right behind you."

"You're sure I'm safe?"

"Yes."

"You're really scaring me now, Tad."

"Call Chantel," he said. "She'll assure you that my request is valid."

"You've talked to her today?"

"I had to tell her I wouldn't be at the High Risk meeting."

Oh. So he *was* leaving. Which didn't explain why she was on her way to a car lot.

And suddenly she didn't want to know. Life without Tad was inevitable. But did it have to happen right now? When the rest of her world could be caving in?

Chapter 25

Tad didn't want to scare Miranda, but his first priority was to keep her and Ethan safe. His first call as soon as he got on the road to Miranda's place that morning had been to Chantel Fairbanks. In short, distinct sentences, he'd told her everything he knew.

She'd been on board immediately. It had been her decision to have Miranda take Ethan to school as usual. She'd assigned an officer who'd be positioned with Ethan in sight until further notice. Until Tad could talk to Miranda, and maybe after that, they were going to act as though Jeff Patrick was in town, looking for his chance to snatch his family back.

While he'd been sitting around the corner from Miranda's house, waiting for her and Tad to leave for school, keeping his eyes on the place at all times, he'd emailed Chantel the documents he had on Miranda. He'd slid the SIM card into his phone only long enough to do that and then returned it to an inside pocket of his wallet. Chantel had already begun a full investigation of Miranda's past.

He followed Miranda into the car lot, parking directly behind her, and, with a hand at her back, walked her inside.

"How much would it cost me to rent a car for a few hours?" he asked the older guy behind the counter drinking coffee and eating a doughnut. "I'll leave you the keys to both of ours, sitting out there…" He nodded toward the lot. Put his keys on the counter and asked Miranda to do the same.

She clicked to unlock her car first, saying, "I need to get my bag…"

Tad flashed his detective badge, a North Carolina detective badge, while Miranda had her head turned toward her car. The badge wasn't technically valid in California, but he didn't figure the guy was going to know that.

"Cost you nothing," the older man said, handing him a set of keys. "As long as you return it in a coupla hours, not wrecked and full of gas. We'll call it a test drive."

Yeah. He could've just asked to take a car on a test drive. Might have if he hadn't been surging with adrenaline.

Not the good kind.

It was a warning to get himself in check. He had to be a cop first.

Their ride was a newer-model lowest-end Cadillac. Blue.

"I need my bag," Miranda said again, going for the hatchback on her car rather than the front seat where he'd assumed she would've left her purse.

Watching the area for anyone who might be watching them, Tad hoped that whoever was following Miranda, if anyone really was, assumed she was on her normal routine. That this person wouldn't know she wasn't until he cruised by the clinic and saw her car missing.

He noticed that she was fooling with the spare tire on her car.

"You need help?"

"No! No," she said, shoving her hand into the front pocket of her scrubs, as though she'd hurt it and didn't want him to see. "I accidentally pulled the tire up when I went for the bag." The duffel had been hidden in the wheel well. He pretended not to notice that he'd noticed. With a quick side trip to the front seat, she got her purse, and put both in the front passenger seat of the Cadillac.

The guy with his doughnut had been watching them the whole time. Let him think he was taking Miranda to a quickie at a motel. Tad didn't care.

On the road again as quickly as possible, away from cars that might be known to them, he drove back into town and straight to the police station.

Frowning, Miranda looked at him. "We're going to the High Risk Team meeting?"

He shook his head, leaning over to kiss her on the lips. He was sure the move was completely inappropriate and equally sure he had to do it.

Her lips lingered on his, kissing him back, and when he pulled away, he said, "Trust me for a few minutes longer and then you'll be fully in the know."

She nodded.

And he hoped to God he hadn't just had her trust for the last time.

Or kissed her for the last time, either.

Miranda knew her way around the police station. She'd been there many times in her scrubs, as she was that Tuesday morning. She'd planned to be there later that morning, for the team meeting. And it felt weird as hell, being shown, with Tad, into a different area. One she'd never seen before.

Various desks dotted the room, and as Tad approached one in particular, Chantel stood up.

She greeted Miranda with a smile, and then said, "You can use this room right over here. It used to be a storeroom, but it's become a place where we can go for quiet conversation among ourselves."

Ushering them into a room with a couple of worn tweed couches in black and beige stripes with scarred wooden legs, and a single equally scarred coffee table, Chantel closed the door behind them.

She was no longer in fear for her life, but Miranda still felt uneasy.

Standing by the first couch, she faced Tad—aware of Chantel's presence just outside the door. "What's going on?" Maybe she and Ethan weren't on the verge of running or dying, but this wasn't good, whatever it was.

Taking her hand, he sat down. "Sit, please."

It was Tad. He was touching her. So she sat.

"I know who you are."

Heart thudding, she felt as though the cereal she'd had for breakfast was coming up. Clogging her airway. Swallowed a couple of times.

"I'm Miranda Blake."

Chantel's smile a second ago had been…compassionate. Was it Sara? She'd told them?

She'd told Miranda not to say anything!

Which could only mean…

"He's here." Shaking, she stood. She had to go. Get out. Now.

Tad pulled her back down. "There's no evidence that anyone's following you," he said. "And no evidence that you're in any immediate danger."

Immediate.

Ethan! She had to get to Ethan. Jumping up, she reached in her pocket for her keys. Didn't have them.

Tad had ditched their cars—the cars someone might recognize as theirs.

"I have to get Ethan."

"Chantel has an officer assigned to him until further notice. It's probably not necessary. But we're taking no chances."

"You don't know my—"

Tad took her hand again. "Dana, it's okay."

Trembling like she'd never trembled before, she couldn't answer him. And wasn't sure she could even stand.

She had to get Ethan. Go.

"Please, just listen to me for a minute?"

She nodded. Mostly because she needed a minute to get herself under control. To figure a way out. She had her bag in the car. Had stashed the money in it.

She didn't have a car, didn't have access to her own.

"There may not be any danger at all," Tad told her. Not at all what she'd expected to hear. Chantel was involved. Ethan was under guard.

She wasn't an idiot.

"You don't know him like I do…"

"We think he's dead, Dana."

"Don't! Don't call me that. My name is Miranda. Miranda Blake."

"You don't have to be! That's what I'm trying to tell you. Chantel's just waiting on final confirmation, but it would appear he really is dead."

Elation flooded her system. And then immense grief. Relief. And…disbelief.

"How?" She could only get out a whisper.

"Overdose."

Fitting, and yet, other than alcohol, her father had never

taken drugs of any kind. Not even aspirin. It had to be another one of his tricks. Playing with her head.

"Dana…"

Her gaze shot from her hands up to Tad's. "Do not call me that," she said through gritted teeth. And then, "I'm sorry. But please, don't ever call me that again. I'm Miranda now."

And then, slowly, her mind started to work. "How did you find out?"

When he looked away, she got scared again.

"What?" she asked.

He took both her hands. Kissed them. "I've known all along," he told her. "Your father, he knew that Jeff was dead, that you were free to come home. He hired me to find you. And then to watch over you until he thought it was time to get in touch with you himself."

Anger smoldered through her. White-hot. Burning her from the inside out. Pulling her hands from his, she jumped up. Ran for the door. Tried to open it, but couldn't get a grip on the handle. Her hands weren't functioning.

"Miranda." Tad was there, his arm around her.

"Don't *touch* me," she screamed, elbowing him away. And then, "Chantel! Detectives!" she cried out.

Chantel was at the door almost instantly, along with a couple of other detectives. She saw them and began to gasp for air. Could feel it slowly filling her lungs again.

"He's… Don't let him take me," she said, motioning to Tad. "He's…"

"Okay." Chantel's tone was understanding and commanding at the same time as she led Miranda away from that little room, down the hall and into a women's restroom. "We're alone here," the detective said, her blond ponytail moving as though to punctuate every word. Miranda focused on that hair. And then let herself look into the brown eyes an inch or so above hers.

"He's working for my abuser," she whispered. "I...invited him into my home. I... I...*slept* with him. I let him near my son..."

Ethan was safe. Chantel had an officer with him.

Tears blinded her, and sobs took her air again as the horror overwhelmed her. Sinking down to the floor, she leaned against the wall, curled in on herself and let the emotion out. She had no power to do anything else.

At some point Chantel sat beside her. Maybe within seconds. The door opened. No one came in, and it closed again. And Miranda cried. She tried to think but was blinded by pain. Mentally and physically.

And then, slowly, the rage of emotion inside her stopped. Calm started to seep in. Maybe just exhaustion that felt like calm.

She had to take care of this. Of Ethan.

"I need a way out of here," she told the detective, looking her straight in the eye. Sara and everyone at The Lemonade Stand trusted Chantel. Dr. Bennet not only trusted her, he was the reason Chantel was in Santa Raquel. They'd been friends for longer than either of them had known their spouses. "I have a bag in the car. And money. I need Ethan, and a way to escape. We can figure out the rest from there."

Shaking her head, Chantel said, "You don't have to run, sweetie. It's over."

"No, it's not," she said, the words surprisingly strong and clear. "Tad's working for my father."

"I know. He told me this morning."

With horror, it dawned on her. They could all be under Brian O'Connor's thumb. He was insidious when he believed he was right about something. He got away with it because most of the time, he *was* right.

"Have you talked to Sara?" Miranda asked. If she had, then Miranda knew she couldn't trust any of them.

"Not yet. I put a call in to her, but she's with a resident who was admitted early this morning."

For a long moment she stared at Chantel. "You were Max's first wife's partner," she said, verifying what the doctor for whom she worked had told her himself.

"That's right."

"You saw her die."

"Yes."

"And your sister-in-law, Julie. She was a victim."

"Yes."

"One who wasn't believed for over a decade because her abuser had a lot of power…"

"Her brother always believed her. And it was her abuser's father who really had the power, but he believed his son."

Chantel was exhibiting patience, seemingly willing to take whatever route Miranda needed to get where they were going in this conversation.

"I can trust you."

"Absolutely."

She hadn't been asking a question. "Tad told you that Jeff was my abuser," she went on, guessing, but sure, too, based on what he'd said in the other room. *Your father, he knew that Jeff was dead.* As if that made her free. No shit he knew. She'd told him.

"Yes, he did." And then, pinning Miranda with a steely look, Chantel asked, "Isn't he?"

She shook her head, then collapsed, and this time it was Chantel who screamed for help.

Chapter 26

"Sam!" Chantel's voice could be heard through most of the detective squad room. Tad, who'd been standing with Detective Sam Larson, locked eyes with the older man for a second before they both ran for the door of the women's restroom, bursting inside without hesitation.

They were all trained in basic CPR.

"Get Ethan," she said. "Bring him here." She was talking to Sam, but Tad was going, too. If something had happened to that boy...

"Tad, stay here." Chantel's command was just that. A command. Not a request. Or open to options.

With a glance at the departing back of the detective, Tad forced himself to stand down. He had to admit he was influenced by Sam's history; he'd just discovered the detective was married to a woman he'd promised to keep safe, only to have her first husband, a noted psychiatrist, find her and beat her almost to death.

"Jeff Patrick is not her abuser," Chantel said, biting the words out with such anger, Tad didn't question her.

"Who is?" The chief was wrong. The chief, who was never wrong.

"Her father." Chantel's words came in the same instant as recognition.

He went cold. Could feel the blood draining from his skin. And nausea forming. He'd led Miranda's abuser to her doorstep.

His worst nightmare coming true.

He looked at her, huddled there, refusing to look back at him. He'd done this.

"I'll be right back," he said, throwing the door open. He pushed into the small bathroom next door, barely made it to the toilet and puked his guts out.

Miranda didn't need Chantel's urging to get up off the floor. To wash her face, pull herself together. Knowing that Ethan was on his way was enough to propel her outside herself and into doing whatever had to be done.

Within minutes of Sam's leaving, Miranda was sitting in a kitchen with Chantel, drinking orange juice.

"I've asked Tad to come in and tell us what he knows," the detective said. "I need you to listen, to corroborate, or not, the things he says. He's our only lead to your father's thinking and we don't have time to waste."

"I can just go, get another identity, start over. It worked before, it can work again."

"Did it?" Chantel asked, staring her down.

For six years, it had.

"Trust us, Miranda. I realize it's a tall order, but you've been in Santa Raquel four years now. You know Lila and everyone at the Stand. You know me. You definitely know

Max. And we know you. We don't know Brian O'Connor. He has no power here."

She wanted to believe that. So badly.

"Give us a chance to get him. To put him away. Give us a chance to give you your life back. A real life. One where you don't have to keep wads of money and emergency bags in your car. One where your son can make friends he can keep for a lifetime if he wants."

She wanted help. God, how she wanted help. She'd been alone for so long. Eleven years old was far too young to take the weight of the world on your shoulders.

But she was her mother's daughter. Had to make her proud. She wouldn't be a victim. Wouldn't let him win.

"Sometimes it takes the most strength to stay and fight." Chantel's words hit her at her core. She'd been fighting for so many years.

But she'd never stood up to her father. She'd only run. To college. And Jeff. To Miranda Blake.

She'd made the right choices then.

Maybe, now, the right choice was different.

"Fine," she said.

At Chantel's urging Tad walked in, sat down. Miranda wouldn't look at him.

The three of them were at a round table with four chairs. Two vending machines lined the wall directly across from him, behind Miranda and Chantel. One held packaged junk food. Chips. Pretzels. Candy. The other, microwave meal choices. Soup. Pasta. The microwave was on the counter behind him. He'd seen it when he came in.

The refrigerator, next to the vending machines, had smudges on the handle. And the Formica floor beneath the table was cracked.

Apologies were choking him in their need to escape. But this wasn't his show. He waited for permission to speak.

"Miranda, tell me about the man you know your father to be."

Surprised that Chantel had turned to Miranda, Tad looked at her, too. He'd been under the impression that he was only going to be allowed to speak about his part in what could turn out to be criminal charges against him.

If someone wanted to try to prove that he'd knowingly aided a man in his attempt to abduct his grandson. Or assault his daughter.

As far as Tad was aware, Brian O'Connor had never had charges filed against him. He'd never even been exposed as an abuser. But he knew that his daughter had fled his abuse. Tad knew none of the details, but he'd put that much together.

"He's insidious." The way Miranda said the word suggested she'd thought it many times before. Like it was just something she knew. "All the great stuff he did, the lives he saved, the volunteering, the caring for the community, it was all real. He didn't fake a bit of it. He can see a burning building falling down at his feet and instinctively know how to save one more person before it collapses completely. And he's got nerves of steel that let him act on what he knows."

Tad nodded. And then stopped himself. He didn't want to admire one damned thing about the man. Was still sick at his own culpability. Still trying to make sense of it all.

Miranda had been lying to protect herself. But the chief had been lying, too. Tad...well, he'd been nothing more than an effing pawn—all puffed up with his own ability to save and protect.

"Your greatest challenge is going to be not to underestimate him," Miranda said, looking straight at Chantel.

"Don't think you're his equal. Assume he'll be outthinking you." Her sentences were clear. Each one a lecture in itself.

"If you need proof, look at what he just pulled off. He takes a strong, powerful detective like Tad Newberry who, it seems, isn't from Michigan, after all, and makes him into a patsy—apparently with very little effort."

He felt the dig clear to his soul. Took it like the man he wanted to believe he was.

"But don't stop there," she continued, still with little inflection. A professor, teaching a class. "He knows me, knows enough about Tad, knows human nature. You can't give him any information. He builds profiles of people from what he learns and intuits about them. He allowed Tad to get close to me in whatever way he could, even if that meant having sex with me."

"I did not, absolutely not, have any kind of personal relationship with you at your father's behest." He hadn't been asked to speak yet, but there was no keeping that one down.

With an eyebrow raised, Chantel glanced at him. The retribution he expected for his outburst didn't come, though. She looked back at Miranda without saying a word.

Miranda did, though. Glaring at him, she asked, "Did he let you know that it would be okay with him if you did?"

His answer was his silence. And with sickness spreading through him, he thought of all the information he'd fed the man over the months he'd been in town. All the little tidbits that would reveal his daughter's current state.

"My father knew I'd fall for Tad," she said, turning back to Chantel. "The plan would be to let me fall in love, to think I'd finally found happiness, only to let me know that it was all his idea, his plan. That he'd been the one to pick my man for me. To show me that he's in control of my life even now."

Tad wanted to blurt out a denial. To prove she was wrong.

He couldn't do that when his instincts were telling him she was right. He'd been played. Thoroughly and completely played.

"Girls usually go for men like their daddies. They don't mean to, don't necessarily even want to, but it's human nature. And human nature is his biggest tool. He knows when and how to cash in on it. Probably helps him save lives."

Because every side had its opposite. Good versus bad. And bad versus good, as well.

"He wants me to know I can't run. I can't hide. And if I'm ever going to be really happy, I need him to watch out for me. His end goal is that I'll feel I have to come home, so I'll bring my son to him. That's who he really wants. Ethan."

She shuddered, and Tad could only imagine what she was remembering. But he was fully confident that whatever it was had to do with the reason she'd run. Whatever final catalyst had prompted her to never let her father near Ethan.

"He truly believes in his own power over others and in his ability to control the world," she said. "In North Carolina, he pretty much is that powerful. He's revered, and it sticks because he's earned the reverence. Everything his admirers know him to be is true. But it's created a man who thinks he's invincible. And that's your biggest challenge. He'll do things you wouldn't expect anyone to try. And he'll succeed."

"Not this time," Tad said. He was going to see the man stopped if he had to give his own life up to do it. If that meant shooting him in cold blood and spending the rest of his life in prison, so be it.

* * *

Miranda couldn't remember when she'd ever felt so tired. Bone-deep, just "lie down and go to sleep" exhausted. Being unconscious for an indeterminate amount of time sounded good.

But she knew she wasn't going to be sleeping anytime soon.

The minute they got Ethan to her, she'd look for her chance to get away. She'd find a "vacation" spot for them until she could figure out the next move. She just needed him to arrive safely.

Talking about her father had reminded her all over again that Chantel, the High Risk Team, Santa Raquel—they couldn't save her from him. Legally, he'd done nothing wrong. Finding her—there was nothing preventing him from doing so. No restraining order. No charges to file. There'd never been a single police report. The broken bones over the years had all been readily explained away as accidents. A lot of kids had bumps and bruises along the way. For the most part, the chief had made certain that hers didn't show.

Except the summer she'd kissed a boy on her father's front porch. Then, he'd just suggested she stay inside until she healed. And she had.

Even if he *was* in town now, had been watching her, which she was certain of now that she knew Tad had turned him on to her, they couldn't arrest him. He'd broken no laws.

He was simply letting her know that she belonged to him. That he could always get to her. That he wanted her back, out of possessiveness, control, vindictiveness. But mostly because he wanted Ethan. The son he'd never had. The son she should have been. The wonder was that it had taken six years...

Because he wanted her to think he'd changed? Had given her a cooling-off time? She might never know the reason, but she was certain he had one. And that it had to do with her doing what *he* wanted.

The whole thing made her sick to her stomach. Ethan should be there any minute. She'd rest better with her hands on his bony little shoulders.

"How certain are you that O'Connor's in town?" Chantel asked Tad.

"I'm not. I've had a colleague of mine, my partner, Gail Winton, checking up on him." Tad's words brought her gaze to him. He'd had doubts?

And how close was he to this Gail?

Were they lovers?

She wanted to ask, to distract herself, but knew she'd come across sounding like a crazy woman.

And it didn't matter, she told herself firmly. Tad Newberry wasn't who she'd thought he was. He'd used her...

Pain sliced through her and she had to stop letting it in.

"She said he's recently been diagnosed with terminal lung disease, asbestos-induced, probably due to fighting fires in older buildings..."

Her father was dying?

She stared at Tad. Was that true? Could it really be true? Dare she believe there'd be an end to this madness? Or was it him, up to something else to get her to come home? Playing on her sympathy?

"He's on vacation, according to his staff," Tad was saying, and fear pounded through Miranda.

"Gail suspects he's actually in for treatment."

He wasn't. He was in Santa Raquel. Following her. Biding his time. She could feel it.

She couldn't look at Tad. And couldn't help looking at him. He knew her father.

Chantel asked for Gail's contact information and Tad gave it to her. "Let me get this to Sam," the detective said, going to the door to call out to her coworker, who came over immediately.

She obviously wasn't leaving Miranda alone with Tad. Before Miranda could process how she felt about that, the thought of being uncomfortable alone with the man she'd trusted with her life, she heard her son's voice.

"Is this where they keep the bad guys?" He sounded curious, maybe a little excited, not at all worried, and her heart leaped. Tears sprang to her eyes, but she blinked them quickly away.

As she watched the doorway, needing him to appear, she could hear a male voice, couldn't make out the words, and then, closer, and louder, Ethan again. "Can I see where they keep the bad guys?"

Standing, she forced herself to remain calm, and when Ethan came into the room, didn't rush to him, didn't grab him into her arms.

"Hi, Mom. Hi, Tad. They said I get to tour the police station today, while you do your meeting that you do here every week. Kinda like school outta school."

They were making sure her son wasn't scared, turning his trip to the station into an adventure. She felt on the brink of tears again, but managed a smile. "That's right. And then you and I, we'll go out to lunch, okay?"

She had to give him normalcy.

"Can I have a hamburger and french fries?"

"I guess."

"Can Tad come, too?"

"I've got some work to do, buddy, but we'll meet up later, okay?" Tad preempted her response, as though he didn't trust her not to diss him to her son. She wouldn't. Not for his sake, but for Ethan's.

The detective who'd brought her son in, Sam, had a couple of quiet words with Chantel while Miranda was speaking with Ethan, and then he led the little boy away.

"There's a room with toys and a television down the next hall. After they show Ethan around a bit, they'll sit with him in there until we're done."

They were done there, as far as Miranda was concerned.

"We've put a call in to Lila Mantle," Chantel was saying, naming the managing director of The Lemonade Stand. "And to Sara Edwin, too. They'll be ready for you and Ethan…"

She wasn't going to The Lemonade Stand. "There's no point," she said. "We'd only be prolonging the inevitable. My father's done nothing actionable at this point. There's no proof of any abuse. It's my word against his— in a North Carolina court because that's where the crimes took place—and his reputation is golden. If I go to the Stand, we'd only be playing a waiting game with him."

It wasn't as though her abuser had recently abused her. They weren't getting her out of his home, and they weren't on a manhunt to arrest him.

"But you'd be safe, both of you," Tad spoke up. Miranda wanted to ask why he was still there. He'd given them the information he had.

This was no longer his business.

And she no longer trusted him.

"Excuse me, Chantel?" The door had opened and a uniformed officer stood there. "There's someone here, asking to speak with the chief."

Frowning, Chantel shook her head. "I don't think he's in…"

"I think you'll want to see this visitor," the young female officer in the doorway said. "He says his name is Chief Brian O'Connor, from North Carolina. He showed his credentials and said he's here to talk to someone about his daughter."

Tad's hand covered Miranda's on top of the table.

She pulled herself free.

Chapter 27

Chantel offered to speak to Miranda's father alone. Miranda shook her head. She couldn't afford to play the victim. She had a son to save. Facing her opponent was the first step in doing that. She had to know exactly what she was up against. He'd taught her that.

"Do you want Tad to join us?" Chantel asked.

She didn't. Wouldn't even look in his direction. But… "Yes," she said. Because she had to see for herself that the two men knew each other. Wanted to hear what they had to say to each other. Masochistic, in a way, and yet she needed the information to take with her into the future. She was going to have to make peace with all of this.

Including the fact that she'd given her trust, her body, even her closed-off heart, to a man in her father's employ.

Tad followed them down the hall, slightly behind Miranda. She felt his hand slide to the small of her back and sidestepped. She wouldn't fall for him again.

Wouldn't be wooed by the false sense of peace and future he'd brought to her world.

She couldn't afford to be weak.

Pausing outside a closed door to a room with no visible windows, Chantel turned to her. "You ready?"

Of course not. She was about to see her father—a man she'd promised herself she'd never have to see again.

A man she still loved. A man she feared even more.

She nodded.

"Dana! Baby! Oh my God, it's good to see you."

Chief Brian O'Connor didn't seem to age. His hair was still as dark as hers, although he was approaching his fifty-fifth birthday. His eyes as blue. Standing up from his chair at a conference table, he reached out to her with both arms, but didn't approach.

She followed Chantel to the other side of the table, taking one of the four seats there, as far from the chair her father occupied on the other side as she could. Tad took a seat at the end. Closest to Miranda.

Playing both ends against the middle?

That was fitting.

Chantel landed right next to Miranda.

Maybe they were protecting her by sitting on either side. Maybe she liked the feeling.

Maybe she didn't need it.

Brian moved closer, taking the seat across from her. They were doing what they'd always done. Communicating with every move, every look, as much as with the words that weren't being said.

He was cat to her mouse.

She could choose her chair, he'd stand back and allow it. And then he'd move in. If she'd been a good girl, a smart girl to his way of thinking, she would've immediately made the right choice, the obvious choice—planting her butt in the seat across from him.

Or next to him, depending on how he wanted this to play out.

Trouble was, she had no idea what he was up to. Other than the ultimate win of getting Ethan to his home in North Carolina.

"You're so beautiful," he said, his hands reaching across the table as he leaned in, looking her in the eye.

She looked back. Said nothing. Her face remained flat, not because she willed it, but because she was on hold. Every system in her body. Holding.

With his eyes narrowing, probably imperceptible to everyone else, he met her gaze for another long, uncomfortable minute, and then turned to Tad.

"Thank you, Detective. I owe you a debt of gratitude. A lifetime of it. You've brought my daughter back to me."

Tad took a breath, Miranda felt it, although she wasn't touching him. She prepared to hear his response, but her father wasn't giving up control of the floor.

"I'd hoped we could have this conversation in private," he said, turning his full attention on Chantel.

"Tad and Miranda have chosen to be here," Chantel answered, pleasantly enough, but without a hint of being willing to give his request consideration.

"Tad, yes, that's fine. But Dana—Miranda—we might be better served if I could have a moment alone with Detective Fairbanks."

What game was he playing? Clearly he knew Chantel wasn't going to give him what he was asking.

So why ask?

"Your daughter has expressed a desire to be here," Chantel said. "Can you tell me why she shouldn't be?"

Brian looked at her again, and for a brief moment, she

thought she saw regret in his eyes. Her heart pounded and her chest grew tight.

He'd loved her once. In her deepest heart, she knew he still did.

Just as she knew that the ugly parts of him, the pained and bitter pieces inside, ruled his relationship with her.

"I'm sorry, sweetie," he said. "I didn't want it to go this way. For your mother's sake, I'd hoped…"

He'd invoked her mom. It was going to be no-holds-barred. Miranda had no idea what was coming, but she grabbed the sides of her chair with both hands and held on, because she knew it wasn't going to be good.

Tad stared at the man he'd revered. In a dark suit and tie, the chief embodied authority with every move he made, every word he spoke. Tad wondered how he, and thousands of others, had so misjudged him?

Could it even be possible?

And yet…he knew Miranda. There was no doubting that her father was the abuser from whom she'd run.

With almost no money, she'd taken her newborn from the small apartment she'd moved into from her dorm shortly before she'd given birth, left behind everything familiar, everyone she knew, everything she held dear, and started a new life for herself and her son. She'd gone to school. Had a well-paying, respectable job she loved. A career, not just a job.

The former he'd found out from what her father had told him in the beginning—that she'd left her apartment in the dark of night. That O'Connor knew for a fact that she'd had little money.

Now he said, "My daughter needs help." Not at all the words Tad had expected to hear from the chief, who sat with a closed manila folder in front of him. "She's mentally…unstable. Has been since shortly after her mother died. She refused to go to school. Threw fits if I tried to make her. Sobbed until she made herself sick. Eventually, I had to get her help."

He pulled a sheet out of his folder, placing it before Chantel. "That's a signed letter from her psychiatrist and it's in her school records, as well. It states that she could have recurring episodes later in life." He looked briefly at Tad and then back at Chantel.

"Her psychiatrist believes that her mother's passing just as Miranda was entering puberty was likely the catalyst that sent her over the edge. Her emotions became too much for her handle, and her psyche invented a way for her to check out. She'll do fine for a while, and then she'll relapse. Often in cycle with hormonal changes. Which is what happened shortly after my grandson was born. She got it in her head that I was going to try to take him from her and so she ran, taking him from me."

The man looked from Chantel, to Tad, and then back, his tone soft, compassionate. "I never intended to take him. A child needs his mother, and it was obvious that she adored him. And that she was taking good care of him. But knowing her…challenges, I felt it was my duty to keep them close by. A newborn baby—if something happened to him, and I knew about her issues and did nothing…"

His voice trailed off, leaving the obvious unsaid.

Maybe for Miranda's sake.

"The night Dana took Jeffrey out of his crib in the middle of the night and fled into the dark, I'd driven to Asheville, stopped by her apartment, asking her to move back home to Charlotte. She was living alone, said the father of her baby was dead, but I couldn't believe her at that point. When she has her episodes, she tells lies that even she believes are true."

Tad listened. Hearing sense. Logic. A tragic, tragic correlation of events.

Glancing at Miranda, he was struck by the lack of emotion on her face. It was as though she wasn't there with them.

And then he saw the whiteness of her knuckles against the seat of her chair.

"She accused me that night of abusing her," the man said. He had Tad's attention. "Said I'd been getting away with it for years, but that it was going to end right then. That her son wouldn't grow up as she had."

"Had you been abusing her, sir?" Chantel's question was nonjudgmental in tone. They were having a conversation. Tad's interrogation skills tended to go in another direction.

"Of course not."

He turned to Miranda. "Did I ever, ever raise a hand to your mother?"

"No."

"And did I ever, ever even look like I might raise a hand to you or speak to you in anger while she was alive?"

"No."

He looked back at Chantel. "I'm telling you, these delusions started after my wife died."

White knuckles against dark wood. They stayed in Tad's peripheral vision.

"When she first went missing and I was out of my mind with worry for her, I called her psychiatrist. Told him what she'd said. He suggested to me that since there'd been no abuse in our home, chances were good she'd suffered it elsewhere. Said it didn't sound like something she'd just made up. We came to the obvious conclusion that it was her ex she'd been afraid of. That she was, in her own confused way, trying to tell me something. That she'd said the guy was dead because she'd wished him to be."

One hundred percent focused, Tad was aware of every crack on the wall, the floor, the scars on the table. Every line on the chief's face.

And those knuckles. Still white.

"You told Tad when you hired him that you'd had recent word that her ex was dead," Chantel said as Tad was reaching a point of no longer being able to hold his silence.

His time would come. When he knew it all.

O'Connor bowed his head, then met Tad's gaze. "I lied to you about that," he said. "I didn't know. I wasn't even sure who he was. I suspected it was that kid she'd hung out with, talked about a time or two, but I never met him. Or knew his name. But I knew about you. Your reputation. And when events happened in such a way that you were out of work, I looked into your record more completely. I knew that if anyone could find my kids, you could."

"You were willing to put them at risk of an abuser possibly finding them through my search? Of me leading him to them?"

"I knew that wouldn't happen. You'd be there every minute, until I could ascertain enough about her mental state to come myself. You'd keep them safe. You always do. Keep those you're protecting safe. You'd give your life if you had to. Because of your sister. Because of Steffie."

He sucked in air at the mention of his sister's name. The man was right. He'd have given his life to protect Miranda and Ethan.

"At the same time, I was doing everything I could to locate Jeffrey's father. You telling me that she'd named the boy after his father—that was my big break. Once I had a name, I could go to Asheville and learn about any Jeff who might have spent time with my daughter."

"That's how you got the coroner's report," Tad said.

Opening his folder, O'Connor pulled out the original.

Along with a death certificate. Cause of death, overdose. Not car accident.

Tad glanced at Miranda. Like a recalcitrant child, she sat quietly, allowing the three of them to talk around her.

"You told me he died because of a car accident," he said, expecting her to ignore him.

Instead, with eyes that had little life in them, she addressed him. "It was an intramural football injury, actually. And an overdose. He'd been told he only had a couple of months to live. He knew it wasn't going to be long enough to see his baby born. So he mixed his pain medication with alcohol and some over-the-counter sleep aid, leaving a note so that I'd understand he wasn't running out on me, but was preventing me from having to care for him at the end. He'd said he was also providing for us financially, in that he wouldn't be eating up what money he had left on his medications and medical care. He left it for me, instead."

Tad wasn't sure what to believe anymore. Had no basis with which to make that decision. Just as Miranda no longer had reason to lie.

Chantel was allowing him the floor, so he turned back to O'Connor. "Why now?" Tad asked, wishing to God he could know what Miranda was thinking.

"Because I was diagnosed with mesothelioma. Time was up. I couldn't go without knowing they were okay. Without seeing them. Without letting her know they were set for life, financially. Without having a chance to teach my grandson some things about being a man.

"But as it turns out, it was a misdiagnosis. I had a biopsy soon after you came out here and what they'd found in the lining of my lungs was nonmalignant."

Miranda's chin tightened.

"So now, I've come to collect my family and take them

home," the chief said, looking at Chantel, as though Miranda wasn't even there.

"Miranda is a grown woman with a successful career. You can't force her to go with you," Chantel said.

"I think I can," the man said. "Actually, I know I can." He opened his file again. "I've been in touch with her psychiatrist and I have here a signed commitment order—"

"It's okay." Miranda shook her head. "You don't need to do this. I'll go with you." She turned to him, tears in her eyes. "You win, okay?"

Brian O'Connor looked almost sad for a second before he reached across the table, holding out his hand.

Tad could hardly believe it when she let go of the seat she'd been clutching and put her hand in his.

Chapter 28

Miranda hadn't had any idea what her father was going to do, but she'd known he'd do something. He never left himself unprepared.

Or left stones unturned.

Briefly, sitting in the conference room with Chantel and Tad, she'd had moments of hope. When her father had confirmed his illness, she'd figured that even worst case, she'd only have to fight him off for another year or two, less depending on how quickly he grew weaker.

When he'd admitted that the illness had been misdiagnosed, she'd known where it was all going.

How it would end.

So she'd play it out.

She asked her father, in front of the others, if she could please have an hour or so back at her house with Tad, so they could clear out her stuff and Ethan's, because she knew that if she asked without the others there, he'd likely say no just to establish that he was the one in charge.

Sitting there, listening to him render her powerless, it was as though she'd become him. If she was going to save Ethan, she was going to have to play her father's game. Know him better than he knew himself.

Her son had his favorite things. She was going to get them for him.

Her lease and so on she'd deal with later.

Reminding her that she could have everything packed and shipped if she wanted to, he said, "I have us on a flight back to Charlotte that leaves in a little over four hours. I'm expected in my office Thursday morning. Will half an hour do?"

If he'd refused outright, he'd have looked bad in front of Chantel.

Five minutes would do. She knew what she was after. The money. And Ethan's things. And couldn't take more than she could easily carry. She'd be leaving it all soon enough, but if she could give Ethan his favorite things, just for the first few days...

She might have to get on the flight. Might even end up in her father's home, where he'd most likely have her under guard, a guard no one would ever see, including her. But when she saw her chance, she'd take Ethan and run.

If she had her way, she wouldn't be leaving Santa Raquel with her father. When Tad offered to bring Ethan in a few minutes, so she could have time to collect his things without having to answer the child's questions, she shook her head immediately.

Tad's tone was so respectful, conciliatory even, she wanted to puke. Or cry.

"I'm not leaving without my son," she said, reacting. Not thinking first.

Tad looked to her father, his brows raised, giving him the last word. He, of course, then said, "Thank you, Detective, thank you. I'd rather the boy meet me in his own home, rather than a police station."

"Okay, then, I'll bring Ethan. I can meet you and Miranda at her house in, say, twenty minutes?"

"You're a good man, Detective."

Instinctively, she wanted to argue, to see her son, but knew that to balk would do her no good. Tad wasn't going to run off with Ethan. Chantel was there. They were all doing their jobs. Pandering to her father was part of that.

While she was with her father, she'd see Ethan again. She just had to play along. To get along.

Until she could snatch her son and get away.

Tad hadn't looked at her since she'd said she was leaving. And why should he? What she'd thought they'd shared—it hadn't been.

He couldn't know, as she brushed past him in the hall, with Chantel as her escort, that the way his hand accidentally connected with the small of her back sent a shock of life into her.

And she hated herself for still reacting to him.

"You know I love you." Brian's words broke the silence in the car he'd rented—a black sedan, no surprise—as he drove Miranda to her home. She might have feared that he'd dump her off a cliff, but since everyone knew they'd left the station together, that he was the last person to see her alive, he'd be the prime suspect.

He'd never allow his reputation to be tarnished like that.

"I know you're angry with me, girl, but I only want what's best for you. You and Jeffrey. You can move in with me for the time being. Get a job. Maybe something at the hospital. And we'll see how it goes."

How *he* decided it should go, she translated.

He told her about the money he'd been awarded. About his new position as North Carolina chief fire marshal. He told her how much he'd loved her mother. And that she'd be glad now, knowing they were all back together.

He talked about coaching Jeffrey's Little League team.

"He likes basketball," she said, and then, at his assessing glance in her direction, wished she'd kept her mouth shut.

She'd just given him something. She wasn't sure what. Some glance into her mind. A tidbit no one else would have noticed.

And she was going to pay for it.

All the way to Miranda's house, Tad kept up a constant stream of chatter with Ethan, asking the boy about his tour of the police station. What he liked best. He wanted to prepare him, but realized he couldn't. He needed Ethan to act as though he knew nothing, and the only way to get a six-year-old to do that was to make certain he knew nothing.

Tad pulled into Miranda's drive in his own SUV, which had been returned to the station, along with Miranda's car, in exchange for their "rental." It took his full strength of mind to let the boy hop out. To run up to the front door, filled with stories to tell his mother.

He'd told Ethan she'd driven separately because they'd come in two cars, and the boy hadn't questioned why he'd been left to ride with Tad. Tad would've made up some story about her not feeling well if he'd had to.

As it was, he was on full alert. He had two goals. First and foremost, get Ethan and Miranda into his car and disappear with them. The second, do it without anyone getting hurt.

He'd take down the older man if he had to. His gun was loaded and in the back of his jeans.

He didn't want Ethan to witness any violence. Miranda

had sacrificed her entire life so her son could grow up free of violence.

As he turned off the car in Park, he felt a second's hesitation. He was risking everything.

The chief *could* be telling the truth. His story had been convincing enough that Miranda had given up. Or maybe she'd given up *because* he'd been telling the truth.

He'd seen the psychiatrist's letter. And the rest of the paperwork her father had left behind in his file.

Miranda had had a psychotic break when she was eleven. And again at sixteen. She'd grieved beyond her ability to cope.

Maybe because her father had been beating her?

There'd been a report of a broken arm. She'd fallen off the monkey bars at school. At the age of twelve.

And the same arm had been broken a second time, in a different place, when she'd missed a step in the dark at sixteen. She'd been going outside to take out the trash and missed the last step. That kind of thing happened.

"Come on, Tad, let's go in! I wanna tell Mom about the cell I got to walk in."

He wasn't so sure Miranda would be pleased to hear her son's excitement at being in an actual jail cell. As a guy, he got it. The boy wasn't imagining himself ever being locked in one. It was just cool to see stuff that was on television. To see where they kept the bad guys after they caught them all.

With one last check to make sure his gun was in place, he followed Ethan into the house.

When Miranda saw Tad and Ethan get out of the car, she zipped up the bag she'd been filling—the backpack from under her bed, which now held more money and her and Ethan's favorite things, in addition to one change of clothes for each of them. The pajamas had to go. As did most of the food. She'd kept the jerky, some applesauce and a package of sandwich meat.

That should all make it through security. If it got that far.

Her father had allowed her privacy to pack, and was waiting for her in the living room.

"You want him to like you?" she asked him as Tad and her son came up the front walk.

"He will."

"You want him to like you, call him Ethan. And let him get to know you a bit before you tell him who you are."

She'd purposely waited to make that suggestion. He'd listen, or not. Without giving him time to assess, she had a better chance that he'd take her advice.

He wasn't a stupid man.

"Mom! Guess what?" Ethan came barreling in the front door with Tad right behind him. And then, seeing Brian O'Connor, stopped.

"Who are you?"

"He's someone I knew before you were born," Miranda said, coming forward to draw her son closer to the man she wanted him farthest away from.

Play the game, she reminded herself. It was the only way to free her son.

"This is Chief O'Connor. He's a fire chief. So now, today, you saw a police station and you get to meet a fireman."

"Cool!" Ethan looked his grandfather up and down. "You're kinda old to slide down poles."

Her father knelt down, reaching out to draw a light hand across Ethan's jaw. "I can teach you how to do it if you want," he said, grinning.

Because she couldn't bear to see the awe on her son's

face, Miranda looked at Tad, expecting to see his beaming approval. If that was the case, she couldn't really blame him. He'd been under her father's influence long before he'd ever met her. And Chief O'Connor told a convincing story with credible "proof."

The truth would come out in the end. She had no doubt of that. If she didn't get away, he'd hit her again. Maybe even kill her.

But then it would be too late to protect Ethan from the residual effect of living with violence. She wanted her son to grow up with the ability to trust others. The cycle of violence stopped with her. She'd promised herself.

Tad wasn't looking at Ethan and her father. He was watching her. Intently.

"Well, if we're ready to go…" the chief began.

"Go?" Ethan asked, frowning at her.

"Remember that vacation I talked to you about?" She said the first thing that came to mind. "You wanted to go to Disneyland or Yellowstone, remember?"

"Yeeaahh."

"Well, how about we go to North Carolina instead?"

"Why?" Ethan frowned again. "And you said a weekend trip. What about school?"

It wasn't that the boy loved going to school. But his life was routine. He expected that.

"I'm going to head to the little boys' room, and then we'll go." Her father took that chance to bug out of the awkward conversation, leaving her to be the bad guy.

As he left the room, he sent a look to Tad, as if to say, *they're in your care.*

Telling Tad to watch them, she was sure.

Miranda had no doubt he'd had someone in California draw up appropriate paperwork to at least get her into some kind of mental health facility for a check. After all, he would've argued, what woman just up and ran, changing her identity, for no reason?

He'd used her earlier trauma, incident-induced and long gone, to lay doubt with others about her current mental state. It was cruel in the extreme.

And he'd already let her know, the night she'd run all those years ago, that in North Carolina, as in most states, grandparents could go to court to be granted visitation rights.

"Mom? What's happening?" For the first time Ethan looked scared.

As soon as the bathroom door shut, Tad grabbed the pack she'd dropped to the floor. "Run this out to my car, Ethan," he said with enough authority that Ethan did as he asked. "Let's go." He didn't touch her. But the look in his eye... He was giving her a choice.

He'd get her out of here if she wanted to go.

She didn't trust him. Didn't even feel she knew him anymore.

But for whatever reason, he'd offered her the chance she'd been waiting for.

Chapter 29

"Marry me."

They'd been driving north and mostly east for a couple of hours. Before they'd even left town, Tad had her take the SIM cards out of their phones. And in some obscure little burb half an hour into the country, he'd traded his SUV for a newer model, complete with a DVD system and drop-down screen for the back seat. He'd told Ethan they were going on an adventure.

"To Yellowstone?" Ethan had asked.

Tad had never confirmed or denied the question, he'd just talked about various natural forests, ones he'd been to, ones he'd liked.

And for the past ten minutes or so, her son, with headphones on and a movie they'd purchased for him at a gas station, had been asleep.

"Marry you," she said, keeping her voice low, but letting her incredulousness seep through.

What she kept to herself was the warm delight that shot through her at the very idea.

"We'll be in Vegas by eleven. We could be married before midnight."

And the world thought she'd lost *her* mind.

"Why would I marry you?" she asked him. "You used me. Set me up. Because of you, I'm having to leave everything I care about and expose my child to a life on the run."

"For one thing, if we're married, he can't force you to go with him for emotional or mental evaluation. Not even for your own good. I'm guessing those papers are signed by a doctor who trusts and believes him and signed based on things your father has reported not on meetings with you, which could put him in danger of losing his license, not to mention jail time, but it's not like you have time to prove all that. If we're married I'd be the only one who could request evaluation."

She hadn't thought of that. If she was married, some of her father's power over her would naturally disappear. Psychiatric papers or not.

She had to think. The future. Ethan.

"We could get married, and then head back to town," he told her. "Take a day to give Ethan his adventure and he could be back in school by the end of the week."

It sounded so easy.

And crazy.

Anything that seemed too good to be true usually was.

"He's not just going to go away, Tad. If it was that easy, I'd never have had to run in the first place."

"You were younger. A lot more vulnerable. Completely alone. You had no training yet, no counseling, to help you stand up to his manipulation. And Lord knows, in North Carolina, you'd had no way to compete with the power he wields. It would've been your word against his."

She stared at him. "You believe me."

"I thought that was established the second you left with me," he said. "The second I asked you to go. Either I was going to trust that you were telling the truth and not delusional, or I wasn't. And either you were going to trust me or you weren't. There weren't a lot of options, and no time to find any more."

She'd had similar thoughts rushing through her mind as they'd driven, but Ethan was right there. She hadn't been free to speak...

"I've never been so thankful to hear a man say he had to pee," Tad said, smiling over at her. "I'd have figured out a way to get you out of there, even if I had to hold the man at gunpoint, but this way Ethan is none the wiser..."

She nodded. Staring out the front windshield. "I left with you because I believed I'd have a better chance of escaping from you than from him."

He'd shared her most vulnerable confidences with her father. Brian O'Connor had made sure that arrow landed on her heart during their conversation at the police station that day. He'd let her know he'd had the power to get Tad to "tell" on her.

"You're free to go anytime," Tad said, totally serious as he looked over at her. "I swore to myself that I'd get you away from him. That I'd undo what I could of the damage I'd done, but you owe me nothing."

She had money. Her emergency pack.

"You want some jerky?" she asked him, reaching into the back seat to retrieve the pack on the floor behind her.

She removed the jerky. He took a piece. She chewed one.

"It could be that all that time you were working for my father, you genuinely thought you were saving me." She told him what she'd realized at some point during that very long day.

"Or that I did what it takes to do a good job. That I was on the payroll and, being off work, needed the paycheck. That, after letting down my peers on that last case, I wasn't going to be disloyal to another man in uniform. Particularly not the state's fire chief."

"On the other hand, it could be that you care more about the end in mind than the means," she told him.

"Or it could be that I went to California to do a job and fell in love, instead."

Her heart jumped. Her stomach jumped. She wanted to be happy. She could feel happiness out there, right in front of her.

"He has the power to see that you won't work as a detective again. Especially now. Taking me away like this…"

"You haven't been declared incompetent. His paperwork only gave him permission to have you examined. You'd have passed with flying colors."

"I never intended to let it get that far."

"I know."

She turned to look at him. "You did? You do?" She needed the honest-to-God truth, whatever that might be.

"Your knuckles, they were white on the chair. You weren't giving in to him. You were pandering to him. Patronizing him."

"I was taking it," she said. "To do anything different at that point would have been stupid."

"You had to get home to get Ethan's things." He said, nodding toward the bag still on her lap.

She'd needed things for Ethan, either way.

"You told him he was going on the vacation you talked about. You'd prepared him. In your quiet, careful, intelligent and completely sane way, you were taking care of your son."

Irritated by the tears that sprang to her eyes, she looked ahead and said, "It's what I do."

"It's what I'd like to do, too."

He reached for her hand. She hesitated.

And then she took it.

"Dearly beloved, we are gathered here today in the Crystal Heights Casino and Chapel to witness the union of this man and this woman in holy matrimony."

The Elvis impersonator even talked like the legend.

"And me, too," Ethan interrupted. "This man and this woman and don't forget me…"

Standing there in his jeans and T-shirt, with Miranda still in her scrubs and Tad in the jeans and shirt he'd pulled on that morning, the boy didn't seem the least bit fazed about the strange turns his life had taken that day.

Pushing his glasses up his nose, he glanced at his mother. "Are you sure Tad really knows what he's doing?"

Grinning, Tad looked at the boy. "I think it's the mom and dad who have to get married first, and then the kids," he said.

"Wait a minute." Ethan took a step back. "*Dad?* I'm going to have a dad?"

"Is that okay with you?" Miranda asked. She'd been handed a cheesy bouquet of flowers when they'd walked in the door. It was shaking in her hands.

"Yeah!" The upward lilt in Ethan's voice left no doubt that Tad had a place in this family if he wanted it.

What Tad wanted was to give her a proper wedding, as soon as their lives settled down. She deserved so much better than this.

What he wanted just as much was to take away Brian O'Connor's power over them.

"I don't mean to be rude, but can we get on with this?" Elvis whispered. "We got people waiting and time is money, if you know what I mean."

A minute later, with two quick *I do*s and no chance even to kiss the bride, they were pronounced husband and wife.

Though Ethan was all about seeing the lights, getting ice cream and visiting a hotel swimming pool, he was asleep five minutes after they were back in their newer SUV.

Pulling off to the side of the road, Tad grabbed a phone she didn't recognize out of the glove box. "It's the burner phone I've been using to communicate with your father so that no one could trace me to you," he said. "Now that the deed is done and we're married, we need to call Chantel. You want to do it or do you want me to?"

"She knew your plan to kidnap us?"

"She knew I planned to marry you if you'd have me." Oh.

She took the phone. Looked at him in the darkness. "What are we doing now?"

Getting out of town safely, getting a car, getting Ethan something to eat when he woke up, getting married…one thing led to another.

And now, here they were, parked on the side of a desert road outside Vegas with no bed to sleep in.

"I say we find a place to stop for the night. And then head back to town in the morning."

"You were serious? We're just going back?"

"Either your father will see the wisdom in admitting defeat on this one, with the hope of one day seeing his grandson, or he's going to lose his temper, in which case,

I'll be there when he breaks the law and we'll have something to charge him with."

She frowned, shaking her head.

"What?"

"I hate what he did. How scared I am of him. I really believe he'd have killed me and somehow justified it. But… he's done so much good, too. He really is a hero to the rest of the world. It's just such a shame that it all has to come tumbling down."

"It doesn't have to. He can go home. Leave you and Ethan alone to live your lives."

"I don't think he's capable of that."

She thought about that last night in Asheville, when he'd come to her apartment. His eyes had been glazed. He'd been like a madman. No one was going to keep him from his wife's grandson.

Not his grandson. His wife's.

"When I look back on the three of us as a family… I think my father always struggled with his shadow side. Whether it was the adrenaline rush from work, the need to be strong and forceful to do what he did, or events from his past… I don't know, but after my mom died, I was always afraid to be alone with him."

"You said he never hit you, or your mother, while she was alive."

"He never did. When my mom was around, he was different. I liked being with him then. It was like she tamed something in him, quieted whatever lion roars inside him. After she died, it all fell apart."

He touched her face and she turned to look at him in the moonlight. "As I went through puberty, matured, he drank more, lost his temper more, got meaner and meaner. He said it was because of my belligerence, my inability to do what was right. But I think it was because I resembled her so much. I'd cringe when people mentioned how much I looked like her in front of him. I was a constant reminder, a stab of pain every time he looked at me."

"Then as far as I'm concerned, he's lost the right to look at you," Tad said softly, leaning over to give her a kiss. It wasn't sensual. Or passionate.

But it made her cry.

In the end, Miranda opted for Tad to call Chantel. There'd likely be plans to make and she figured the two detectives were better suited to do that than she was.

That was the moment Tad knew she'd placed her trust in him.

Chantel suggested they hole up in a safe but off-the-grid hotel for the night. And call her back in the morning.

"She said they're watching your dad," Tad relayed to her as they looked for a place. "He drove around like a maniac for hours, she said, checking every place you've been in the past week."

"He was there all that time, watching me."

He thought so, too.

"And then he bought a bottle of whiskey and is holed up at your place. He has to realize you aren't going back to the cottage with him there."

"I've given up trying to figure out what he knows. My guess is he's planning. And has to have somewhere to sleep. He believes he owns us, so he owns my house, too. Believes he has a right to be there. Could be he's searching through all my things, looking for whatever he can use to get to me."

"He did that a lot, didn't he? Find out what hurt you, what you cared about, what made you vulnerable, and then used it against you."

"He used it to get me to go along with him."

It would be best if the chief caught a plane to North Carolina and then hoped that Tad never had cause to return to the state.

"I'm going to put my house in Charlotte on the market," he told her. It was something he'd thought about doing. "Have everything packed up and shipped out here."

She stared at him in the half light. "This marriage. It was just to get me away from him. You don't have to go through with it."

He'd spotted a motel and pulled in. Turned to her. "I want to go through with it," he said. "If you do."

She touched his face, studied his eyes. "I do, Tad. But I'm scared. I'm just so scared."

He nodded. Started to tell her he was afraid, too, but went inside to get them a room instead.

The sun was shining when Miranda woke up the next morning. She didn't know where she was at first, and then felt a leg brush up against hers.

She was in her jeans. On top of a bed with a blanket over her. Tad was lying there next to her, watching her.

Turning her head, she saw Ethan, still in his clothes, asleep under the covers of the other bed.

"Guess we didn't have to worry about shocking him," Tad said, glancing over at the boy, who was so zonked his mouth hung open and drool trailed from his mouth down to his pillow.

She wanted to say that she was there, in that hotel room, married, for Ethan's sake. That she was doing it all for him.

"I want a life," she said softly, looking back at Tad. "I love him so much, I'd give my life for him, but I want a life, too. I want a partner, someone I can talk to when I'm scared or worried or so proud of Ethan I could burst. I want to make love on a regular basis. To not sleep alone.

I want to be able to open my heart and love. Really love. Without fear."

He traced her lips with his finger. Ran his hand along her neck.

"I want all that, too," he told her. "But only if I can have it with you."

She could feel a tear drip from her eye down to the pillow. She was crying so much lately, as though all the emotion she'd bottled up for so long couldn't be contained anymore. There was no room for it.

She'd taken on as much as she could.

Clasping his hand, she brought it to her lips. "I love you."

"I love you," he said. "And Ethan, too, in case you hadn't figured that out yet."

His love for Ethan wasn't anything she'd worried about. Strange how she could accept it for her son, but was struggling so hard to allow it for herself.

"I suspect the fear's become a part of you," Tad said. "It's like you said, when you grow up with it…"

She nodded.

"But it's a part of you that makes you who you are," he told her. "You're more aware, more compassionate. You don't take things for granted."

She took a deep breath, and then took a huge leap. "You don't think it makes me crazy?"

He didn't gush. Or exclaim. Either would have been hard to take.

"Do you think I'm crazy for diving through that door and saving that little girl?" he asked.

"Of course not! You saved her life."

"I acted, at least in part, because of what had happened to my sister. In the process, I put others' lives at risk."

"That's understandable, Tad. Not crazy."

"Exactly."

* * *

"We should probably wake him up and get going." As much as Tad wanted to lie in bed talking with Miranda, his wife, he couldn't do that easily until he knew they were settled. That Brian O'Connor was either on a plane or in jail. Miranda could request a restraining order against the man, that would probably be granted on a temporary basis, until she could get proof that her father had obtained papers to have her evaluated without her actually having been examined in the last ten years. At that point she'd probably be granted a full restraining order. For a period of time.

She couldn't prove prior abuse, but she could testify about it to a judge for a restraining order.

He'd talked to her about it the night before, and it was already on their agenda for that day.

They had breakfast at a diner up the road and then Ethan was settled in the back. He'd chosen the third seat this time, and he was watching another movie as they headed back across the desert.

"I was thinking… I'd like to go into private detective work," he told Miranda as they drove, and it occurred to him that if their marriage was real, he wasn't alone anymore. He should include her in life-changing decisions. "Not regular PI work, that's not me, but working domestic violence cases, you know, for the High Risk Team. Maybe hire myself out to police departments. The Lemonade Stand. Individuals. As long as I'm licensed in the state, I could do any of it."

The plan was fluid. But he was liking it so far.

"I think it's a great idea," Miranda told him. And then asked, "Would you want to move? Into a different place, I mean?"

He'd been thinking about that, too.

"All those things you said last night," he began, "about

what you wanted... You didn't mention babies. Do you want any more?"

He hadn't thought he did. Or ever would. But he'd been wrong about a lot of things.

"With you? I'd have one tomorrow if we could," she told him. "I did it all alone, with Ethan."

He took her hand. "Then yes, I'd want to move eventually. We'll need a third bedroom, at least. But I'd like to stay in Santa Raquel, if that's what you're asking."

She nodded.

And as he turned onto the highway that would lead them the rest of the way across the desert, he felt something he'd never expected to feel again.

Like he was going home.

They'd just stopped for lunch and were about an hour from home when Tad's burner phone rang. He'd asked Miranda to wait to put her SIM card back into her phone, and he hadn't put his in, either. Not until they knew more about her father's plans.

Their plan, as determined mostly by Chantel, was for Tad to take Miranda and Ethan to The Lemonade Stand, where an attorney would meet her to fill out paperwork for a restraining order, while Chantel tried to talk to Brian and get him to leave town willingly.

She listened while Tad talked, surmising from the conversation that it was Chantel. And then realized, when he mentioned North Carolina, that it wasn't. He was talking to a woman; she could hear enough of the voice to know that. And didn't like how proprietary she felt.

Or how threatened.

"That was Gail," he told her as he hung up. "Good news!"

She'd gathered that from his tone of voice. "Chief Fire

Marshal Brian O'Connor is back in North Carolina," he said. "Apparently he chartered a plane, and just landed."

Right. Her father was a millionaire now. He could charter planes. She didn't care about his money.

"He left," she said, hardly believing it. "Gail's sure? Someone's physically seen him?"

"He's at his office right now."

"Chantel told him we were married," she guessed.

As she said that, his phone rang again. This time it was Chantel. She explained that she hadn't wanted to call until she knew the chief had landed on North Carolina soil, but now it was confirmed, Tad relayed when he got off the phone.

"Apparently he saw reason in Chantel's point that if he ever hoped to have a chance to talk you into seeing him again, and letting him see his grandson, he should go home and wait for you to contact him," Tad said.

She couldn't believe it.

She'd won?

"Maybe seeing me reminded him why it was best that he not spend a lot of time around me," she said. "He's happier without the constant reminder of my mom. Or maybe seeing his grandson really does matter more." Loving Ethan like she did, she got that.

"And maybe seeing you again reminded him how much he loves you, and with the health scare giving him a new perspective, he doesn't want to grow old alone."

"He could get away with beating me up, manipulating and controlling me back then. He could do it without risk to his reputation. He'd never get away with kidnapping Ethan. I guess his need to do good in the community really is the stronger part of him." She wanted to hope so.

"He wasn't always an abuser," Tad said, as though wanting to help her believe that her father could change.

Time would tell.

"If I ever see him again, or introduce him to Ethan as his grandfather, we aren't going to do it alone," she said. "You're there or it doesn't happen."

His expression was serious as he looked over at her. "You love me."

"Yes, I do. More than I ever thought I'd be able to love anyone but Ethan."

"I love you, too. With all of me."

They were words she trusted.

* * * * *

*If you enjoyed this great romance,
keep an eye out for the next book in the
Where Secrets are Safe miniseries,
available in March 2020!*

COMING NEXT MONTH FROM

H HARLEQUIN®
™

ROMANTIC suspense

Available October 1, 2019

YOU CAN FIND MORE INFORMATION ON UPCOMING HARLEQUIN® TITLES, FREE EXCERPTS AND MORE AT WWW.HARLEQUIN.COM.

HRSCNM0919

Get 4 FREE REWARDS!

We'll send you 2 FREE Books plus 2 FREE Mystery Gifts.

Harlequin® Romantic Suspense books feature heart-racing sensuality and the promise of a sweeping romance set against the backdrop of suspense.

FREE
Value Over
$20

YES! Please send me 2 FREE Harlequin® Romantic Suspense novels and my 2 FREE gifts (gifts are worth about $10 retail). After receiving them, if I don't wish to receive any more books, I can return the shipping statement marked "cancel." If I don't cancel, I will receive 4 brand-new novels every month and be billed just $4.99 per book in the U.S. or $5.74 per book in Canada. That's a savings of at least 12% off the cover price! It's quite a bargain! Shipping and handling is just 50¢ per book in the U.S. and $1.25 per book in Canada.* I understand that accepting the 2 free books and gifts places me under no obligation to buy anything. I can always return a shipment and cancel at any time. The free books and gifts are mine to keep no matter what I decide.

240/340 HDN GNMZ

Name (please print)

Address   Apt. #

City   State/Province   Zip/Postal Code

Mail to the **Reader Service:**
IN U.S.A.: P.O. Box 1341, Buffalo, NY 14240-8531
IN CANADA: P.O. Box 603, Fort Erie, Ontario L2A 5X3

Want to try 2 free books from another series? Call 1-800-873-8635 or visit www.ReaderService.com.

"I appreciate you coming," he said.

"You said it was important."

Paul nodded as he gestured for her to take a seat. Sitting down, Simone stole another quick glance toward the bar. The two strangers were both staring blatantly, not bothering to hide their interest in the two of them.

Simone rested an elbow on the tabletop, turning flirtatiously toward her friend. "Do you know Tom and Jerry over there at the bar?" she asked softly. She reached a hand out, trailing her fingers against his arm.

Her touch was just distracting enough that Paul didn't turn abruptly to stare back, drawing even more attention in their direction. His focus shifted slowly from her toward the duo at the bar. He eyed them briefly before turning his attention back to Simone. He shook his head. "Should I?"

"It might be nothing, but they seem very interested in you."

Paul's gaze danced back in their direction and he took a swift inhale of air. One of the men was on a cell phone and both were still eyeing him intently.

"We need to leave," he said, suddenly anxious. He began to gather his papers.

"What's going on, Paul?"

"I don't think we're safe, Simone."

"What do you mean we're not safe?" she snapped, her teeth clenched tightly. "Why are we not safe?"

"I'll explain, but I think we really need to leave."

Simone took a deep breath and held it, watching as he repacked his belongings into his briefcase.

"We're not going anywhere until you explain," she started, and then a commotion at the door pulled at her attention.

Don't miss
Reunited by the Badge *by Deborah Fletcher Mello
available October 2019 wherever
Harlequin® Romantic Suspense
books and ebooks are sold.*

www.Harlequin.com

HRSEXP0919

Love Harlequin romance?

DISCOVER.

Be the first to find out about promotions, news and exclusive content!

Facebook.com/HarlequinBooks

Twitter.com/HarlequinBooks

Instagram.com/HarlequinBooks

Pinterest.com/HarlequinBooks

ReaderService.com

EXPLORE.

Sign up for the Harlequin e-newsletter and download a free book from any series at **TryHarlequin.com.**

CONNECT.

Join our Harlequin community to share your thoughts and connect with other romance readers!
Facebook.com/groups/HarlequinConnection

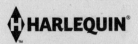

HARLEQUIN®

ROMANCE WHEN YOU NEED IT